BATTLEGROUND

Recent Titles by Alan Savage from Severn House

THE PARTISAN SERIES
PARTISAN
MURDER'S ART
BATTLEGROUND

THE COMMANDO SERIES
COMMANDO
THE CAUSE
THE TIGER

THE SWORD SERIES
THE SWORD AND THE SCALPEL
THE SWORD AND THE JUNGLE
THE SWORD AND THE PRISON
STOP ROMMEL!
THE AFRIKA KORPS

BATTLEGROUND

Alan Savage

This first world edition published in Great Britain 2002 by
SEVERN HOUSE PUBLISHERS LTD of
9–15 High Street, Sutton, Surrey SM1 1DF.
This first world edition published in the USA 2003 by
SEVERN HOUSE PUBLISHERS INC of
595 Madison Avenue, New York, N.Y. 10022.

British Library Cataloguing in Publication Data

Savage, Alan
    Battleground
    1.   World War, 1939-1945 - Campaigns - Yugoslavia - Fiction
    2.   Yugoslavia - History - Axis occupation, 1941-1945 - Fiction
    3.   War stories
    I.   Title
    823.9'14 [F]

    ISBN 0-7278-5890-4

Typeset by Palimpsest Book Production Ltd.,
Polmont, Stirlingshire, Scotland.
Printed and bound in Great Britain by
MPG Books Ltd., Bodmin, Cornwall.

PART ONE

THE HUM

From camp to camp, through the foul womb of night,
The hum of either army stilly sounds.

William Shakespeare

One

The Gathering

With screaming sirens the dive-bombers swooped out of the clear early morning sky. It had rained during the night, but the clouds had now gone, leaving a day of bright and sharply etched images; at six o'clock on a May morning the sun was already high. It shone directly on to the eastern slopes of Mount Lerlija, and on the walls and rooftops of the little town of Foca that nestled at its foot, fronted by the swiftly flowing River Drina. The mountain had always provided an element of protection from the air, and even now the Junkers dared not come straight down on their target, but they could get close enough, and the riverside was already a mass of flames and craters, while the small craft moored along the bank were being reduced to driftwood as the water about them leapt and churned to the raucous music of the exploding bombs.

Tony Davis rolled out of bed and ran to the window to look down the sloping street at the destruction; his billet was at the back of the town, high above the river. Still only twenty-eight years old, he had seen a similar sight just over a year ago. Then he had stood at his window in the British embassy in Belgrade and watched the first Nazi bombers soaring over the city, introducing Yugoslavia to modern warfare. Just a year, but it seemed an eternity. He sometimes thought that the sound of bombers overhead would stay with him for the rest of his life.

But the important fact was that he was still alive, although

3

his naked body bore the scars of three quite serious wounds. The first had been suffered two years before in Flanders during the bitter retreat of the BEF from the River Dyle to the beaches of Dunkirk, only a week before the 'miracle'. That wound, which had caused him to be returned to England before the evacuation had begun – just as its situation, in his leg, had left him with a permanent slight limp – had also caused him to be seconded from his regiment, the Buffs, to the supposedly sedentary position of one of the military attachés in the then neutral city of Belgrade. He had resented his fate then, less for the secondment than for the indication that he was considered unfit for combat duties. Instead, he had spent the last year engaging in the most serious fighting he had ever experienced, and picked up two more wounds – this time on behalf of the Yugoslav Partisans, led by the Communist Josip Broz, who called himself Tito.

Tall and dark, with a saturnine sense of humour to match his aquiline features, Tony Davis was now prepared to find his recent career an amusing twist of fate, no matter that he had spent much of that year living like a bandit, murdering the enemy when necessary to survive. Besides, there had been ample compensation – Sandrine.

The Frenchwoman had also been awakened by the bombing, and now joined him at the window, her body still warm from the bed as she leaned against him and clutched his arm. 'They have found us out.'

'I reckon they always knew we were here,' Tony said. 'They were just waiting for winter to end. The question is, is this just a raid, or the start of an offensive?'

Sandrine listened to the screams and shouts from the bottom of the hill, watched the smoke billowing upwards. 'Should we get out?'

'I don't think they'll trouble us up here; we're too close to the mountain. But we'd better get dressed. They'll need us down there.'

She went into the tiny bathroom without hesitation. The

same age as Tony, she had been a Paris-bred sophisticated journalist on the staff of *Paris-Temps* in Belgrade before last April – and also the mistress of a German officer, who, like Tony, had been a military attaché. With her diminutive five foot four-inch body, her straight yellow hair, and her classically beautiful features, she had in every way been quite unsuited for the desperate existence into which she had been thrust by the Nazi invasion. Cast adrift by the realization that her boyfriend had suddenly become an enemy, and then losing her best female friend to that enemy, she had been in danger of drowning in the intensely masculine world in which she had found herself and in which any woman was a potential victim, even of those officially on her side, and the only rule was kill or be killed.

Tony had rescued her – inadvertently, in the beginning – from both rape and murder, and since then she had clung to him with a passionate devotion. And more than that. She had never handled a weapon in her life before the German assault on Belgrade, but on that frantic first day she had possessed herself of a tommy-gun, and over the past year had become as deadly a guerilla as any man, while her mental toughness had been displayed during the weeks just before the last Christmas when she had been a prisoner of the Gestapo; Sandrine had survived with neither physical nor mental scars because she had done whatever had to be done, said whatever had to be said, accepted whatever had to be accepted, to ensure that survival. Thankfully, Tony and Tito had managed to arrange her exchange for the prize they had captured in turn, the daughter of the Nazi governor-general.

Now she was again happy to be at Tony's side, obeying his every command. Neither of them knew how they would fare after the war. Both knew they had hardly more than a fifty-fifty chance of survival, and neither knew how soon, or if ever, the war would end. But in each other they could always find safety and contentment, however fleeting.

He stood behind her as she brushed her teeth, putting his

hands round her waist to cup her breasts – surprisingly and delightfully large for so small a body – while he drew her bottom against his groin and nuzzled her sweet-smelling hair. After a year he still found her the most exciting of women. As she knew. She turned her head for a kiss. 'Will we fight them?'

'We'll do whatever the general tells us to do. But we'd better see how the girls are taking it.'

They dressed themselves and hurried down the hill. The bombers had gone by now, and the narrow streets of the town were filled with anxious people, wailing children, barking dogs, and bleating goats. Tony and Sandrine, as the only two foreigners in the Partisan army, were well known and greeted on every side as they pushed their way through the throng to where groups of men and women were attempting to put out the flames, or to rescue precious food supplies.

Many of the women wore the Partisan 'uniform' of blouse and pants and sidecap, and worked under the immediate command of their captain, who now saluted as her colonel and adjutant approached. 'Bastards!' she commented.

Her name was Sasha Janitz, and she was a tall, strongly built young woman with handsome features and long black hair, which she wore tucked into the collar of her blouse. She had been one of the first of the women accepted into the Partisan army, as Tito had sought to recruit wherever volunteers could be found who were willing to fight, and if necessary die, for their country. She and Tony had shared their moments during the period when the Frenchwoman had been supposed dead, but, although Sandrine on her return had reasserted her prerogatives where the Englishman was concerned, there was no suggestion of hostility or embarrassment between them. Tony had been placed in command of the women's regiment, and had led them to glorious if bloody victory on more than one occasion. Sasha, as one of his company commanders, had considered it her duty in Sandrine's absence to share his bivouac during the long retreat from the town of Uzice during the winter. And Tony, however grief-stricken he had felt in his supposition that he would never hold Sandrine in his arms again, had found Sasha's eager sexuality both comforting and therapeutic.

At her side, as always nowadays, was the girl Jelena Brolic. Tony was not sure theirs was an altogether healthy relationship. Jelena's father had conspired with the Partisans the previous October to provide a site from which the new governor-general could be assassinated. That had gone disastrously wrong, and as a result the entire family, save for the eldest son, had been arrested. Tony knew that both the mother and father had been savagely tortured. He did not know what had happened to the younger son and the daughter, but no one could spend several weeks in the hands of the Gestapo without suffering. Jelena had no visible physical scars, but he could not be certain about her mind.

She had been part of the exchange the previous December, the one which had brought Sandrine home. But by then another catastrophe had overtaken her family. Her older brother, after escaping from Belgrade, had joined the Partisans and proved himself a good soldier. But his fanatical hatred of the Germans, who he had supposed had executed the rest of his family, had led him to disobey orders in the face of the enemy, and Sasha, commanding his unit, had shot him. Officially it had been given out that he had died in battle, but there could be no doubt that the event lay heavily on Sasha's mind, especially since the rest of the Brolics had been rescued. Thus she had taken Jelena under her wing, as it were, inducted her into her own company and treated her almost as a sister. Or something more. Tony did not know and did not wish to find out their true relationship; certainly the young woman, who was just sixteen, had slimmed down from the rather overweight girl he remembered – thanks to Sasha's strict training methods – as well as gained in height, and was now a lean and attractive guerilla, her somewhat tight features enhanced by her long brown hair. She seemed to worship Sasha, and followed her around like a pet dog. What worried Tony was how she might react should she ever discover the truth of her brother's death. But hopefully that would never happen.

Now he asked, 'Casualties?'

'We have not suffered any ourselves. But there have been some. Will they attack us?'

'I imagine they will. You'd better get your women together. Take command, Sandrine.'

He left them, and went in search of Tito.

The general was also surveying the damage, and the dead bodies arranged in a row before him, with a grim expression. He was a heavy-set man, shorter than Tony, but with powerfully handsome features. He exuded charisma and the pleasure of command, even in the most difficult circumstances.

He and Tony had liked each other from the moment they had first met, when Tony and Sandrine, fleeing the uncertain hostility of the Cetniks – the pro-monarchist guerillas commanded by the erstwhile chief of the Yugoslav general staff, General Draza Mihailovic – had stumbled into the Partisan camp. In those early days, Mihailovic had been, and should have remained, the natural leader of the Yugoslav resistance, at least in view of his rank and experience. But his aim had been the freedom of Serbia and the well-being of the Serbs, not the survival of the Federation as a whole, and while Tony had been able to sympathize with his determination to restore the pre-war monarchy, he had been unable to stomach his ethnic hatred of people like the Croats, the Bosnians, the Slovenes, the Montenegrins, or the Albanians, who composed the population of this unrealistic nation, or the contempt he had expressed for the large Muslim minority in the country. Even less had he been able to accept Mihailovic's determination that the Germans were best left alone, at least until it could be seen how the war was going to turn out.

By contrast, Tito was everything that Tony, as a British

soldier, should have rejected. He was unashamedly a Communist, and if he did not ram his political ideas down his people's throats, as the long-standing secretary-general of the Yugoslav party he openly took his orders from Moscow, and no one could doubt that he personally had little interest in restoring a monarchy which he saw as too Serb-oriented and which had made him an outlaw before the war. But as far as the war went, he was determined to fight, and win, no matter the cost. And although he was a Croat he fought for Yugoslavia, and would accept in his ranks anyone prepared to join him in that fight, regardless of nationality, ethnic background, religion or sex. An experienced officer in the British army, however irregular his personal life, had been a godsend; together they had transformed his ragtag band of followers into a proficient fighting force.

Now he greeted Tony with a hard smile. 'A nasty business. But it had to happen.'

'Will they put in ground forces?'

'I imagine they will, when they feel we have been sufficiently softened up. Well, we always knew they would stir themselves when the weather improved. What happened today is not going to cripple us. But we must strike back. We cannot just lie down and be slaughtered.'

'Say the word, General.'

Tito grinned. 'Your women are anxious for some more action. Well, you shall have it. If our so-called masters would re-arm us . . .'

His tone was bitter, but Tony could understand that; he felt the same way. It had taken the British some time to realize the possible value of a Yugoslav resistance movement, and when they had, with their weakness for doing everything by the book, they had elected to give their support to Mihailovic as the ranking officer on the ground and to treat all other groups as subordinate to his orders. Thus what supplies of arms and ammunition had been available had always been dropped to the Cetniks.

Granted that these supplies had in any event been scanty. Until last July Britain had been fighting alone, and every gun and bullet had been needed for the defence of either their island or the Suez Canal, while since last July all spare munitions had been channelled to the Soviet Union. But it was the principle that rankled. From his position as inadvertent liaison officer with the Partisans – a situation apparently accepted by GHQ in Cairo – Tony had tried to change this point of view, without success; both Cairo and London held Tito and himself responsible for the murder of the governor-general's wife, and they had been given no opportunity to defend their innocence.

On the other hand . . . 'What about the arms promised us by Moscow?' he asked.

Tito grimaced. 'They say they are doing all they can to get them to us, but there are difficulties, delays . . . Who can say they are not right?'

Tony suppressed a sigh. If Tito had a weakness, it was his slavish acceptance that whatever Moscow said or did – or in this case, didn't do – had to be right.

'But there are developments,' the general said. 'Come.'

They left their people working at clearing the rubble – the fires had all been put out – and climbed the hill to Tito's headquarters, where, despite the early hour and the bombing raid, secretaries were already busy, some typing, others monitoring the huge radio set, and others working the portable printing press which accompanied the general wherever he went – because of his training as a Communist early in his life, when he had lived in Russia, Tito could not suppress his continuing inclination to churn out endless manifestos, exhortations, and newsletters, even when they were directed at people many of whom could not read.

He sat behind his desk, and gestured Tony to a chair. 'This came in last night.' He handed over a sheet of paper. Tony scanned the radio transcript.

*I wish to inform you, General Tito, that the men commanded
by Major Matovic, who attempted to betray you to the Germans
last December, were not under my command, and were indeed
traitors to the cause of Yugoslavia, for which we are both
fighting. I congratulate you in dealing with this matter so expe-
ditiously, and assure you of my wish to assist you wherever
possible. If you will inform me of your requirements as regards
weapons and ammunition, I will do my best to re-equip you.
Mihailovic, Commander-in-Chief and Minister of Defence.*

'He does give himself airs.' Tony handed the letter back.

'Apparently he has actually been appointed Minister of
Defence by the government-in-exile in London,' Tito said, and
made a face. 'I doubt those fools regard me as more than a
nuisance.'

'And it has taken him a while to admit that it was his people
involved in that attempted ambush. He also makes no men-
tion of the death of Major Curtis.'

'Because Curtis was murdered by Matovic, for whom he
has disclaimed responsibility. For all of these lapses there has
to be a reason,' Tito agreed. 'I would say that pressure has
been brought to bear on him from London to patch up his dif-
ferences with us. I may say that I have received a communication from Moscow suggesting that I drop the title I have
given us – the Proletarian Brigade – and revert to plain
Partisans. They are afraid that revealing open Communism
will offend the democracies.' He grinned. 'I am sure this is
one matter in which you agree with Moscow. As for Major
Curtis's death, I'm afraid suspicion still lies on us, as he was
with us when he was killed, and I imagine Mihailovic is quite
happy to have London continue to hold us responsible. We
will have to work on it. *You* will have to work on it, Tony.
But right now we have more important matters to worry about.
I have no reports of any large German troop movements in
Bosnia. But I cannot believe this raid was just an isolated
attack. I need information.'

'Such as a visit from old Malic,' Tony suggested.

Tito sighed. 'I doubt we shall see him again. His source was his daughter, who was Angela von Blintoft's personal maid when her father was govenor-general, was she not?'

Tony nodded.

'So now that Fräulein von Blintoft has gone off back to Germany to marry that bastard Wassermann, Rosa Malic has no means of obtaining information. We shall have to look closer to home.'

'Sasha?' Tony asked.

'Well, she has been into Sarajevo several times over the winter, has she not?'

'Oh, indeed. She is a Bosnian, and speaks the local dialect.'

'And she has always brought us back some useful information. I have never asked you before how she gets this.'

'Ah . . . I believe she has a friend.'

Tito raised his eyebrows. 'A boyfriend? I thought . . .'

'That is history,' Tony said. 'Since Sandrine came back. This friend is a woman. Frankly, she is what we in England call a "madam".'

Again Tito raised his eyebrows.

'She runs a brothel. A very exclusive brothel, for the use of German officers and important citizens only. It is, or can be, a very useful source of information. Men have this weakness for wishing to impress their bedmates, even when such bedmates are whores. Anyone with a little bit of skill can extract quite a lot from her current partner.'

'And this madam is a supporter?'

'Not quite to the extent we would like. But she allows Sasha to use the brothel when she is in town. They were apparently friends as children.'

'Do you mean that Captain Janitz prostitutes herself?'

'She's built for it. She's big and strong and good-looking, and very sexual.'

Tito scratched his head. 'And you are happy about this?'

'As I told you, sir, there is no longer an attachment between

12

us, other than she likes having me as her commanding officer, and I like having her serve under me.' This was not altogether true; he still ranked Sasha very highly as a woman, a companion and a lover. But he knew that Tito did not believe in allowing personal feelings to interfere with the business of fighting the war, and so merely added, 'I know her worth, both in battle and in other fields.'

'Yes,' Tito said drily. 'I wonder if you know women as well as you think you do, Colonel. However, you feel she will be willing to undertake this mission?'

'Certainly.'

'The point she must appreciate is that whereas in the past she has brought us such snippets of news as she may have picked up, this time we wish specific information regarding German troop movements in Bosnia. That is to say, it will be far more dangerous than usual, as she will have to ask questions instead of merely listening. You must put this to her.'

'I will.'

'But you still think she will do it?'

'I have no doubt of it,' Tony said. 'And she will succeed, too. She will be in no danger. There is no one in the whole German army who knows her by sight, save for that fellow Ulrich, who was Wassermann's right-hand man in charge of the local Gestapo. And he is not likely to return to Bosnia in a hurry after the way in which we humiliated him.'

'Then I will leave the matter in your hands, Tony. And Sasha's hands, to be sure. Just get me that information as rapidly as possible. We must have the time to prepare a counter-strike.'

Captain Hermann Ulrich stamped up and down the platform at Belgrade Central. He was in a state of some agitation. This was at least partly because he could not help remembering previous occasions he had stood here. One had been eight months ago, when he had waited for the arrival of the new governor-general, only minutes before the general's wife had been cut down by a sniper's bullet. The Partisans, he knew, claimed that it had been an accident, but nonetheless it had sparked a series of quite horrific events. Another had been in December, when he had stood here to see off his commanding officer, Major Wassermann – gravely wounded as a result of those events – and his fiancée, the daughter of the governor-general. And less than an hour later that train had been blown up!

Miraculously, Wassermann, even with his wound, had survived the blast. Even more miraculously, as some would have it, he had officially recovered from his dreadful injuries in only six months, and far from being given a desk job, was being returned to his old post of policing Yugoslavia.

Ulrich regarded this development with mixed feelings. For the past six months he had been acting commander of both the Gestapo and the SS detachment in the conquered country, and he had not enjoyed it. This was because he had quickly realized that he lacked the capability for the job. Before the war had sucked him into the armed services, he had been a simple police officer in Hamburg. He reckoned he had been good at his job there, and his ability as a detective had been highly praised. That praise had resulted in his being inducted into the branch of the SS which dealt with conquered territories. The powers that be seemed to assume that a man simply had to be given a black uniform with a death's head badge on his cap and he would immediately become a cold and unemotional upholder of the Reich. There had been considerable training as well, of course, both physical and professional, but while the physical had done him a world of good – he had always had a tendency to plumpness – the mental training had appalled him. But there had been no way out.

Thus he was very happy to have a new commander coming to take over, even if he was disappointed not to have received a promotion to major for his efforts. But this was not a new commander. It was again Wassermann, just about the most cold and ruthless upholder of the Reich that could be imagined. It was Wassermann who had ordered the execution of five thousand men and boys at Kragujevac during the previous autumn's campaign. Ulrich had felt physically sick as he had watched; Wassermann had merely smiled his cold smile.

And soon afterwards he had been cut down by a Partisan bullet. He was hardly likely to be returning in any more of a humane mood.

What was worse, he would be accompanied by his wife, General von Blintoft's daughter Angela, who had been captured by the Partisans after the train wreck and been subjected to God alone knew what indignities – certainly Ulrich knew she had been raped at least once, because she had told him so. And even before that horrifying experience she had revealed a quite demonic character in her hatred for the people who had gunned down her mother. Her return too was not going to make the atmosphere in Belgrade any the lighter, especially as she would no longer be the governor-general's daughter – her father had been retired for his incompetent handling of the situation – but merely the wife of the police chief.

Ulrich stood to attention as the train pulled into the station. There was no guard of honour and no band, such as had been turned out the day the Blintofts had arrived last October. Just half a dozen people on the platform, including himself and two orderlies to take care of the luggage. The train puffed to a stop, doors opened and shut, and Ulrich hurried forward.

Angela Wassermann was in front of her husband. Whatever her ordeals, both at the hands of the guerillas and in having to marry a half-dead man, she had outwardly changed very little since last he had seen her, six months ago. She was of average height, with smooth black hair which she wore straight to her shoulders, a trim figure, and bold features. She moved gracefully and had long fingers encased in black gloves. Although the May morning was by no means cold, she wore a pale mink coat with a matching hat. The dress beneath, so far as he could deduce from the visible hem, was dark blue.

'Captain Ulrich!' Her voice was low and melodious. Her expression arranged itself into a smile, which did not extend to her eyes. But her nostrils flared as she spoke, in that so well remembered manner, leaving him unsure what message she was trying to convey to him, which of the various traumatic experiences they had shared were to be kept secret from her husband.

'Frau Wassermann! I trust you had a pleasant journey?'

'It was more pleasant than the last time I used this line, certainly,' she said.

Ulrich had a sense of relief. At least she could speak of it without visible emotion. But now she was turning, and he looked past her at the carriage door; Wassermann was just then appearing.

The first thing Ulrich noted was the stick, which tapped the steps down which the colonel hesitantly came, watched by his wife . . . with contempt? The Wassermann he remembered had been tall and strongly built, his physique enhanced by the black uniform, his handsome face a mask of cold disdain. The height was the same, as was the uniform, now decorated with the Iron Cross First Class with the Oak Leaf Cluster – his reward for so-called heroism in the pursuit of the Partisans – but it covered a clearly emaciated body. The face was the same as well, save that it was thinner, and the eyes were colder than ever, while he had developed a slight twitch at the corner of the flat mouth. Ulrich wondered whether that was a result of his wound or a nervous development. 'Herr Colonel! Heil Hitler!' Ulrich saluted, and then extended his hand.

'Heil!' Wassermann also saluted before taking the offered fingers. His grip was limp.

'May I offer my congratulations on your recovery, Herr Colonel.'

'Thank you, Ulrich. It is good to be back.'

His wife gave him an incredulous glance.

'You have a car for Frau Wassermann?'

'Yes, indeed, sir. But . . .'

'I will come directly to the office.'

'Will you not see me home?' Angela asked.

'I will come home for dinner. I am sure there is a great deal waiting for my attention.'

Angela was clearly tempted to protest, but changed her mind. She turned to Ulrich. 'The house . . . ?'

'Well, obviously, my dear, it will not be the royal palace,' Wassermann said. 'We have a new commanding general now, eh?'

Angela's face twisted at the jibe, but she did not riposte. 'I merely wished to ask the captain if it is adequate.'

'Oh, it is very adequate, Frau Wassermann. Very well appointed, situated in a nice area . . .'

'And away from possible snipers, eh?' Wassermann asked.

Angela walked away from him towards the waiting cars while the orderlies carried their luggage behind her.

'Yes,' Wassermann said, sitting behind his old desk and surveying his office. 'It is good to be back.'

Certainly the staff at Gestapo Headquarters, situated in the grounds of the General Command, had given him a rousing welcome, lining the corridors down which he had felt his way behind his tapping stick – almost as if he were blind, Ulrich thought – and clapping their hands and cheering. Even the prisoners awaiting interrogation in the tram, that dreadful room where those accused or even suspected of crimes against the Reich were forced to sit rigidly upright on backless benches for hours on end, had managed to get some enthusiasm into their 'Heil Hitler's. Although possibly, Ulrich reflected, they had just been glad to be given the opportunity to stand and stretch their cramped limbs.

'Now,' Wassermann said. 'Bring me up to date. Oh, sit down. Sit down.'

Ulrich seated himself before the desk. He knew he was going to have to choose his words with care. 'There has been little activity over the winter,' he said. 'It has not been possible to carry out any large troop manoeuvres with so much snow and ice and rain. But now that the weather is improving, I believe a fresh offensive is planned, into the Bosnian mountains. It is known that Tito has made the town of Foca his headquarters. It is difficult to access, but I believe it was bombed yesterday morning. I have not seen the damage reports.'

'What was the purpose of this raid?'

'I am not in the confidence of the governor-general, Herr Colonel. But I would assume that it was intended to soften up the Partisans with a view to a ground assault.'

'That is the most utter rubbish. Soften them up? It will merely have alerted them that we mean to attack.'

'That is possible, sir.' Ulrich had no intention of being caught in any possible conflict between his immediate boss and the new governor-general.

'What is the Partisan force in Foca?'

'It is not known exactly, sir. However, we may be sure that they have spent the winter recruiting, and, where possible, re-arming. I would suggest that there may be several thousand of them.'

'We had them in our grasp last year,' Wassermann said. 'And we let them get away. *You* let them get away, Ulrich.'

'With respect, sir, when you were hit, I considered it my first duty to get you to safety.'

'Wars are not won by taking people to safety, Ulrich. Even your superiors.'

'Would you rather I had left you to die, Herr Colonel? And in any event, we did not have the whole Partisan army in our grasp. It was only a couple of under-strength regiments. One of which was that women's regiment we have heard so much about.'

Wassermann's mouth twisted. 'I have sometimes thought, over these past few months, that it would have been far better *had* you left me to die.'

'Oh, come now, sir,' Ulrich protested. 'You have everything to live for. You are a national hero, you have a beautiful and loving wife . . .'

18

Wassermann snorted. 'Loving? She hates me. She only married me because Berlin expected it and her father forced her to go through with it. She has told me this. Married to a cripple, she says when she is angry. Can you imagine a worse fate than that?'

Ulrich desperately tried to think of adequate words. 'She will grow out of that mood, sir. And meanwhile . . .' He bit his lip.

'And meanwhile I have the use of all of that beauty, eh? I am impotent, Ulrich.'

Ulrich stared at him in consternation.

'That bullet did more than rip up my gut and shatter my ribs,' Wassermann said. 'It went further than that. And by the time they had finished sewing me up, there was very little left.'

'I am so very sorry, sir. But . . .'

'Oh, the marriage was consummated. I saw to that before we were even engaged.'

Ulrich looked at the floor. Himself a man who lived to the strictest moral code, it would never have crossed his mind – or that of his wife, waiting for him in Hamburg – to have sex before their marriage.

'Now the only pleasure I can have is by beating her,' Wassermann reflected.

Ulrich's head jerked. That was something else he would never have dreamed of doing to his wife.

'But enough of my personal problems,' Wassermann said. 'So that bunch of Partisans got away. The women's regiment. One of whom undoubtedly fired the shot that hit me. Do you have any idea which one it was?'

'No, sir. We have never taken any of the women prisoner.'

'Never? Surely some were wounded in that battle? And they retreated, did they not, leaving us in possession of the field?'

Ulrich coughed. 'Wherever possible, they carry their wounded with them rather than allow them to fall into our hands. And on the odd occasion when we have come upon one of them still breathing, she has invariably blown herself up with a grenade before she could be secured.'

'Barbaric,' Wassermann commented. 'But is this regiment not commanded by the Englishman Davis?'

'Yes, sir.'

'Then he must be regarded as responsible for everything they do, including shooting me. He must be about the most wanted man in Yugoslavia, after Tito himself. And now he is no doubt safe in Foca. Another failure. As for that doxy of his . . . You had her here, Ulrich. You had her in this office. And you let her go.'

'Well, sir, you had given me instructions that she was not to be harmed until you could interrogate her personally, and then, when you were hit, there was so much confusion . . . And Fräulein von Blintoft – I beg your pardon, Frau Wassermann – personally repeated your orders to me when she came to the cells.'

Wassermann frowned. 'My wife met Fouquet?'

Ulrich perceived that he might inadvertently have stepped into a trap. But he had no intention of sacrificing himself for Angela Wassermann. 'She insisted upon it, sir.'

'You were present at this meeting?'

'I was present at the first meeting, sir. Not at the others.'

'Others?'

'Your wife called upon Fouquet's cell quite regularly, sir. I could not prevent it. As she reminded me on more than one occasion, she was the governor-general's daughter, and could do whatever she wished. I could only beg her to do nothing rash.'

'And?'

'I do not know if she took my advice, sir. When I escorted Fouquet to the place of exchange, she appeared to be quite unharmed.'

'The place of exchange,' Wassermann said bitterly. 'All my work gone for nothing.'

'Ah . . . the exchange was insisted upon by General von Blintoft, in order to regain his daughter. Your wife.'

'Yes,' Wassermann said, getting a load of inflection into the word, intimating that in this personal matter Blintoft had been as incompetent as in the way he had tried to run the country. 'The point is that now the whole business will have to be done again. Are we still in contact with Matovic?'

'No, sir. Major Matovic, and several other Cetniks, were killed by the Partisans when they tried to support us at the exchange.'

'Damnation. What a foul-up.'

'With respect, sir, can we not now leave the destruction of the Partisans, and Davis and Fouquet, to the Wehrmacht? If they intend to carry Foca by force . . .'

'There is still no guarantee that they will take Davis and Fouquet. That pair have more lives than a couple of cats. And I doubt the Wehrmacht has the slightest idea how important they are, both to the Partisans and to us. No, we must be down there when the town falls. *You* must be down there, Ulrich.'

'Me, sir?'

'You. I would come if I could, but I am no longer capable of action. If you wish to advance, on my recommendation, you will have Davis and Fouquet kneeling on that floor begging for mercy.'

Ulrich gulped.

'So, in the first instance, you will go to Sarajevo.'

'Sarajevo,' Ulrich muttered.

His only memory of Sarajevo was of staggering back there, on foot, with the remnants of his command – and Angela von Blintoft, to be sure – after they had contemptuously been let go by the victorious Partisans.

'I will telephone the commander on the ground – General von Demmich, isn't it? – and inform him that the Gestapo has an interest in this business and that you wish personally to interrogate all prisoners that are taken when Foca falls. It would be most unfortunate were Davis or Fouquet to be shot or hanged before we can get hold of them.'

'It is a matter of sufficient men, sir. We are short-staffed as it is . . .'

'I understand that there is a Ustase unit based in Sarajevo. I will inform the general that you will be making use of them.'

'Ustase,' Ulrich said uneasily. The Ustase was a Croatian terrorist organization which officially aimed at securing the independence of their country from the Federation, if possible with an Italian prince as king, but which dealt in murder; one of their agents had carried out the assassination of King Alexander in 1934, a crime which had precipitated the series of events which had led up to the German invasion. Since then they had served under their new masters as executioners, carrying out a succession of brutal massacres of any group considered enemies to the Reich, regardless of age or sex. 'I would prefer not to employ them.'

'They are our allies, Ulrich. And they are useful.'

'Yes, Herr Colonel,' Ulrich said sadly. 'When should I leave?'

'I wish you to leave within the hour, Ulrich.'

'Who are you?' Angela Wassermann demanded. She stood in the entry hall of her new home, looking around with distaste. As a result of her previous residence in Belgrade she spoke sufficient Serbo-Croat to carry on a conversation.

The woman, tall and raw-boned, gave a slight bob, which might have been intended as a curtsey. 'I am Madame Bestic, your housekeeper, Frau Wassermann.'

Angela looked her up and down, her distaste evidently growing. 'It is not much of a house to keep.'

'This house belonged to a wealthy man before the war, madame.'

'And where is he now?'

'I do not know, madame.'

'Well, show me to my room.'

The housekeeper gestured at the stairs. 'If you will come this way, madame.'

Angela followed her up the stairs to a landing, and then up some more steps to a corridor, off which there opened several doors. 'This is the master bedroom.' Madame Bestic opened the first door, and Angela stepped past her into the room, which was surprisingly large. 'You'll see that the windows open on to the garden,' Madame Bestic said hopefully, as Angela's expression had not softened.

Angela went to the window, surveyed the overgrown lawn and the beds of weeds and dead flowers. 'That is a garden?'

'Well, it has been neglected over the winter. I am sure it can quickly be put right.'

'Then see that it is done. Now, where is my maid?'

'Madame?' Madame Bestic looked at the door, as if she expected to see someone standing there.

'My maid,' Angela repeated. 'Have you not provided one for me?'

'You mean an upstairs maid? She comes in every morning.'

'I mean a personal maid, you stupid woman.'

Madame Bestic decided not to take offence, even if she had a strong temptation to take this unpleasant young woman, place her across her knee, and give her a good thrashing. 'Ah . . . nothing was said of a personal maid, madame.'

'I would have thought it was obvious that I must have a personal maid. Obtain one, immediately. No, wait. When I was here last year, I had a maid. Her name was Rosa Malic. I had to let her go when I returned to Germany, as I did not expect to come back to Belgrade for some time. Now I wish to employ her again. Find her, and send her to me.'

'She will undoubtedly have found other employment, madame.'

'Then she will have to leave it. I have given you an order. Kindly see that it is carried out.'

'Very good, madame. Shall I have your bags sent up?'

'Not at the moment. You may close the door.'

Madame Bestic gave another of her brief bobs, and left the room. Angela took off her coat and hat, draped them over a chair, then tested the bed. Predictably, it was hard. She got up, took off her dress and kicked off her shoes, then lay down in her underwear. She closed her eyes, suppressing a desire to scream and scream and scream.

She had often had such a desire over the past six months, and from time to time had given in to it. What had she done to deserve such a horrible fate? Coming back here had awakened every memory, from the ecstatic to the dreadful.

When she had first arrived in Belgrade the previous October, it had been as a totally contented eighteen-year-old, protected at once by the loving care of her mother and by her father's rank and position. She had intended to enjoy herself. Belgrade was the city where her parents had honeymooned back in 1922, and she was being allowed to stay with them for a couple of months before she embarked upon the serious business of being a woman in Nazi Germany. And on her very first day, on virtually her very first footstep on Yugoslav soil, she had watched her mother shot down at her side.

The desire to enjoy had been replaced, instantly, by the desire to hate, and to avenge. And in her father's police chief she had found the very man to encourage her in her determination to bring her mother's killers to justice, a man who in addition had been handsome and dominating, the sort of man she had dreamed of all her life, the man she had willingly allowed to transform her from a girl into a woman, who had pandered to her irregular erotic tastes, a man to whom marriage had promised a lifetime of physical fulfilment. And then a man who had suddenly turned into a cripple, but who, for political reasons, she had still been forced to marry. One did not break off one's engagement to a national hero, certainly when one's father was in disgrace.

So what was left? With Wassermann only half a man, she could never be a mother. Actually, she had no wish to be a mother. She wanted love, and desire, and passion, not the time-consuming nuisance of rearing a child. The real tragedy was that she thought she had found those things, in the days

after the dreadful train crash but before she had been ordered
back to Germany with her wounded fiancé. Then she had
experienced passion, but it had been an utterly distasteful,
horrible passion, which had left her loathing all things masculine. And it had been followed by that dreadful fortnight
when she had been in the hands of the Partisans. She had
not known whether she would survive, whether someone
would thrust a pistol into the back of her neck and pull the
trigger, while always she had been at the cruel mercy of a
fearsome woman named Sasha Janitz. She would never forget
that coldly handsome face. Sasha had reduced her to the
level of an animal, and smiled as she had done it. That was
an experience she had never confessed to anyone, not even
Wassermann.

The love she had sought and thought she had found was
gone forever. What did she have left but hate?

She did not know how long she lay there. She fell asleep,
and awoke with a start when her bedroom door opened. As
there had been no knock, she knew immediately that it was
her husband.

'Exhausted, are we?' Wassermann asked, closing the door
behind him and leaning his stick against the wall.

Angela sat up. 'Bored.'

'So very quickly? We shall have to do something about
that.'

She caught her breath. 'No, Fritz. Please. I am not in the
mood.'

'Am I concerned with your moods, my dear?' He sat beside
her on the bed. 'Tell me about the woman Fouquet.'

Angela's head jerked back. 'Have you caught her again?'

'No. Nor are we likely to, now. You never told me that you
had visited her when she was in our cells.'

Angela shrugged. 'It was not important.'

'You visited her several times.'

'She . . . interested me.'

'She was part of the squad who murdered your mother. You

told me once that you wanted to hear her scream. Did you make her scream?'

'She does not scream easily. And you had left orders that she was not to be harmed.'

'So what did you do during these repeated visits?'

'We talked.'

He gazed at her so intently that she lowered her eyes. 'My wife,' he said at last. 'And a Partisan *woman*!'

'I did not mean it to happen. I wanted to make her scream. But she is so very lovely. So . . . poised. So in command of herself. And I thought you were dying.'

'And you actually think she returned your love?'

Angela sighed. 'No. I knew she did not. She sought only to survive. She would do anything to survive.'

'And she got what she wanted, thanks to you. She made a fool of you. Tell me, was the whole thing arranged? The train sabotage, followed by the exchange? You for her?'

Her eyes widened. 'Of course not.'

'But you were the only person who got out of that train and survived. Was that not part of the deal?'

'Deal?' Angela shouted. 'Do you know what *happened* to me?'

'I know what you *say* happened to you.'

'My God!'

Wassermann reached behind her to unfasten her brassiere and let it fall to the bed. Angela shuddered and tensed her muscles, for his caress was not in the least gentle, and she knew where it was going to lead.

'If,' he said, 'there were to be any suggestion of collusion between you and the Partisans, I would have to hand you over to the Gestapo.' He smiled, a frightening elongation of the tight lips. 'But I control the Gestapo here in Belgrade. I would have to hand you over to myself, for interrogation. Isn't that an attractive thought. And then, perhaps, even for execution. I should enjoy that.'

Angela was panting. 'You would not dare.'

'Do you think your father would intervene? Do you think that poor deflated windbag *could* intervene?'

'There was no collusion.' The low voice had risen into a wail.

He continued to stare at her for several seconds. Then he stood up, and she gasped in temporary relief. 'Do you know, my dear, I think I will believe you. For the moment. But I am still disgusted by the idea of your forming a ... *relationship* with a Partisan murderess.' He returned to the door and picked up his stick. 'You will have to be punished. You know what to do.'

Angela hesitated for a moment, almost as if considering resistance, then she rose and slid her knickers down her thighs, stepped out of them, and lay on her face across the bed, buttocks clenched, arms extended above her head so that her fingers could grasp the bedposts tightly. She heard him cross the floor and stand above her. 'Please don't hurt me, Fritz,' she begged. 'Please be easy.'

Wassermann swished his stick. 'But my dear, hurting you is all the pleasure I have left in life.'

Angela held her breath in anticipation of the first blow. Instead, she heard a grunt and then a moan. She released the bedposts and turned on to her side; her husband was slowly sinking to his knees, chin sunk on to his chest.

'Help me,' he whispered. 'For God's sake, help me.'

She knew he was in agony. The doctors in Berlin had warned him to avoid stress as much as possible; any tensing of his interior muscles could trigger excruciating pain in his still healing wounds.

She swung her legs out of the bed and he clutched them, resting his head on her thighs while gigantic shudders tore through his body. She stroked his head. 'Poor Fritz,' she said, looking past him to smile at herself in the wardrobe mirror. 'I am so sorry that you are in pain. But you know that I cannot help you. You will just have to be very brave, and bear it. Soon you will be well again.'

27

Two

The Women

'You understand the dangers?' Tony asked Sasha.
'Pish! Have I not been in and out of Sarajevo several times already?'

'Yes, but this time you are looking for specific information. You will have to ask questions, and the answers can only come from reasonably senior officers.'

'So it may take me a little longer than usual. I will take Jelena with me.'

'Eh?'

'She wants to come. And two are better than one.'

'But Jelena . . . well . . .'

'She will have to lie with men. This is something she wishes to do. Oh, she is a virgin. But it is a condition she is anxious to be rid of.'

Tony looked at Sandrine. Who gave a wicked smile. 'I would go myself, if the Germans had not plastered my picture all over the place.'

Tony tried another tack. 'Can she be trusted?'

'I would trust her with my life. I am doing that.'

'I meant, can she be trusted to go through with it, no matter what is involved. If she has never had a lover . . .'

'She will go through with it,' Sasha promised. 'I have taught her what to expect. I will be back in a week.'

'Well,' Anna Sabor said. 'I wondered when I would see you again.' She was a tall, forcefully handsome woman. Although

28

now past forty, her hair was still long and black, and she was still as much in demand as any of her girls. But she only serviced the very best, and charged double. 'And who is this?'

'Her name is Jelena Brolic,' Sasha explained. 'And she is my friend.'

Anna looked Jelena up and down. 'She is very young.'

'She is old enough.'

'Well, let's have a look at her.'

'Strip,' Sasha said.

Jelena looked at her, and then at Anna, and then around the small room in which Anna kept her desk and her files. The door was open, and from the rest of the house there were gentle sounds, all of them feminine. 'If she is afraid to undress in front of me,' Anna remarked, 'how will she get on with a man?'

'She is just shy,' Sasha said. 'Come along, Jelena. Madame Sabor only wishes to look at you.'

Slowly, cheeks pink, Jelena took off her blouse and then her shoes, then her pants and her drawers, and stood before the two women, hands hanging at her sides.

'Her tits are small,' Anna commented.

'She is only sixteen,' Sasha pointed out. 'Turn round, Jelena.' Jelena obeyed. 'She has a lovely ass,' Sasha pointed out. 'But more than that: she is a virgin.'

Anna pinched her lip. 'You are certain of this?'

'Yes, I am certain.'

'She needs a bath,' Anna pointed out.

'We both need a bath,' Sasha said. 'We have just walked thirty miles.'

By the time they had bathed, the house was stirring. Lunch was early in the brothel, as their doors were open for clients at two o'clock. But first there had to be a fitting. Sasha and Jelena's masculine Partisan clothing was set aside, and they tried on a variety of close-fitting long gowns, each with a deep décolletage and skirts slashed to above the knee. When attracting clients they wore no underclothes.

'When she grows a little she will be of some value,' Anna commented, walking round Jelena. 'You understand, as she is a virgin, I will auction her off the first time. At the present, it is the best she has to offer, lovely ass and all.'

'We understand,' Sasha agreed. Jelena rolled her eyes. 'But there is something we need to discuss,' Sasha said. 'Go and have lunch with the others, Jelena.'

'Remember,' Anna said. 'No garlic, and only one glass of wine. We cannot have you falling asleep on a client.' She closed the door. 'This time you want a cut.'

Sasha sat down. 'No. Our deal stands for her, too. Whatever we earn is yours.'

'She knows this?'

'She does what I tell her to do. No, this time I need something specific. I wish you to give me to someone important. A general.'

'Generals do not come here,' Anna pointed out. 'They send for girls when they wish them.'

'That would be better yet.'

'But it does not happen very often.'

'Well, in the meantime, a colonel, or at least a major.'

'Why is this?'

'There are things I need to find out.'

Anna took a turn around the room. 'You understand that this is very dangerous.'

'War is a dangerous business. And you are in less danger than almost anyone else. Men always need women, alive and healthy and without blemishes or inhibitions. Your house has the reputation of being the best in all Yugoslavia.'

'That is not to say they would not hang me if they found out I was letting Partisans use my house for spying.'

'How are they to find that out? You have not told any of your women who I am?'

'Of course I have not.'

'Well, then, it is our secret. Do I not earn you good money?'

'Of course you do. When you are not here, they are always asking for you.'

'What do you tell them?'

'That you are a married woman who can only come to me when her husband is away.'

Sasha smiled. 'I like that. So what is frightening you?'

'Three things. First, that girl. *She* knows who you are. She is one of you.'

'For that reason she is absolutely trustworthy. She worships the ground on which I walk. She would do anything for me.'

'I still think a secret shared by three people no longer exists as a secret.'

'And I tell you there is nothing to worry about. What are your other problems?'

'You say you wish something specific. That means you will not just be listening; you will be asking questions.'

'They won't know they are questions.'

'It would be a grave mistake for you to suppose that German officers are stupid. Have you ever met one?'

'Have I not been here several times?'

'I meant outside of the house. Someone who may not have been interested only in getting between your legs.'

'I met an SS captain once, very briefly. Now he was a complete blockhead.'

'No one can be a captain in the SS and be a complete blockhead. What was his name?'

'I think it was Ulrich. As I was pointing a gun at him at the time, he was anxious to leave.'

'You have not got a weapon with you now?'

'There is a pistol in my bag. But I don't intend to use it unless I have to.'

'Shit, shit, *shit!*' Anna complained. 'Don't you know that the Germans have made it a capital offence to possess a firearm?'

'I told you, I don't intend to use it. It is to protect us on the road to and from Foca, in case we encounter any Cetniks.'

Anna sighed. 'And I suppose your little friend has one as well. I feel as if I am already standing on the platform with the rope round my neck.'

'You have become a nervous wreck. Did you have another problem?'

'The worst one. Did you know that there is a Ustase group situated in the town?'

'Ustase, in Bosnia?' For the first time Sasha was concerned. 'What are they doing here?'

'They are everywhere. The Germans use them to support the Gestapo.'

'So? Why should they interfere with you? You operate under German auspices.'

'They are controlled by the SS. If they were ever to be turned loose upon us . . .'

'Is there an SS office in the town?'

'No.'

'Then there is absolutely nothing for you to worry about.'

'Then why have they come here at all?'

'I would say that they have come here to be on hand to follow the Germans into Foca – if they can capture the town.'

'Are the Germans going to attack Foca?'

'That is what I have come here to find out. Just let me get on with my business. I will earn you good money, and then I will leave you in peace.'

Anna sat beside her and put her arm round her shoulders. 'I love you, Sasha. I have loved you ever since I played with you as a little girl in Wicz, even though you were so much older. I would hate anything to happen to you. The thought of you in the hands of the Ustase turns my stomach.'

Sasha kissed her. 'Nothing is going to happen to me.'

By the early evening, the salon was crowded. In the main the clientele was composed of German officers, but there were a few businessmen as well, mainly Serbs who had made their peace with the invaders. Sasha and Jelena sat together with the other girls in a row along the wall while Anna and her two senior women circulated, talking, making sure all the men had a drink. Then Anna stood in the centre of the room and clapped her hands for attention.

'I have a treat for you tonight,' she announced. 'I have procured, at great expense, the services of this young lady . . .' She beckoned Jelena, who rose and went to join her.

Her cheeks were again pink, but she moved easily and gracefully. She wore a white gown, as befitted her status. The décolletage revealed the faintest of curves but the material clung to her thighs and bottom, and was sheer enough to reveal the outline of her vee. The men gathered round, and the bidding began.

Sasha was able to survey the room at her leisure. Several of the officers were above the rank of captain, and as they all wore uniform, she was able to study their insignia as well; her heartbeat quickened when the recognized the badges worn by one major as belonging to the Panzer corps. She had seen no tanks either in Sarajevo or on her approach, but if a squadron commander was in the town, his command had to be somewhere close, and panzers were neither defensive nor peace-keeping weapons.

Jelena was carried off, by a colonel, to great applause. Sasha watched them leave the room for the stairs to the bedrooms, Jelena giggling girlishly. Then she caught Anna's eye.

'Have you chosen?' Anna asked, coming over.

'That one.'

'He wants head. He has only been in Sarajevo a few days, but he has been here every night, and it is always head.'

'So tell him I give the best head in Yugoslavia.'

'Do you? I never knew that.'

'I never knew it either. I have never done it before. But I will please him.'

'You take too many risks,' Anna complained, but she went across the room and tucked her arm through the major's, bringing him back to where Sasha was now standing.

'Major Gruber, I would like you to meet Sasha,' Anna said.

Gruber obviously liked what he was looking at. Sasha's crimson gown showed off her heavy breasts and long legs to perfection, while her thigh-length silky black hair was always an attraction. Well, she reflected, he was not bad-looking himself, in a crisply Aryan manner. 'I have not seen you before,' he remarked in uncertain Serbo-Croat.

'Sasha is not always available,' Anna explained. 'But she is the best I have.'

Again Major Gruber looked her up and down. 'And she accepts specialities?'

'I deal in specialities, Herr Major,' Sasha said.

'She is the very best,' Anna repeated.

'Well, then . . .' Gruber freed himself from Anna. 'Will you drink?'

'Thank you.'

Gruber escorted her to the bar and the barman set two glasses of 'champagne' in front of them. 'What do you do when you are not available?' he asked casually.

'I look after my husband.'

He raised his eyebrows. 'He is a lucky man. You are a very beautiful woman.'

'You are very kind, sir.'

'But he lets you out now and then, is that it?'

'No, sir. He goes to Belgrade on business – now and then.'

'Ah.' He stretched out his hand, touched her throat with his forefinger, and slowly drew the finger down her flesh into the valley between her breasts. He was taking possession. 'And how long do these business trips take?'

Sasha shrugged, allowing the finger to move up and down. 'A few days. Sometimes a week.'

'It is possible that I might wish to see you again. Will you be available all of this week?'

'I might be. But I will come again. You will catch up with me.'

'There is no chance of that. I am only going to be here for the next fortnight.'

'You are returning to Germany?' Sasha asked innocently.

He studied her for several seconds. Then he said, 'I am leaving Sarajevo.'

'But you have only just come.'

'I am passing through.'

Sasha finished her drink. 'With all of your tanks?'

'How do you know I have anything to do with tanks?'

Sasha realized she had been too impetuous. 'You look like a panzer commander. You look so romantic.'

He held her hand and led her to the stairs. 'Let us find out if you are as good as you say you are.'

'So, when are you leaving us again?' Anna asked the next morning at breakfast when the other girls had left the room.

'I think we will stay another few days,' Sasha said.

Jelena stared at her with her mouth open.

'Did you not find out what you wanted?' Anna asked.

'Not enough. Besides, Hans wants me to stay.'

'You certainly seemed to please him. And will Jelena be staying, too?'

'Of course. She could not possibly make the journey back to Foca without me. I doubt she could find the way.'

Jelena knelt in a hot tub. Sasha undressed and stooped beside her. 'Have you douched?'

'Yes. It was horrible. And she gave me something to drink. It tasted foul.'

'Well, you really don't wish to get pregnant. Not by a German, anyway. And it is only for a few more days.'

'Why do we have to stay here for a few more days?' Jelena asked. 'Is it not very dangerous?'

'Sit down and I will wash your legs.'

'I do not wish to sit down. It is too painful.'

'Then stand up. We are staying a few more days because I

have not yet completed our task. There is no danger. We are protected by being in Anna's house. Why are you in such a hurry to leave?'

'That man beat me.'

'Some men do like beating women. And having paid so much for you, I suppose he wanted his money's worth.'

'It hurts. And then he made me . . . *suck* him. Ugh.'

'It's called giving head. You didn't refuse?'

'I bit him.'

Sasha was aghast. 'You *what*?'

'I didn't mean to,' Jelena protested. 'I didn't know anything about it. He pushed his prick into my mouth and told me, suck, suck. And when I tried to do so, he suddenly jerked, and my teeth must have touched his flesh.'

'My God! What did he do?'

'He shouted, and cursed me, and then beat me again. My ass is raw.'

'Let me see it.'

Jelena turned round, and Sasha stroked her buttocks. 'It is certainly bruised. And cut. What did he use?'

'His belt. A great big heavy thing. And then he made me kneel, just like this.'

'It is the best way,' Sasha said.

'I felt as if he was tearing me apart. First with his hands and then with his prick. It was terrible. I screamed, so he beat me again.'

'It was painful because it was the first time, goose. Come out.'

Jelena obeyed, and Sasha wrapped her in a towel, massaging her dry.

'But if we stay here, won't I have to do it again?'

'You'll enjoy it more the next time. Do you mean you only had one trick last night? He kept you the whole night?'

'It was a long time. When he had climaxed he kept playing with me, hitting me, pulling my nipples, putting his fingers into my sex . . .' She shuddered. 'It was terrible. When he left me, I couldn't move. When Madame Anna came in, I begged her not to sell me again, and she agreed. She let me come to bed instead.'

'She has a soft heart,' Sasha agreed.

'Will I have to do it again?'

'We are here as whores, my dearest girl. We must *be* whores, for our own protection. As I said, it will be better from here on.' She dropped the towel and got into the bath herself. 'Wash me.'

Jelena knelt to obey. 'Did your trick not beat you?'

'No, because I did not bite him.'

'You sucked him?'

'Again and again and again. That was all he wanted. But he talked too. Now listen very carefully. Just in case something happens to me . . .'

'What is going to happen to you?' Jelena's voice rose in alarm.

'Nothing is going to happen to me. But just in case something does, you must get back to Foca and report to the colonel. Tell him that the Germans are concentrating a large force of both panzers and infantry to the west of Sarajevo. They are doing this slowly and in as much secrecy as possible. No one is allowed to approach their camp. They are putting out that the concentration is for manoeuvres, but it is actually to storm Foca. At the present time I think there are two tank brigades and four battalions of infantry. But more are coming in. The assault will not commence until the concentration is complete. I have not yet found out exactly when this will happen, but I know it will not be for another fortnight. I hope to find out more when next I go to Gruber. That is why we are staying a few days longer. Can you remember all of that?'

'I think so.'

'There is more. This is for the colonel and Sandrine, *alone*. Major Wassermann is back in Belgrade.'

'Major Wassermann?' Jelena's voice rose an octave. 'He arrested me once. Why has he come back?'

'Because he is again the commander of the SS in Yugoslavia – and also the Gestapo. Colonel Davis shot him and he was laid up for a long time, but now he has recovered, and has been promoted; he is a colonel himself now. He has come back to Yugoslavia, together with his wife.' His wife, Sasha thought. She had once had Angela von Blintoft as her prisoner. For two weeks she had been able to vent her spleen on the miserable German girl. She had enjoyed that, even if, in view of the impending exchange, she had been unable to mark her victim as she would have liked. Certainly, after such an ordeal, Sasha would never have expected her to dare return to Yugoslavia. Some people were just gluttons for punishment. But she was interested. While she knew that the Brolic family had been prisoners of the Gestapo for several weeks, she had not known that they had been arrested by Wassermann personally. 'Why did he arrest you?'

'He thought that Mama and Papa were involved in the shooting of Frau von Blintoft.'

'As they were. What did he do to you?'

'Nothing.'

Sasha raised her eyebrows. 'You were not tortured?'

Jelena shook her head. 'I was just locked up. But the guards . . .' She shuddered.

'They raped you? But you are a virgin. Or you were, until last night.'

'These were female guards.'

'Ah.' Sasha ruffled her hair. 'I bet you really enjoyed it. Anyway, you are very unlikely ever to see Wassermann again, as we are not going near Belgrade. But the colonel and Major Fouquet will wish to know this. They too are old enemies. Can you remember *that*?'

'I think so.'

'Be sure that you do. And when you go with a man this evening, remind yourself that you are doing it for Yugoslavia.'

Ulrich stepped down from the train on to the platform at

Sarajevo Central and was saluted by the waiting lieutenant.
'Heil Hitler!'

'Heil!' Ulrich said.

'There is a car waiting, sir.'

'Where am I staying?'

'At the officers' mess, sir. But the general hopes you will
dine with him tonight.'

'It will be my pleasure.' Ulrich accompanied him to the
waiting Mercedes while his orderly followed with their bags.
He surveyed the houses as they were driven away from the
station. He supposed that, however much he disliked the
place, Sarajevo was a very attractive town. Situated in the
narrow valley created by the Miljacka River at the foot of
Mount Trebevic, it retained many indications of the years of
Turkish rule, from the innumerable mosques to the archi-
tecture of many of the houses – despite the fact that it had
been burned by Prince Eugene of Savoy in 1697. After that,
the town had attracted a large number of Jewish immigrants,
but these had either moved on or been arrested since the
Nazi occupation.

It was also, of course, the place where the Archduke Franz
Ferdinand of Austria had been assassinated by Gavrilo Princep
in July 1914, thus starting the Great War. Without which there
would not have been this war, Ulrich thought sadly. He could
have been at home in Hamburg, investigating the odd murder
case and enjoying the company of his wife, the pleasures of
his garden, the good fellowship of his circle of friends. Instead
of hunting people from one end of this benighted country to
the other for the pleasure of his superior's vengeance.

At least, for the time being, it was a peaceful place.

He had a bath, and dressed for dinner. The other officers
using the club greeted him courteously enough when he
entered the bar, but always seemed to have somewhere to go
in a hurry. His black uniform was the only one of its kind in
the club, and no one wanted to be seen to be too chummy
with an officer in the SS. He was relieved when the car came

to take him to the house the general had appropriated for himself.

'Ah, Captain ... ?' General von Demmich was a large, heavy man with a red face and a bluff manner.

'Ulrich, Herr General.' The bastard, Ulrich thought. He would certainly have been informed of the name of the visiting policeman.

'Ulrich. Of course.' Demmich shook hands. 'All the way from Belgrade, eh? Meet Colonel Emmerich and Colonel Wolff.' Ulrich saluted and shook hands. 'And this is Captain Vorster, my adjutant. He will also be dining with us.' His inference was obvious; if he had to entertain one captain to dinner, he might as well have two.

Again Ulrich shook hands, feeling very much like a sheep in a gathering of lions. But then he reminded himself that in the eyes of these men, indeed of the whole world, he was the lion and they were the sheep. 'And this is Captain Kronic.' Demmich's tone was now definitely derogatory. 'Colonel Wassermann's message said that you wished to meet the local Ustase commander. He speaks German,' he added contemptuously.

The Croat, a small, dark man who wore a moustache, did not look the least concerned at the general's tone. 'My pleasure, Captain,' he said. 'I have long wished to work with the SS.'

An orderly presented a tray of brandies, and they toasted the Reich, then Demmich gestured them to chairs. 'Now tell me what the Gestapo wish of us in Sarajevo. Since I have been here this has been the most peaceful place in Yugoslavia.' He seemed to take the credit for this himself.

'You are to be congratulated, Herr General. We are interested in the proposed assault on the Partisan stronghold at Foca.'

'Attack on Foca? What attack on Foca?'

'There has been idle talk,' growled Colonel Wolff.

'It is the job of the police to know everything, Herr Colonel,' Ulrich said.

'Hm,' Demmich commented. 'Well, just supposing there were to be an assault on Foca, Captain, of what special interest is it to you?'

'There are certain people amongst the Partisans whose capture is very important to us. To the Reich.'

'You are thinking of this fellow Tito?'

'Him, certainly. But also one of his commanders, the Englishman Davis. And the woman Fouquet.'

'People for whom a reward has been issued, eh?'

'The reward is not important to us, sir. Whichever of your people captures any of those three will have the reward. We wish them for interrogation.'

'For the pleasure of hearing them scream for mercy, you mean, when your thugs get them into your cellars.'

Ulrich refused to be rattled. 'There is an ongoing inquiry, Herr General, into the murder of Frau von Blintoft. All the evidence we have been able to gather points to Davis and Fouquet. It is our business, our responsibility, to bring these assassins to justice.'

'Hm,' the general commented again. 'Well, Ulrich, you are welcome to accompany my people into Foca, if that is what you wish. Just be sure to keep your head down, eh? How many men have you brought with you?'

'Only my orderly, sir.'

Demmich raised his eyebrows.

'I will use the Ustase squad that is here in Sarajevo,' Ulrich explained, glancing at Kronic.

'I will be happy to assist, Herr Captain,' Kronic said.

Demmich snorted. 'You mean you intend to carry out a systematic murder of our prisoners. I will not have it.'

'I did not come here to murder anyone, Herr General. I came here to arrest certain people whose capture is of great importance to the Reich. For that I need the assistance of Captain Kronic and his men. But they will at all times be under my command. What you do with the rest of your prisoners is up to you.' Kronic nodded his agreement.

41

'Hm. Well, that is enough shop talk for one evening. We are here to enjoy ourselves, eh? Vorster, telephone Madame Anna and tell her that we require her six best girls this evening. You will send a car for them at ten o'clock. Tell her I wish her to be one of them. I like women with flesh on their bones.'

'Yes, Herr General.' The captain left the room.

'Girls?' Ulrich asked uneasily.

'Do you not feel like having a woman, Ulrich? I always feel like having a woman. We shall dine, and then we shall let our hair down, eh?' He gave a shout of laughter. 'No, no, we shall let *their* hair down! Drink up, man. Drink up.'

'With respect, Herr General, I would beg to be excused.'

'It is up the stairs and on the right.'

'I meant from the evening's entertainment, sir. It has been a long journey from Belgrade, and I—'

Demmich pointed. 'Captain Ulrich, you SS people are too stiff by far. In the wrong place, eh? Ha ha. I command you to enjoy yourself, just for a change.'

'Do you expect Major Gruber again tonight?' Sasha asked. Having been in constant demand since two o'clock, she had escaped the salon to have a quick bath, and was brushing her hair. Anna had followed her.

'Probably. But something more important has come up.'

'Nothing can be more important than Gruber. He knows what I have to find out.'

'I thought you were more interested in a general.'

Sasha put down her brush. 'There is a general coming here tonight?'

'No, no. I told you, our general does not come to us. But when he entertains, he wishes us to go to him. I have just had a telephone call from General von Demmich's adjutant saying that his car will pick up six of us at a quarter to ten.'

'Who is General von Demmich?'

'He arrived here about a month ago. He is the commander of all German forces in Bosnia.'

If the general had only arrived a month ago, he had to be in charge of the coming attack, Sasha thought. 'Then you must let me go. He will know even more than Gruber.'

'Certainly. But you will be careful.'

'I am always careful.'

'And you understand that this general's idea of entertainment is on the boisterous side.'

Sasha made a face. 'Don't tell me I have to be whipped?'

'No, no. It is we who will do the whipping.'

'Eh? You are coming too?'

'By special request. He likes me. But I will try to make sure he gets you. It should not be difficult, as he will never have seen you before.'

'And what do I have to suffer?'

'I said, it is they who like to suffer. At his last party, all the men stripped naked and went down on their hands and knees, and we had to ride them around the room, whipping their bare asses. This apparently puts them in the best shape for a prolonged fuck.'

'One day you must write your memoirs,' Sasha suggested. 'But the idea appeals to me. You must take me.'

'And the child?'

'Ah . . . no. It is best she stays here. She is not yet ready for the worst of men. She found her colonel of last night a little trying.'

'So she told me. She will have to get used to it.'

'I am sure she will,' Sasha said. She dressed and went downstairs, where she managed to catch up with Jelena in between tricks. 'Are you all right?'

Jelena grimaced. 'Are all men like this?'

'I do not know. I have only had two men outside of this brothel.'

'Your husbands?'

'Silly girl. I have never been married. One was my brother, when I was very young. The other was the colonel. *Our* colonel.'

Jelena stared at her with her mouth open, less concerned

about the confessed incest than Sasha's second claim. 'You have slept with Colonel Davis?'

'Several times.'

'But . . . is not Major Fouquet his woman?'

'Major Fouquet was away at the time.'

'But she knows?'

'Certainly.'

'And you are still friends?'

'We are grown women, not children. The sooner you become a grown woman as well, the better. Now listen, I am going out.'

'You cannot leave me here by myself.'

'You are not by yourself. You have all these other women to look after you. And I shall only be gone a couple of hours. But remember what I told you. I hope that we will be able to leave here tomorrow morning. But if by any chance I cannot, you know what you have to do.'

Jelena nodded, slowly. 'Do not fail me in this,' Sasha said. 'Or I will never speak to you again. Why, Captain . . .' She smiled at the officer who had approached them. 'This is just the girl for you.'

The captain clicked his heels. 'I would prefer you, Fräulein.'

'But I am required by General von Demmich,' Sasha said roguishly, and kissed him on the cheek.

'Have you ever thought that people may remember you when the war is over, driving around in a general's car like this?' Sasha asked as she sat beside Anna in the back of the command car. With two of the girls also in the back, it was very crowded. The other two girls were in the front beside the driver. As they were following the street beside the river, the rushing water shrouded her voice; besides, she spoke in Bosnian, which the driver, from his stumbling Serbo-Croat greeting, obviously did not understand.

'When the war is over, Yugoslavia will be a permanent German province,' Anna said.

'That is if the Germans win. But suppose they lose?'

'How can they lose? They have the greatest army in the world. They hold all of Europe, except England and the Iberian Peninsula, and the conquest of Russia will be completed this summer. Who is going to beat them? America? America has its hands full with Japan. And anyway, America is not interested in what happens in Europe.'

'If you are so sure they are going to win,' Sasha argued, 'why are you helping me?'

'I allow you to use my house because you are my oldest friend. But I think you are crazy. If you would give up this stupid business and come in with me full-time, I would make you a wealthy woman. Listen, I will make you a partner.'

'I will think about it,' Sasha said. Now was not the time for a discussion of the future; they were pulling into the gate of the general's residence, and only the present mattered.

The car drove through extensive gardens, heavily patrolled by soldiers, and drew to a halt before the front steps; the two sentries presented arms. A young officer was waiting for them. 'Madame Anna.' He looked over the other women. Like Anna and Sasha, they were all in evening dress. 'I have not seen you before,' he said.

'She is the very best I have,' Anna explained. 'Sasha, this is Captain Vorster.'

Sasha simpered as the captain kissed her hand.

'I brought her especially for the general,' Anna said. 'I know he likes big tits.'

'I also like big tits,' Vorster said regretfully. 'But I can wait for the general to be satisfied. Come along.'

He led the way up the steps. The doors were open, attended by two footmen, and he led them into a wide, high-ceilinged entry hall.

'This used to belong to our president,' Anna whispered.

'I know,' Sasha said.

Now they could hear raised voices and loud laughter from

beyond the double doors to the drawing room. 'I am afraid the gentlemen are drunk,' Vorster said.

'Not too drunk, I hope,' Anna said.

Vorster grinned, and opened the door. 'Madame Anna,' he announced. 'And friends.'

The officers, having completed their meal, were sprawled on various chairs and settees, drinking brandy. Now they turned, and blinked at the six women framed in the doorway. For a moment no one moved, then Demmich stumbled to his feet. 'Anna! How good to see you.' He tripped and would have fallen had she not caught him. Her reward was a bear hug and a kiss on the mouth. 'And what have you got for us tonight?'

'Something very special, Herr General. This is Sasha.'

Demmich blinked at Sasha; her cleavage seemed to reach to her waist. 'But she is splendid. Splendid. I congratulate you.' He disengaged himself and half fell into Sasha's arms, his face for a moment lodging between her breasts. 'Splendid,' he said, struggling up to kiss her mouth as well. 'You and I must have a conversation. Gentlemen . . .' He swung round, turning Sasha as well, so that her back was to the room. 'Choose your partners. Enjoy yourselves.'

His hand was inside Sasha's gown now, clutching her breast and then sliding down towards her crotch. Anna blew her a kiss as she stepped past her, and Demmich swung round again, turning Sasha with him. 'A drink!' he announced. 'You shall have a drink.' He began half carrying her towards the sideboard. Sasha wondered if she would get anything worthwhile out of him, he was so drunk. Perhaps she would do better with one of the others. She looked left and right . . . and found herself staring at Hermann Ulrich.

Although she had only ever seen the SS captain once before in her life, and that had been six months ago, it had been an unforgettable occasion.

With Wassermann wounded, Ulrich had been in command of the German side of Sandrine's exchange for Angela von

Blintoft, just as, with Tony wounded, Sasha had been in command of the Partisan side. Thus they had faced each other as the exchange was about to be carried out. It had been the Germans who had turned it into a shooting match. But they had been out-gunned by the Partisans, Sasha's own regiment of women, despite the interference of the Cetniks. Caught in the middle, having lost his pistol, Ulrich could have expected only death as he had looked into her eyes. But Sandrine, standing beside him, had commanded her not to shoot. Apparently, Ulrich had been kind to her when she had been a prisoner of the Gestapo. Sasha had never learned the truth of that matter, because Sandrine would not speak of it. But she did not doubt that Ulrich remembered the occasion – so triumphant for her and the Partisans, so humiliating for him and the Gestapo – every bit as clearly as herself.

And here they were, again facing each other. The captain was obviously as drunk as the other officers, but he was blinking, trying to remember, as well as trying to stay on his feet. Sasha realized that she might have only a few minutes to live. 'Please,' she told the general. 'The bathroom. I must go to the bathroom.'

'Ha ha,' Demmich shouted. 'You wish to pee. I will come with you, and we will pee together. I love watching women pee.'

Still half carrying her, he headed for the door. But Ulrich had reached his feet. 'Stop!' he shouted. 'Herr General! Stop.'

Demmich looked over his shoulder. 'What the devil is the matter with you?'

Ulrich pointed. 'That woman. She is a Partisan. She is a captain in the Partisan army!'

Now Demmich goggled at Sasha, and she realized her time was up unless she acted very quickly and ruthlessly. She drove her elbow with all her considerable strength into the general's stomach. He gasped and let her go, and she stepped away from him. He recovered and clutched at her gown. The material ripped easily enough, and she stepped out of it; it would only have hampered her, in any event.

She ran at the doors, which had been closed. Vorster still stood there, for the moment confounded by the sight of a naked woman charging him. When she got up to him he raised his hands, but she used the unarmed combat skills Tony had taught her, and with a twist of her wrists she threw him to the floor, leaping over him and pulling the doors open. There was a footman in the hall, but he was as taken aback by her appearance as Vorster had been, and she was past him before he could react. Now she was at the foot of the stairs, but even in her dire condition her brain was still working with ice-cold clarity. Up there was a dead-end. She swerved past them, ran down the hall, and burst through the swing-doors into the kitchen.

Here there were several men, but they were, like all the others, astounded at the sight of her, and she was past them before they recovered, pushing one man hard against the still hot stove to bring forth a scream of pain. Then she was through the back door and into the darkness of the garden.

Ulrich had not really believed his eyes. Sasha's was a face he could never forget, but when last he had seen her she had been dressed like a man and carrying a sub-machine gun. That she should suddenly appear before him, beautifully clad and groomed, in the guise of a whore . . . He had initially supposed she was a brandy-induced vision – but a vision who, like the woman he remembered, dealt in extreme violence.

He staggered forward to help the general regain his balance while Vorster scrambled to his feet. The other officers had also risen, utterly bewildered. As were the women. They were looking at Anna, hoping to discover what she had got them into, while Anna was trying to look as bewildered as anyone.

'Fetch her back here,' Demmich commanded. 'Fetch her back! Vorster!'

'Yes, Herr General.' Vorster ran into the hall and began shouting.

'She hit me,' Demmich complained. 'The bitch hit me.'

Ulrich helped him to a chair. One of the other officers

brought a glass of brandy. 'You knew her,' Demmich said to Ulrich. It was almost an accusation. 'How did you know such a woman?'

'I encountered her once before, sir,' Ulrich said. 'She is under the command of the man Davis.'

'Davis,' Demmich muttered. Like every other officer in the army of occupation he had heard of the Englishman. His voice suddenly took on a note of anxiety. 'You think he is here?'

Tony's reputation as a ruthless killer of Germans was equally well known.

Ulrich looked at Anna. 'I think the madam will have to tell us that.'

'Me?' Anna asked. 'I know nothing of that woman.'

'She came here with you,' Ulrich pointed out.

'Yes, but . . .'

'Shut up.' Demmich heaved himself to his feet. Having been thoroughly frightened he was now thoroughly angry. 'You will explain this, Anna.'

Anna licked her lips, and was temporarily relieved by the return of Vorster.

'The woman has disappeared, Herr General,' he panted.

'Disappeared? This house is full of German soldiers. How could she have disappeared?'

'Well, sir, you see, she had no clothes, and the servants thought she was part of . . . well, whatever it is we were doing.'

'We were doing nothing except being tricked by these bitches. Lie down,' Demmich commanded. 'All of you.'

The women looked at Anna, but there was no help or advice coming from there; Anna was trembling. They dropped to their knees.

'On your bellies!' Demmich shouted.

They lay down.

'You too,' Demmich commanded.

Anna joined her women on the carpet.

'Pull your skirts up. Round your waists. I am going to beat the living daylights out of all of you.'

One of the girls burst into tears. Ulrich felt physically sick; he almost regretted having fingered the Partisan. 'With respect, Herr General,' he said, 'should we not concentrate upon finding the woman first?'

'My men will find her. But for these whores . . .'

'What instructions shall I give the men, Herr General?' Vorster asked.

'For God's sake, you idiot, find the woman. She has no clothes. And there is a curfew. Surely your people can find a naked woman where no woman is supposed to be? Find her!'

Vorster again hurried from the room.

'Now,' Demmich said, going to a stand by the door to select a stout walking stick.

Another of the women burst into tears as they lay in a row, naked backsides trembling.

'With respect, Herr General . . .' Ulrich said.

Demmich glared at him. 'What is it now?'

'Ah . . .' Ulrich looked at Kronic for support.

Kronic did not fail him, even if he misunderstood his motive for interfering. 'Captain Ulrich is correct, Herr General. This is a serious matter.'

'Do you suppose I don't know that? This is an affront to the Reich!'

'I mean, on more than a personal level, Herr General. This woman has clearly been using the brothel for the benefit of the Partisans. That she was here tonight may be of less importance than discovering what else she has been doing, and perhaps accomplishing.'

'And how do we do that?'

'That she has been able to use the brothel at all has to be because Madame Anna has permitted it. I think Madame Anna will be able to tell us a great deal about this Partisan.'

Demmich snapped his fingers. 'Yes. You are right, Kronic. You! Get up! Kneel!' Anna rose to her knees, shivering. 'Well?' Demmich demanded.

'I know nothing of her,' Anna gabbled. 'She came to me,

looking for work. Well, she is good-looking and healthy, so I hired her.'

Demmich looked at Kronic. 'Do you believe her?'

'No, Herr General. With your permission, I would like to take her to my headquarters for interrogation.'

'No!' Anna screamed. 'Please, Max, no!'

Demmich's head jerked at her use of his Christian name. 'Yes,' he said. 'Take the bitch. Beat it out of her.'

Kronic took a pair of handcuffs from his jacket pocket, pulled Anna's arms behind her back, and clipped her wrists together. Then he put his hands in her armpits and lifted her to her feet. Anna was now shaking from head to foot.

'You cannot permit this,' she said. 'He will destroy me!'

'If you knew what that woman was up to, you have destroyed yourself,' Demmich told her. 'Take her, Kronic.'

Kronic looked at Ulrich, who was trying desperately to decide which would be the more unpleasant scenario. 'And these other women, Herr General?'

'Oh, as they are here, we may as well enjoy them. But we shall beat them first. And . . .' He pointed at Anna. 'We will not pay for them.'

Ulrich made his decision. If he had to watch women being beaten, he preferred it to be one rather than four; besides, once they got out of this room he would be the senior officer, able to control events. 'I think it would be best if I accompanied Captain Kronic, Herr General. The madam may have information regarding the people I am after.'

Demmich waved his hand. 'Make her squeal, Ulrich. And now, gentlemen, which one shall we deal with first?'

Three

The Plan

Sasha knew she had only a few moments before there was a general alarm. Naked and unarmed, there was only one way out for her: she had to reach the river before the hunt began.

For a moment she was still bathed in the light from the open kitchen doorway, and behind her there were shouts, but these were mainly of confusion. She ran into the shelter of the trees and bushes – just in time, for as she did so one of the garden sentries, alerted by the racket, hurried up the path. He ran by without noticing her.

She crouched for a few seconds to get her breath back, and her blood chilled when she heard the barking of a dog. But the animal had not yet been loosed. She pushed through the bushes, ignoring the odd scratch, crossed another path, then tripped and plunged head first into a flower bed. This contained rose bushes, and a thorn ripped open her right forearm. She ignored the pain, regained her feet, which were now sore from the rough ground, parted some more bushes, and saw the river in front of her, faintly reflecting the lights of the city. The general's mansion was upstream of the quarter in which the brothel was situated, so she would be carried by the flood. If she could just reach it . . .

She tensed her muscles to cross the open circumference path, beyond which was a low fence before the water, and checked as another sentry appeared. His tommy-gun was slung on his shoulder, with a thumb hooked through the sling, and he also had a pistol on his belt as well as a bayonet on his left thigh. But he was walking slowly, as yet apparently unaware of what had happened at the house. In another few moments he would be gone. Sasha crouched in the bushes and willed herself to be patient . . . and then there was the wail of a siren and a number of floodlights came on, splashing through the darkness.

The sentry stopped, and turned, looking up at the distant lights. He was facing her, although he had not yet seen her. But now she heard the barking of several dogs, and she reckoned they had been loosed. She could wait no longer. Her fingers curled round a large stone, and she stood up and stepped on to the path, her hands at her sides. The soldier blinked at her in consternation but not alarm; perhaps, she thought, it had always been his dream to have a handsome naked woman suddenly appear to him out of the darkness.

Holding the stone, she swung her right hand and crashed it into the side of his unprotected face; with his helmet slung on his hip, he was wearing only a sidecap. Blood flew, and he gasped, and half turned away from her. Sasha stepped against him, plucked the bayonet from its scabbard, and drove it into his ribs. He gave a muted shriek, lost in the cacophony from above them, and fell to his knees, then on to his face, coughing blood.

Sasha knelt beside him. She would have liked to take the tommy-gun, but she felt it might hamper her in the water, so she unfastened his belt and passed it over her right shoulder before restrapping it beneath her left arm. It settled neatly between her breasts, although the holstered Luger and its attendant cartridge pouch weighed heavily on her back.

The barking of the dogs and the shouts of men were coming closer. Sasha climbed over the fence, dropped to the ground on the other side, and a moment later was in the water. The cold took her breath away, but she swam vigorously into the middle of the stream, where she was out of range of any shoreside lamps, and within a few minutes she was out of sight of the house and in comparative darkness. She passed under the bridge, and then moved towards the shore, clambered up the bank and crouched in the shadows, shivering. In front of her the street was deserted, thanks to the curfew, but she knew there would be German patrols. Yet Anna's house was only a block away.

She crept forward, standing in doorways whenever she heard any movement. A car passed her, its headlights scouring the street but not reaching her. Then she was at the house, and again climbed a fence to reach the back garden and kitchen door. This was unlocked, and she stepped inside, bringing a chorus of oohs from the women there.

'Sasha?' the head cook asked. 'Where are your clothes? And you are all wet. And that belt . . .'

'I am also very cold,' Sasha snapped. 'I need to get up to my room. Listen, give me your dress and apron. And cap.'

'Me?'

'Just do it.'

The cook undressed reluctantly. 'But what happened? Where is Madame Anna?'

'All hell has happened,' Sasha said. 'As for Madame Anna . . . I do not know where she is.' She had to assume that the Germans would almost certainly be coming here next, but she didn't want to excite the staff by suggesting that. She took off her gun belt and put on the borrowed dress. Then she restrapped the belt and put the apron over it, adding the cap to her wet hair. Her feet remained bare but she didn't intend to hang around long enough for anyone to notice that. 'I will leave these upstairs.'

'But what are we to do?' The cook looked incongruous in her underwear.

'Nothing. Act as normal. Pretend nothing has happened, and nothing *will* happen. At least to you.' If you are lucky, she thought.

Cautiously she stepped into the corridor. To her left was the bar and reception room, from which there came a great deal of noise. To her right the stairs led up to the bedrooms. The stairs were at present empty, but as she reached their foot a couple came down, one of the girls and a Yugoslav businessman. The girl looked at Sasha with her mouth open, and Sasha gave a hasty shake of the head. The businessman, still fondling his partner, did not appear to notice her at all. A moment later she was in her room, stripping off her borrowed clothing and towelling her hair dry; the rest of her had already dried, leaving her cold and clammy. She would dearly have liked a hot bath, but she knew that she was still operating very much on borrowed time. The sensible – and most responsible – thing for her to do would be to get out now. But she would not abandon Jelena, so she put on a long gown and went downstairs.

Major Gruber was at the bar. 'Why, Sasha,' he shouted. 'I was told you were not available tonight.'

'I am always available for you, Hans,' she assured him, her gaze sweeping the room. Damnation, she thought: Jelena was not there. She had deliberately not gone straight to the girl's room, because if Jelena was there she would be entertaining a client. But she really could not waste any more time.

'Have a drink,' Gruber said, 'and then we will go upstairs.'

Sasha did some very quick calculating. She did not have a watch, but she knew it had to be very nearly an hour since she had fled the palace. Everything depended on how long the general's people spent searching for her, and how soon Anna would tell them exactly what she had been doing – and what Jelena was doing as well. She would not in any way blame her oldest friend for doing that; it could not be considered an act of betrayal, for if she did not talk they would make her suffer – that concept made Sasha's skin crawl. But either way, there could only be minutes left, both to get rid of this rather charming man and to locate and extract Jelena. 'I would rather have my drink after we have had sex,' she said.

'Ha ha!' he said. 'That is how I like my women to speak.

Come along, then.' He held her hand to climb the stairs. They had reached the upper corridor when two of the bedroom doors opened at once. One of the girls and her partner emerged from the first, Jelena and her man from the second.

'Sasha!' Jelena cried. 'I thought you were with the general?'

Sasha bit her lip. Nothing was going well. In the presence of three German officers she could not convey anything to her protégée, not even to warn her not to take on another john for the next fifteen minutes. So she merely said, 'I am home, as you see,' and walked on.

'General?' Gruber asked. 'You were with the general tonight?'

Sasha opened her door. 'Briefly,' she said. 'He did not like me.'

'Demmich?' Gruber gave a shout of laughter. 'I always knew he was short a few marbles. All in the wrong places.' He closed the door behind himself. 'And now, dear Sasha, my good boy has dreamed all day of the touch of your sweet lips.'

'Then we must not keep him waiting,' Sasha said, and pushed him on to the bed, bending over him to open his tunic and release his breeches.

'He is not in that much of a hurry,' Gruber said. 'I wish to feel you, kiss you, experience you again.' Because he liked oral sex at both ends.

'As you wish, sir,' she said, and turned away from him to release her dress and let it slide down her thighs to the floor. With her back to him, she faced the dressing table, on which the Luger she had taken from the sentry lay concealed beneath her shoulder bag. She stepped forward, away from the bed, while Gruber sighed with contented anticipation. She remembered that he usually closed his eyes at moments like this, and picked up the gun before turning to face him again.

Her knees brushed his leg, which dangled over the edge of the bed, and he opened his eyes, for a moment not registering, then widening as he saw the gun. 'Sasha?' He sat up.

'Lie down,' she commanded.

'Have you gone mad? Do you know how to fire that thing?'

'Yes. Down, Herr Major.'

'Do you know what they will do to you? What *I* will do to you?'

'If you ever have the opportunity, yes.' She levelled the gun.

He licked his lips. 'You cannot fire that in here. The noise will bring the entire house up.'

'That will be of no assistance to you if you are dead. I told you to lie down.'

Slowly Gruber sank back on to the mattress. 'But why? Have I not been kind to you?'

'Yes. That is why I am sparing your life. Roll over.'

Gruber hesitated a last time, then turned on to his face. Sasha stepped up alongside him, reversed the pistol to grasp the barrel, and crashed the butt down on to the back of his head. Blood flew and his entire body jerked before subsiding. She wondered if she had indeed killed him; she had not meant to, but in any event she could not wait to find out.

She laid down the pistol for the moment, pulled on her dress, and hurried along the corridor to the stairs. But she had only reached the top when there was a crash from below her, which she recognized as the front doors being violently thrown open. There was a chorus of screams from the women and exclamations from the men, then a voice shouted, 'Hands up, all of you! Not you, gentlemen. Please stand away from the whores. Against the wall.' More exclamations and a shuffling of feet. Sasha remained still, biting her lip, and knowing utter despair. She was too late – by a matter of seconds.

'Now,' the voice said. 'We have come here to arrest two of you. Their names are Sasha Janitz and Jelena Brolic. Stand out, those two.' If the soldiers knew their full names, then Anna had told them everything they wanted. And Jelena was lost. Sasha could either die with her or escape and hope to avenge her. One day. 'Very well,' the voice said. 'If you do not hand them over, we will shoot you, one by one.'

'Her!' a woman shouted. 'This is the woman Brolic.'
Jelena screamed.

Sasha had an overwhelming urge to run back to the bedroom,
seize both pistols – her own was also a Luger – and run down
the stairs, firing left and right. But she knew that the soldiers
would be armed with sub-machine guns, and no matter how
many she managed to hit, she would herself be killed, no
doubt along with several others. That would help neither her
nor Jelena, and it would be a total dereliction of duty. If only
she had done as Jelena wished, and left yesterday . . .

She gathered her skirt and ran back along the corridor to
her room. At least only the kitchen staff and one or two of
the girls besides Jelena knew that she had returned. She had
a few minutes. She dropped her dress on the floor and put on
her Partisan uniform. For a moment she contemplated hitting
Gruber again; he was groaning and stirring. Instead she slung
her shoulder bag with both pistols in it, opened the window,
and was checked by a shout; it had not occurred to her that
the house might have been surrounded.

She let go and dropped. It was only about ten feet to the
ground, but the jar had her staggering, and she watched a
soldier running towards her across the back yard. He was
waving his arms rather than his gun; recognizing her as a
woman – her hair was loose and fluttering – he had probably assumed she was one of the inmates trying to escape.
But there was nothing for it now. Sasha drew one of her
guns and shot him through the chest. He fell backwards with
a scream. The sound of the shot brought more shouts and
the blast of a whistle, but she paused long enough to snatch
his tommy-gun before running for the back fence. Someone
shouted at her to stop, and she did so, long enough to send
a burst in his direction. He also went down with a shriek,
and then she was over the fence and into the gloom of the
city.

*   *   *

'Come on, come on,' Draga Dissilivic shouted. 'Get those feet moving.'

The women ran, or stumbled, down the rough road leading from the mountain into Foca; they were already exhausted from their run up the hillside, but they responded well enough. This was partly because they feared Draga's wrath; the captain was tall and powerfully built and exuded an almost masculine aggression. But it was also because they were accompanied on their run by their two commanding officers, Colonel Davis and Major Fouquet, legendary figures who had seen more action than the rest of the regiment put together, and who had more than once survived situations indicative of imminent death.

Sandrine panted as she matched Tony stride for stride. She was proud of her fitness, of her ability to equal her lover at almost everything. And she was the first of them to see the tattered figure staggering out of the bushes. 'Sasha!' she gasped.

'Sasha?' Tony waved his arm. 'Take over, Captain Dissilivic.' The women trotted by, casting curious and concerned glances at their senior captain, so clearly far more exhausted and dishevelled than they. 'My God! Sasha!' Tony ran to her, and she fell into his arms. He sat her on the ground.

Sandrine stood above them, staring at the blood on Sasha's clothes. 'Are you wounded?'

Sasha shook her head. 'Some scratches. I am exhausted. But I had to come straight to you.'

'Is Jelena all right?'

Sasha shuddered. 'Jelena is in the hands of the Gestapo. All my friends are in the hands of the Gestapo.'

'But . . . were you betrayed?'

'Yes,' Sasha said fiercely. 'They were betrayed. I betrayed them.'

Sandrine and Tony looked at each other in consternation. 'You?' Tony asked. 'I don't understand.'

'It was that man, that SS captain,' Sasha said.

'Ulrich?' Sandrine asked. 'You have seen Ulrich?'

Sasha told them the events of that dreadful evening.

'When did this happen?' Tony asked.

'Two nights ago. The whole country around Sarajevo is alive with soldiers. I could only move at night. I have not eaten for two days. I am starving.'

'Then you must eat, and rest.'

'Will you not shoot me for what I have done?'

Tony remembered that, with her division of life into strictly black and white, she had assumed he would shoot her on more than one occasion during the previous year's campaign, whenever she had not fully carried out his orders. 'Sasha,' he said. 'What happened is not your fault. It was sheer bad luck. I am sorry about Jelena.'

'Jelena,' she muttered. 'She was like a sister to me. And to think of her in the hands of the Gestapo . . .'

'Rest,' Sandrine advised. 'Come on into town. Come to our billet. You will feel better when you have eaten and rested. I will prepare a meal, and then you will sleep.'

Sasha caught her hand. 'You were in the hands of the Gestapo, for three weeks. You survived. How did you survive, Sandrine?'

Sandrine's mouth twisted, and she looked at Tony; she had no secrets from him. 'I survived because Wassermann wanted to have sex with me. But he was hit before he could do it. So I was left in the care of Ulrich. And Angela von Blintoft, to be sure. They both fell in love with me.'

'Wassermann,' Sasha muttered. 'Listen. When I was in Sarajevo, I learned that Wassermann is back.'

'Wassermann?' Tony asked. 'I thought he was crippled.'

'Perhaps, but he is back.'

'And his wife?' Sandrine asked softly.

'Oh, she is back, too.'

Again Sandrine looked at Tony. 'Belgrade is a long way away, sweetheart,' he reminded her.

'Listen,' Sasha said. 'I have just remembered. I have

important information for the general. What you sent me to find out. That is why I had to abandon Jelena. Otherwise I would have stayed and fought – and died – at her side. But I had to come.' Again her eyes filled with tears.

'You carried out your orders,' Tony told her. 'That is all any soldier can be expected to do. You are a heroine. Now, let's get you into town, and give you something to eat and drink, and then we will see the general.'

'Four battalions of infantry, and two Panzer regiments,' Tito mused. 'And you say there is more to come?'

'I think at least as many again, sir,' Sasha said. She had taken a hot bath and changed her clothing and had something to eat, and although still in need of sleep was again alert.

'Was there any time-scale for the arrival of the rest of the troops?'

'Approximately a fortnight, sir.'

'Very good. You have done well, Captain Janitz. I commend you. Dismissed.' Sasha saluted, glanced at Tony, who with Sandrine stood with the other assembled senior officers, and then left the room. 'So,' Tito said. 'They are paying us the compliment of assembling an army to defeat us.'

'Will we attack them, sir?' asked Major Ivanovic. Young and eager, he was always spoiling for a battle.

'No,' Tito said. 'They are already too strongly concentrated. If we are caught in the open by the panzers, we will be destroyed.'

'But when they come against us here, it is we who will do the destroying.'

'Not this time, Major. As I said, they are sending an army against us.'

'But they had an army at Uzice,' Ivanovic protested. 'And we fought them there.'

'And were defeated, as was inevitable.'

'But we pulled out successfully.'

'That is because we were able to do so. An evacuation in

the face of the enemy will not be possible here. Foca is more defensible than Uzice, certainly, but that is simply because the mountain prevents us from being attacked in the rear. Unfortunately, that impassable barrier also prevents us from retreating as an army. Any withdrawal from Foca has to be done now, otherwise we will find ourselves having to vacate the town under the guns and tanks of the enemy, in which event, as I have said, we will be destroyed.'

'Where will we go?' asked Colonel Astzalos. 'Back into Serbia?'

Tito shook his head. 'We are not strong enough to do that. We will go west, further into the mountains.'

His officers stared at him in consternation. 'But there is nothing there,' Astzalos said. 'There are no towns, no villages, no people . . . no food.'

'You are being pessimistic,' Tito remarked. 'There *are* villages. There are even towns scattered about.'

'But will they support us? When they see us fleeing through the mountains, they will know that we have been defeated.'

'We will have to convince them otherwise. Gentlemen, and ladies . . .' He smiled at Sandrine. 'We have no choice. I had hoped to launch a counterstrike, but they have been too quick for us, and they have managed to conceal their plans too well. That we have received a warning at all is thanks to that gallant woman. Now we must act. Prepare your people to move out.'

'And the people of Foca?' someone asked.

Tito sighed. 'It will be hard for them. Those who wish to can come with us, although they must understand that they will have to share our hardships. Those who do not wish to abandon their homes will have to make their peace with the Germans, convince them that we were here as an occupying power, and that they are happy to see the back of us.'

'There will still be reprisals.'

'I have said, it will be hard. War is hard. To have one's country occupied by an enemy is hard. Our business is to maintain the army in being so that when the opportunity arises we can strike back. That is our prime, our *only* duty to Yugoslavia, and to history.'

His officers shuffled their feet. He had addressed them in this vein before, and while the promised day of victory looked more remote than ever, they knew that he had certainly kept the army in being.

'Thank you, gentlemen,' Tito said. 'I repeat, muster your people and prepare to move out. Colonel Vladic, I put you in charge of closing the town. No one is to leave Foca without permission from me. The Germans must not learn either that we know their plans or that we are evacuating.'

'And the Cetniks?'

'I think that it would be best for you to treat any Cetniks you may encounter as enemies,' Tito said. 'Thank you, gentlemen. We begin to move tomorrow morning. Colonel Davis.'
Tony waited, as did Sandrine.

'This is a major crisis,' Tito said when the last of the officers had left the room. 'But it is also one that I have anticipated. It was clear that the Germans could not afford to leave us here in comparative comfort, especially in view of the successes we have had against them. But what Astzalos said was perfectly true. Our withdrawal may be a strategic necessity, but to our enemies, and even to neutral opinion, it will be a resounding defeat. Our disintegration will be regarded as a matter of time. Those opinions we can ignore. Only two matter. One is the British government. We have had no success in obtaining their recognition. They regard us as a disruptive element in the Yugoslav resistance movement. This point of view is obviously encouraged by Mihailovic's people. They also still hold us guilty of Frau von Blintoft's death, and now that of Major Curtis as well. I am not blaming your people, Tony. They can only make their judgements on the information they receive. I may say that I have discovered that even Moscow has been reporting some of our victories as Cetnik triumphs. That will come out, as you English say, in the wash. The important point is that we cannot hope to retrieve our position without British aid, at least in the matter of munitions. So, as I say, we cannot take offence; we must put up with it and persuade them that we are the only viable resistance fighting force in Yugoslavia.'

Tony nodded. 'I'll keep trying.'

'No,' Tito said. '*I* will keep trying. You have more important things to do – if you will accept the task.'

'Just name it.' He already had an idea what his commander was going to require of him.

'You will have to volunteer, because what I am going to ask of you will require a devotion to duty of the highest order. A devotion which, I am proud to say, you have revealed several times in the past. We have to convince the British, and the world, that what we claim is true. Moreover, we have to convince our own people. Morale is going to suffer during this retreat because, to the rank and file, that will be all we are doing, retreating. And it is going to be hard. There is little sustenance to be had in those mountains, and we must expect to be harried by the Luftwaffe as well as ground forces every inch of the way. Thus I need to leave someone behind. Someone who will command a picked force of volunteers, who will carry out active guerilla warfare against the German lines of communication, against the Germans themselves, someone who will hit and run and hit and run, and cause all possible harm to the enemy in as public a direction as possible.'

'Yes, sir.'

'You are willing to volunteer for this assignment?'

'Yes, sir.'

Tito looked at Sandrine. 'I also, sir.'

'You understand that you will be entirely on your own. I will not be able to give you any physical support, in either men or munitions.' He gave a grim smile. 'Or food. You will have to exist on whatever you can carry out of here – and you will have the pick of everything we possess – or what you can glean from the enemy.'

64

Tony nodded.

'And, of course, you face certain death if you are captured – after some unpleasantness first.'

Now both men looked at Sandrine. 'I do not believe that lightning ever strikes twice in the same place,' she said.

'Very good. How many people do you think you will need?'

Tony had already been considering that. While he wanted a strong squad, he was not required, and was not intending, to take on any large German unit in a pitched battle, so the size of his unit was dictated by their logistical situation and the necessity of having only the best. 'Twenty, apart from Sandrine and myself.'

Tito raised his eyebrows. 'That will be sufficient?'

'Perhaps not. But twenty devoted men' – he grinned at Sandrine – 'and women, will be more effective than fifty, one or two of whom may have doubts. Twenty also means that all of my people will have maximum firepower and, hopefully, sufficient to eat. It will certainly be easier to feed twenty than fifty.'

Tito nodded. 'That is clear thinking. You will recruit your people this afternoon. You will tell them that they are volunteering for a special, secret, and highly dangerous mission. You will not tell them what that mission is until you are ready to strike, and you will remain in Foca until the army has moved out. That way they, and any fifth columnists who happen to be in the town, will assume that you have remained behind to carry out various demolitions. Once the army has moved out, you will leave the town and commence your operations. I am not going to ask you what targets you intend to hit, or how you intend to do it. Yours is an entirely independent command. But your overall task is to maintain a position as close as possible behind the advancing Germans and do all you can to disrupt their communications, and, wherever possible, obtain propaganda successes. When you have assembled your team, you may then requisition whatever weapons and ammunition supplies that you think you will require.'

'Understood.'

Tito stood up and shook hands with both of them. 'I wish I could stay and fight with you. Sadly, I have taken on the responsibility of this command, and I will see that through. I regret very much that I may be sending you to your deaths, but I have chosen you because I believe that you are two of the most determined, the most experienced, and the most ruthless members of my army, and I wish you to know that whatever happens, your names will always be honoured in the annals of the Partisan army. Report to me tonight with your specifications.'

'So,' Sandrine said. 'Now we go out in a blaze of glory.'

'You don't have to.'

'You think I want to live without you?'

'Snap.'

'Bah,' she said. 'If I am killed, you would always have Sasha.'

'I don't think the Sasha I once had still exists.'

'Oh? I was going to suggest she join us. She is the best.'

'Agreed. And I am going to invite her to join us. What I meant was that although she was always fairly ruthless, I think that is her whole character now.'

'Then will she not be the more useful?'

'Again, agreed. But not in bed.'

'Of course I volunteer,' Sasha said. 'That is all I have left to do. Kill Germans.'

'Will any of your women join us?'

'Draga, certainly.'

Draga Dissilivic had accompanied them on their last secret mission, and had proved herself invaluable. 'I leave it to you to sound her out. Any others?'

'I will see. What do I tell them?'

'That we have been deputed to fight a rearguard action.'

'How many do you wish?'

66

'My total force is to be twenty, apart from Sandrine and myself. I want fourteen men. That leaves six women, including yourself.'

Sasha pulled her nose. 'You are going to fight a rearguard action against a German army with twenty people? I do not believe you.'

'You will believe me, Sasha, until I tell you something different.'

Sasha grinned. 'I will wait.'

Tony made the rounds of the various battalions all afternoon. Having fought with most of these men for the past year, he knew quite a few of them by name, as he also knew their capabilities. Some who would have volunteered had to be rejected because they simply weren't fit enough, either mentally or physically. Some others, who he would have liked to have along, declined. Fighting shoulder to shoulder was one thing; embarking on a suicide mission was another.

But he was delighted when Ivanovic appeared in the office he was using. For all his youth, the major had actually commanded the rearguard at Uzice, and knew all about desperate situations. 'I will be your second in command,' he declared.

'Correction. You will be my third in command.'

Ivanovic frowned at him. 'Who is coming that is senior to me?'

'Me,' Sandrine said.

'You? You are a woman!'

'She is my second in command, Major. Take it or leave it. A third of my command are going to be women, and they will be considered the equal of any man, because I know they *are* the equal of any man in combat.'

Ivanovic considered, and then grinned and shrugged. 'It should at least be an interesting campaign,' he said on his way out.

'Do you think he will make trouble?' Sandrine asked after the major had left.

'No one is going to make trouble,' Tony told her. 'We cannot afford discord.'

That night Tony reported to Tito. 'I have my squad, General.'

'Excellent. Equipment?'

'I have the list here. I wish every person in my command to be armed with a tommy-gun, with as much extra ammunition as can be spared, with a pistol, ditto, and with a long-bladed knife. I also wish three of our best sniper's rifles, with ammunition, and I wish every one of my command to be equipped with two strings of grenades. I will also require all the available gelignite and detonators. We will commence with a week's rations—'

'And when that is used up?'

'We will forage.'

'You will remember my orders, that it is essential we remain on good terms with the civilian population. Hopefully, we will come back this way one day, and we want to return to friends, not enemies. You had better requisition some of that store of gold coins we brought from the bank in Uzice so that you can pay for what you need, at least as long as possible. What about medical stores?'

'We will have our first-aid boxes.'

'I doubt that will be sufficient. You must accept that you will take casualties. You will require a stock of bandages, antiseptics and morphine.' He grinned. 'And brandy. Just remind your people that it is for medicinal purposes. You have also not mentioned a radio.'

'I am trying to avoid unnecessary encumbrances.'

'I regard a radio as a very necessary encumbrance. You must have one, to keep in touch with us.'

'Very good, sir. There is just one thing. You have placed me in command of this venture. I take it that means you have faith in my judgement.'

'I have more faith in your judgement, Tony, than in that of any other man in my command.'

'Thank you, sir. Then I must ask you not to expect any spectacular results, certainly in the first instance. We will need to reconnoitre the situation very carefully before we strike, and when we do strike, it is obvious that should we be successful, the enemy will not be in any hurry to publicize that fact. I will try to keep you up to date, but that may not always be possible.'

Tito nodded. 'I understand that. I have just said that I have entire confidence in your judgement.'

'Then there is one last point. How long is this operation to continue?'

'It will continue until you are completely out of munitions, or – we must face possible facts – you have lost too many personnel, either through death or capture, to remain a viable force, or the German pursuit of our people is called off, or I am able to inform you that we have found a safe base, at which time you will rejoin the army just as quickly as possible.'

'Have you any sort of a time-scale in mind? I may need this to maintain morale amongst my people.'

Tito indicated the map on his table. 'I am thinking of the town of Bihac. There. You see that it is situated on the far side of the mountains, where they debouch on to the Grmec Planina. It is remote enough from any German concentration, and it is difficult of access to armoured vehicles, certainly from the south and east. If we can establish a base there, we will be able to spend next winter recruiting, and hopefully re-arming. When you decide that you can do nothing more here, you will make for Bihac. You understand that I am telling you this in the strictest confidence: no one else knows of my plan, nor must they. That includes your own command, even Sandrine.'

Tony nodded.

'Now, as to time, Bihac is approximately two hundred and forty kilometres from Foca. I would hope to be able to re-establish a base within a couple of months. I cannot be more specific than that, but that is the time-scale you may give your people. Until then, I can only wish you good fortune and the success that should go with it.'

'Can we really survive for two months behind the enemy lines?' Sandrine asked as she snuggled against Tony in bed that night.

'You and I survived for two months in the very middle of the enemy. At Divitsar, last summer.'

She gave a little giggle. 'They didn't know we were there. This time . . .'

'We have to keep reminding them that we are there.'

He ran his fingers up and down her spine, as he knew she liked, and she gave a little gurgle of satisfaction. But she said, 'I will not let them take me again, Tony.'

'Was it so very bad?'

'In the beginning. You know it was Maric?'

Tony nodded.

'I did not know he had betrayed us that day in Belgrade. I thought he had died, gallantly, covering our retreat. When I saw him, alive and unharmed, I was overjoyed. I greeted him as a friend. And he and his people seized me and threw me to the ground.'

Tony held her close. She had not told him this before. 'Did he . . . ?'

'He was prevented by Matovic, who wanted to sell me to the Germans for the reward.'

'And that was worse.'

'No. Really, it was not bad at all. I think it was the apprehension of what *could* happen. Wassermann . . . he tried to rape me as well, you know. But he could not.'

Tony frowned into her hair. 'You mean because of his wound? He captured you before I shot him. And sadly, he seems to have made a full recovery, if he is back on duty.'

'I know. But he could not, even then.'

'You mean he is impotent?'

'I do not know. He did not look impotent. But he could not make it. He could not even enter me. He did not think he was impotent, except on a temporary basis. That is why he sent me off to Belgrade to be locked up until he returned from the campaign, with orders to Ulrich not to harm me in any way. He wanted to deal with me personally. But that harpy of a wife . . .' She shuddered. 'I could not let myself be captured again.'

He hugged her. 'And you will not be captured again. Just remember, as I said, that Belgrade is a very long way away.'

Next morning the army began its evacuation. Tony and Sandrine stood with their little group to watch them go. Tito shook hands with each of them. 'We will meet again,' he said. 'At which time your deeds will be honoured.'

The townspeople also lined the streets to watch the Partisans march out; only a few were going with them. Those that remained obviously had mixed emotions. Most of them were patriots. Had they not been, the Partisan force could not have existed in their midst for several months. At the same time, they had all known that with the Partisan presence, they were living on the slopes of a volcano, and this had been typified by the previous week's bombardment; there had been two more raids since, and the waterfront was still wrecked, several houses had been damaged, and there were too many fresh graves in the cemetery.

In that sense they were glad to see the fighting men and women depart. But now they were also aware of a very real fear of the future. The Germans were hardly going to look on them as friends. Thus they were now regarding Tony's group with some hostility. Like everyone else, and as Tito had intended, they assumed this desperate and heavily armed band had remained to blow up parts of the town as the enemy approached, and that could only bring immediate reprisals.

But there was nothing they could do about it, in view of the firepower possessed by the Partisans.

71

'Now,' Tony told his people. 'We stick together at all times, and this especially means right now. We will move out tonight, and take up a position in the hills overlooking Sarajevo. That way we will be able to monitor the German movements.'

'When do we attack?' asked Draga Dissilivic.

'Not until we have established the enemy intentions. We are hyenas, eh? We follow, and we scavenge, and we strike whenever it is possible to do so without endangering our purpose, which is to remain in being, as a thorn . . .' He grinned at them. 'Twenty-two thorns, in the flesh of the Wehrmacht.' Obeying Tito, he did not tell them that he had already chosen their first target, and intended to strike as soon as possible.

'They will come after us,' Corporal Davidovic said, 'as soon as they know of our presence.'

'Which will be as soon as they enter the town,' agreed Private Soejer.

'That is very true,' Tony said. 'But if they come after us instead of pursuing the army, then we have achieved a large part of our purpose. If they only send small squads to look for us, these will be easier to destroy. But they still will not know where to look for us. Nor do I believe they will be very interested in a group of twenty-two – until we start hitting them. So, ladies and gentlemen, let's allocate all this gear.'

PART TWO

THE TRAP

And fliers and pursuers
Were mingled in a mass.

Thomas Babington Macaulay

Four

The Conspiracy

On a Sunday morning in June the sun shone brightly and warmly. It should be a time for relaxation. Ulrich wished that it could be so.

Having been shown through the house by that formidable Madame Bestic, he stood on the edge of the freshly cut lawn – the remainder of the garden still suggested a jungle, although work had clearly been started on restoring it – nervously clearing his throat. Wassermann, wearing an open-necked shirt, trousers, and slippers, lounged in a deckchair, a drink on the table at his elbow, on which there was also a bottle of schnapps, an ice bucket, and several more glasses. Angela was wearing slacks and a loose blouse; she was kneeling by a flower bed, weeding. Both turned their heads at the intrusion.

'Ah, Ulrich!' Wassermann said. 'Welcome back. Have you heard the news?'

'What news, Herr Colonel?' Ulrich asked cautiously.

'From Prague. That Heydrich has been murdered.'

'I did hear a rumour, Herr Colonel.'

'It is not a rumour. It is fact.'

'But that is terrible, sir.'

'Yes. There is no crime to which these thugs who call themselves patriots will not stoop. At least in Prague they are being made an example of.'

'Sir?'

'As punishment, an entire village is to be wiped out. A place called Lidice. All the men are to be shot, the women and children sent to concentration camps. That should teach the swine a lesson.'

'Yes, sir,' Ulrich said, thanking God he had not been sent to Czechoslovakia.

'No doubt they will now allow us to use the same methods here,' Wassermann remarked. 'Now tell me, are all these reports true?'

'What reports, Herr Colonel?' Ulrich asked, more cautiously yet.

'Why, that Demmich has achieved a great, a *decisive* victory.'

'That is a matter of interpretation, Herr Colonel.'

Wassermann sat up. 'What do you mean? Is it not true that he has captured Foca? Destroyed the Partisan army?'

'The general has captured Foca, Herr Colonel. But he has not destroyed the Partisan army, because it was not there. The town was evacuated several days before we attacked. The Partisans apparently knew we were coming, even the day we were coming, and our strength. So they simply packed up and left.'

'Left? To go where?'

'They seem to be retreating into the mountains of western Bosnia. A pursuit is being mounted, of course, and the Luftwaffe has been called in to assist, but it is difficult country.'

Angela had stopped weeding. 'If it is difficult for our troops, will it not be equally difficult for the guerillas?'

'Oh, undoubtedly, Frau Wassermann. I merely meant to indicate that it may be some time before we can again bring them to a decisive encounter.'

'They slip through our fingers like water,' Wassermann grumbled. 'You say they knew we were coming? Well, that senseless bombardment will have told them that. But even the day? I thought this was to be a top-secret exercise. Has there been treachery?'

'I do not believe there was intentional treachery. But there can be no doubt that the Partisans have an elaborate spy system. They have been using a ... ah ...' – he gave Angela an embarrassed glance – 'a house of ill repute, as an intelligence-gathering centre. This has apparently been going on for some time, without anyone suspecting it. It would be going on still, had I not been there.'

'Then you are to be congratulated,' Wassermann said, and smiled. 'Did you find it necessary to visit this house yourself to ascertain what was happening?'

'Ah, no, Herr Colonel. It so happened that I was dining with General von Demmich and some other officers, and the general wished to be entertained after dinner. So' – another apologetic glance at Angela – 'he sent to this, ah, brothel, to request that six of the, ah, ladies be sent to his house.'

'And you indulged, Ulrich? A dry stick like you?'

Ulrich flushed. 'I had no intention of indulging, sir, as you put it. But I could not leave without offending the general. This was perhaps fortunate, as it turned out, for when the young ladies arrived ... You will not believe this, Frau Wassermann, but one of them was that Partisan commander who behaved so treacherously at the exchange.'

Angela had remained standing by the flower bed, apparently about to resume weeding. Now she came towards the men, stripping off her dirty gloves. Her face, as usual, revealed very little expression, but her eyes were glowing. 'You have captured Sasha Janitz? Where is she?'

'Well, you see, Frau Wassermann . . .'

Angela looked as if she would like to seize him by the throat. 'Where is she?' she shouted.

'Would someone kindly explain to me what this is all about?' Wassermann requested. 'You know *this* Partisan woman?' Not another one! his tone suggested.

'When I was their prisoner, she was my gaoler.' Angela's words were like drips of vitriol. 'For those two weeks she treated me like dirt. Worse than dirt. She made me clean the floor with my tongue. She said that was what the Nazis had done to the Jews in Vienna, and that I should learn to understand how they felt.'

'You did this?' Wassermann was amazed. 'You licked the floor with your tongue?'

'When I attempted to refuse, she whipped me. She stripped me naked, tied my arms above my head, and flogged me. If you have her, Captain Ulrich . . .'

'Unfortunately . . .'

'You let her get away?'

'*I* did not let her escape,' Ulrich protested.

'You will have to explain what happened,' Wassermann said mildly. 'You say this woman was one of a group of six introduced into the general's house? How many other officers were present?'

'Five, including the general.'

'And you recognized this woman. What did you do?'

'I called for her arrest.'

'You identified her and denounced her, in front of five other officers, and yet she got away? Was she armed?'

'Not at that moment, sir. In fact . . .' Another flush. 'Well, she was naked. But so violent. She simply burst through us, and got out of the house. Sadly, most of the officers were the worse for drink.'

'So she got out of the house. Are not the general's grounds patrolled?'

'Yes, sir. But she managed to reach the river. We believe one sentry tried to stop her, and she killed him.'

'Just like that? Is this woman a monster?'

'Yes,' Angela said. 'She is a monster.'

'But if she came with a bunch of whores, then she must have come from the brothel. Did she not return there?'

'Yes, sir. And we went there after her. But she escaped again. She killed two more soldiers and hurt Major Gruber so badly that he is in hospital.'

Angela sat down on a vacant deckchair, shoulders hunched.

'And, of course,' Wassermann said sarcastically, 'you have not captured Davis or Fouquet either.'

'No, sir. There was some talk that they remained behind in

Foca after the Partisan army left, but this is unconfirmed.'

'And the whorehouse?'

'Well, sir, I wished to close it down, but General von Demmich would not do so. It is apparently a very popular place with his officers.'

'What a way to fight a war! Are you telling me that you managed to arrest no one at all?'

'We did arrest the madam, the woman who runs the brothel. She was obviously in collusion with the Partisans. I mean, she must have known that this woman Janitz was one of them. In fact, she admitted this under interrogation, and confessed that she and Janitz had been friends as children.'

'Under interrogation?' Angela asked, her voice back to its normal softness.

Ulrich had forgotten how interested this ghastly young woman was in watching other people suffering. No doubt hearing about it was the next best thing. But he had no desire to humour her perverted tastes. 'I handed her over to the chief of the local Ustase. You told me to use them, Herr Colonel,' he reminded Wassermann.

'Yes, I did. Who was this commander?'

'A man named Kronic. He called himself a captain. If I may say so, sir, he is an unmitigated thug.'

'But does he know his job?'

'If you mean does he know how to ill-treat people, sir, yes. The whole business was utterly distasteful.'

'Oh, come now, Ulrich. You are an officer in the SS. Kindly act like one. You were present at this interrogation?'

'I felt it necessary that I should be, sir. I did not wish the Ustase to be in possession of any information we did not also have.'

'That was absolutely correct. So?'

'It was too horrible to repeat, sir.'

'Ulrich, your squeamishness does you no credit. Tell me.'

'Well, perhaps if Frau Wassermann were to withdraw . . .'

'I do not wish to withdraw, Captain,' Angela said.

'Well . . .' Ulrich licked his lips.

'Come along,' Wassermann said. 'You will not shock her, I assure you.'

Ulrich was sweating. 'This Kronic tied her to a table, naked, and poured petrol on to her . . . her pubic hair. Then he struck a match and said he would set it alight if she did not answer all of his questions.'

'The man has an original frame of mind,' Wassermann said. 'Although I would not have said the method is entirely satisfactory. I mean, it could only be used once.'

'Once was enough,' Ulrich muttered.

'You mean she actually defied him? So he set her alight? My God! What happened after that?'

'She screamed and screamed and screamed. So he put the flames out, and she told him.'

'What did she tell him?'

'Well, she identified this woman as a captain in the Partisans.'

'But as you had recognized her as such, you already knew that. So,' Wassermann said scathingly, 'you arrested this woman, and tortured her, and she told you absolutely nothing you did not already know. I cannot say that reveals a high level of competence. Where is this woman now?'

'Ah . . . she has been hanged.'

'What?'

'Oh, there was a trial, a very brief military affair, and she was condemned as a terrorist. I did not wish this to happen. I was going to bring her back here for further investigation. But General von Demmich insisted upon it. He was very angry. It appears that he had, well, been using this woman ever since his arrival in Sarajevo, and had formed the impression that she was loyal to the Reich, and to him in particular. He felt a sense of personal betrayal. I also suspect that he may have been concerned that further questioning, on a wider front, as it were, might have revealed some private weaknesses of his own, or even that it might come out that he had revealed classified information to her while' – another apologetic glance at Angela – 'in the throes of passion.'

'This has been the most utter foul-up,' Wassermann commented. 'We have made absolutely no progress towards either destroying the Partisans or bringing Davis and Fouquet to justice.'

'I did make one other arrest,' Ulrich ventured. 'Thanks to the information that woman gave us.'

'Some other whore?' Wassermann asked contemptuously.

'She was pretending to be a whore, certainly, sir. But she is actually a Partisan. She was Janitz's partner, who failed to escape from the brothel.'

'Well, that is at least positive. *She* may be able to tell us something worthwhile. Have you questioned her?'

'Only briefly, sir. I thought you would be interested in doing this yourself.'

'Is she good-looking?'

'I would say she is good-looking, sir. But it was not her appearance that interested me. It was her name. Jelena Brolic.'

'Brolic?' Angela awoke from her reverie with a start.

'Brolic,' Wassermann said thoughtfully. 'There is something familiar about that name.'

'Brolic,' Angela said again.

'Yes,' Ulrich said. 'You may remember' – this time his glance at Angela was anxious – 'that the murder of Frau von Blintoft was carried out from an attic window in the house belonging to Josef Brolic, a dry goods merchant. His complicity was obvious, so we arrested his entire family – well, all that we could get hold of. This girl was his daughter.'

Wassermann snapped his fingers. 'I remember. An overweight child of about fifteen.'

'She is now sixteen, sir, and has lost her excess weight.'

'How the devil did she get from our cells into the Partisan army?'

'Well, sir, the entire family was part of the exchange set up by General von Blintoft,' Ulrich said, then hastily added, 'to regain possession of Fräulein Angela . . . Frau Wassermann.'

Wassermann glanced at his wife, his expression indicating that that had to be another example of her father's incompetence. 'I shall enjoy interrogating her. Have her prepared for me tomorrow morning.'

'Brolic,' Angela said again. 'Jelena Brolic. Was there not a brother?'

'There were two brothers. One was arrested and later exchanged along with his parents. You may remember them.'

'I saw them,' Angela said. 'Briefly. I am speaking of the other brother. The older one.'

'Ah. He escaped before he could be arrested, and joined the Partisans. Presumably they are both still with them.'

'No,' Angela said. 'Did you say that the girl was Janitz's partner in this spying business?'

'In more than that. The woman Sabor told us that the two were almost like sisters. That is why I feel that what she has to tell us may be useful, even if it is only about conditions in the Partisan camp.'

'Sisters,' Angela muttered, and turned to Wassermann. 'Fritz . . .'

Wassermann held up his hand; they could hear the telephone ringing inside the house. 'A policeman's work is never done. Yes, Bestic, what is it?'

'It is a call for you, Herr Colonel,' the housekeeper said. 'From Sarajevo. General von Demmich.'

Angela watched her husband limp into the house. 'You had better sit down, Captain,' she invited. 'Help yourself to a drink.'

'I am on duty, Frau Wassermann.'

'No one is on duty on a Sunday morning,' Angela pointed out.

'Well . . .' Ulrich poured himself a schnapps, and took a seat on a deckchair.

They sat in silence for some minutes, both trying, unsuc-
cessfully, to overhear what might be being said in the house.

'He'll get over his disappointment,' Angela said at last,
observing Ulrich's apprehension. 'Certainly when he hears
what I have to tell him.'

'Ah . . .' Ulrich turned his head as Wassermann reappeared,
and swallowed. Angela also tensed; it was obvious that whatever the telephone message had been, it was not good news.

'So,' Wassermann said, standing above them. 'Tito's men
all fled without a fight, eh? There is no news of Davis and
Fouquet, eh? I am surrounded by fools.'

'What has happened?' Angela asked. Ulrich did not dare
open his mouth.

'That was General von Demmich on the phone,'
Wassermann said. 'A very angry General von Demmich. At
four o'clock this morning, the railway track from Belgrade to
Sarajevo was destroyed by an explosion, just as the overnight
train was passing. The train was derailed. It was carrying several companies of soldiers, as well as a cargo of weapons and
ammunition. The derailed train was then attacked by a large
number of people armed with automatic weapons and hand
grenades – at least a hundred, it is estimated – and our people
were shot up while the supply wagon was raided and looted.
What these bandits could not carry away was then blown up
in a separate explosion.'

'You think they were Partisans?' Angela asked.

'Of course they were Partisans, you stupid bitch!'
Wassermann shouted. 'What is more, they were commanded
by Davis and Fouquet. You said some of the bandits were supposedly left behind, Ulrich. You were damned right. This is a
picked squad. A hundred men and women, led by the two
most dangerous people in the country!'

'Ah . . . we have positive information on this, Herr Colonel?'
Ulrich ventured.

'Yes, the information is positive. They were recognized by
one of the surviving officers, who had seen their wanted

posters. And with them, sharing the command, was a tall woman with black hair who was shooting everyone in sight. Now, who do you suppose that was? General von Demmich has no doubt at all that it was the woman Janitz.'

Ulrich bit his lip. 'Sasha Janitz,' Angela said in a low voice.

'The general is convinced of it. He wants something done about it. Do you know what he wants? He wants me, *me*, in Sarajevo, to find and destroy these vermin. I told him that I was no longer considered fit for active service, and he would not accept it. So I am to go to Sarajevo. I'm sure you will like Sarajevo, my darling.'

'Me?' Angela cried.

'Do you think I would leave you behind? To get off with another prisoner? Another *female* prisoner? This girl Brolic? No, you will not do that. I intend to settle her ass before we go.'

'Listen . . .' Angela said urgently.

'No protests. I have made up my mind.'

'I will be proud to look after Belgrade for you, sir,' Ulrich said, again profoundly embarrassed, this time by their exchange on so intimate and, to him, unimaginable a subject.

'You? Oh, no, no, no. You are coming as well. Halbstadt can mind Belgrade. You got us into this mess, Ulrich, and you are going to get us back out.'

'But how?' Ulrich's voice was almost a squeak. 'In those mountains, surrounded by their friends, a small group of Partisans will be almost impossible to find.'

'I am sure you will think of something.'

'I know how they can be found, and how they can be destroyed, too,' Angela said.

Both men looked at her, Wassermann impatiently, Ulrich hopefully.

'That girl,' Angela said. 'Jelena Brolic. She is the key.'

'That is nonsense. According to Ulrich, she was taken a fortnight before the attack on Foca. She can have known nothing about any large-scale guerilla activity. Is that not correct, Ulrich?'

'That is correct, Herr Colonel.'

'You don't understand,' Angela said. 'Just shut up and listen.' Now both men goggled at her; she did not usually address her husband so brusquely. 'Let me ask you something first, Captain Ulrich,' she said. 'You have told us that this woman you executed told you that Brolic and Janitz were like sisters. Do you believe she was telling the truth?'

'I have no doubt of it. She was in agony, and she was ter- rified that Kronic would burn her again. She did not realize that she was going to be hanged anyway.'

'And they were really close?'

'She said that Brolic was a virgin, brought to the brothel by Janitz. That Brolic did everything Janitz told her to, was only happy when in her company. She said they were more like lovers than officer and subordinate. I have spoken to the girl on this matter also, while we were returning here. She would not admit that they had been lovers. Instead she told me that Janitz was so upset by what had happened to the Brolic family, including her older brother, who was killed in action fighting with the Partisans, that she took her under her special protection and has looked after her ever since.'

Angela's nostrils flared in that so well remembered manner. 'That is what I wanted to hear.'

'That does not sound like the destructive monster this woman has been described as being,' Wassermann remarked.

'Even destructive monsters need to love and be loved,' Angela pointed out. Wassermann flushed. 'Now listen,' his wife said. 'You remember that when that train was blown up last November, and I tried to get out—'

'Leaving me behind,' Wassermann said bitterly.

'That was lucky for you. If I had got you out you would have been killed. I was captured by the Partisans, and raped.'

Wassermann snorted.

'I know you don't believe me, but it is true. I was raped, and the man was going to murder me. That man was named Brolic. This girl's older brother.'

'How can you possibly know that? You engaged him in conversation while he was raping you?'

'He told me who he was, yes, while he was raping me, because he knew who *I* was. He told me he was going to kill me because my father had murdered his parents. He did not know they were actually alive and in your cells.'

'So you would like to torture this girl personally. Very well. You can be there.'

'I have no interest in this girl, personally,' Angela lied. 'But like you, I wish to get Davis and Fouquet, and this Janitz. Especially Janitz. Don't you see? The terrorists wanted me alive and unharmed so that I could be exchanged for Fouquet. Davis commanded that attack, with Janitz as his second in command. But he was wounded, so she took over. And when she saw what Brolic had done and was intending to do, she shot him.'

Both men stared at her. 'And you think this girl knows that?' Ulrich asked.

'I am positive that she does *not* know it. You know what the Serbs are like. They regard it as a sacred duty to avenge the death of their loved ones, and when it is an older brother . . . and when, in addition, this Jelena realizes that for the last six months she has allowed herself to fall in love with his murderess, she will not rest until she has avenged both him and herself.'

Wassermann stroked his chin.

'What is more,' Angela went on, 'her hatred will extend to Davis and Fouquet as well, because but for them the train would never have been blown up, nor her brother killed.'

'So, you think she could be persuaded to return, rejoin the Partisans, and kill them? That is a tall order. She is a sixteen-year-old girl. And they are probably the three most dangerous people in Yugoslavia.'

'I think she can be persuaded to cooperate with us to bring about their destruction. If you set her loose with information on a very tempting target which they will be unable to resist attacking, and it is a trap, well then . . .'

Wassermann looked at Ulrich.

'It could work,' Ulrich said. 'It will have to be a very tempting target.'

Wassermann looked from face to face, and then gave a shout of laughter. 'You think they would go for it? For me?'

'With respect, Herr Colonel, I would say that you must be the most hated man in Yugoslavia. As well as the most feared.'

Again Wassermann looked from one to the other; he had no doubt at all that neither of them would shed a tear were he to die. In fact, they might both be very happy were that to happen. Because, quite apart from the fact that they both hated him, in the period between his wound and the train wreck, this pair seemed to have worked very closely together, with Angela paying regular visits to Gestapo Headquarters, ostensibly to see Fouquet, but who knew what else she had gone there to do? He found it quite unacceptable that his wife would have had an affair with this tremulous little twerp. But knowing Angela as well as he did, he knew that when she got herself worked up she would have sex with anything. It would, of course, be a mistake to let them know his suspicions. Better to let them hang themselves. Besides, it would be interesting to discover just how far they intended to go, so he said, 'It would have to be very carefully prepared.'

'It shall be,' Angela said. 'Tell me about this girl, Captain Ulrich. Is she intelligent?'

'I would say so.'

'Educated?'

'She went to school here in Belgrade, and she is well spoken.'

'Was she tortured when you had her in your cells?'

'Ah . . . not seriously. We were under orders from your father, Frau Wassermann, that she should be unharmed when she appeared in court as a witness against the people who murdered your mother.'

'You mean against Davis and Fouquet.'

'Well, this has never been proved. Our investigations led

us to believe that the shot was fired by someone else. The man Kostic, who is now dead.'

'I know this is what they claim. But they were *there*; anyone who was there is equally guilty. What do you mean when you say that she was not seriously tortured? Is it possible to torture someone unseriously?'

'She was not tortured at all. That is, she was never placed under interrogation. She may have been beaten from time to time. You know what those guards are like.'

'They are harpies,' Angela commented with feeling. 'Did they abuse her?'

'I have no idea. She never complained of it.'

'Because she knew that if she did she would just receive more beatings. But you say she had never known a man when Janitz made her go to the brothel?'

'That is what the woman Sabor told me, yes. And I do not think it is true to say that Janitz forced her into the brothel. She went of her own free will, simply to be with Janitz.'

'Again, that is what this madam told you.'

'I have seen or heard nothing to make me believe it is not true.'

'As you say. Very well. I wish this girl brought to me, here.'

'Eh?' Wassermann frowned.

'It would be better here than in those dreadful cells.'

'This woman is a Partisan. A trained killer.' Wassermann looked at Ulrich.

'Well, she would have to be guarded, of course,' Ulrich said.

'No guards,' Angela said. 'That would be counterproductive. You must release her into my custody. I must win her trust.'

'Well, I suppose if you were present, Herr Colonel . . .'

'No,' Angela said.

'Just what are you trying to do?' Wassermann demanded.

'As Ulrich has said, Fritz, you are the most feared and hated man in Yugoslavia. Do you suppose this girl doesn't know that? For God's sake, you arrested her back in October, and you tortured her parents. If my plan is going to succeed, I must win her heart and her mind. She has to believe me, and *in* me, completely. Your presence would make that impossible to achieve.'

'You are making this sound like a long-term operation.'

'It could take a few days.'

'I am required in Sarajevo tomorrow.'

'You will have to leave me here. I will bring her to you as soon as I am sure of her.'

'And when she murders you and escapes?'

'She will not do that.'

Wassermann looked at Ulrich. 'It is a risk,' the captain conceded. 'But if Frau Wassermann is prepared to accept that, and if it might help to bring these terrorists to justice . . .'

'And it is not *your* risk,' Wassermann remarked drily. 'On the other hand, my dear, it might be a good idea for you to contribute something to the war. And I know that you will enjoy amusing yourself with this toy. But you do understand that when this coup has been successfully completed, the girl will have to be disposed of? We do not want anyone out there who knows too much about our methods.'

Angela returned his gaze. 'I understand that, Fritz. Anyway, once our coup has been brought to a successful conclusion, there will be no reason for her to live. But if I do this for you, I wish something in return.'

'Yes?' He was suspicious.

'I wish the right to . . . *interrogate* Fouquet and Janitz.'

'Both of them? You are a glutton.'

'Both of them. Do not worry, you may have them when I have finished with them.'

Wassermann considered for a few moments, then smiled and nodded. 'You may have them on loan. Well then, let us get down to details.'

Wassermann finished his coffee, and put down the cup. He was wearing uniform, and looking both smart and powerful.

Angela thought that he looked better sitting down than standing up, because then his weakness became apparent. His weakness, she thought, and suppressed a shudder. Last night had been worse than usual, because he was going away, and because . . .

He looked at his watch. 'I must go. My car leaves in half an hour. I look forward to seeing you again, my dear.'

'Thank you.'

'Triumphant, eh?'

'I will have Brolic with me when I come to Sarajevo.'

'And how many times will you have her before that, eh? Ha ha.'

'Ha ha,' Angela agreed. 'I will do whatever is necessary to turn her into the weapon we wish.'

He studied her for several seconds. 'While indulging your little perversions.'

She would not lower her eyes. 'Whatever I do is for the Reich, and the memory of my mother.'

He stood above her. 'Be sure that you succeed, or I shall be very angry. The girl will be delivered to you this morning. Will you not kiss me goodbye? Or would you rather be kissing Jelena Brolic?'

Angela turned up her face for his lips. Yes, she thought, I would far rather be kissing Jelena Brolic.

The command car drew to a halt outside the house. 'We are to go in here, Fräulein,' Lieutenant Halbstadt said.

Jelena Brolic glanced at him, and then at the house. She had no idea what she was doing here, what was about to happen to her.

When she had been arrested last October, she had constantly feared the worst. But it had never happened. Certainly she had been manhandled, had been forced to sit in the tram for several hours with nothing to eat or drink, unable to relieve herself. She had only been beaten once, when she had stumbled and fallen after being commanded to stand up in respect to the then governor-general, who was visiting the Gestapo Headquarters. That had been incredibly painful, but not damaging in the long run. And after that, she had been locked in a cell for two months, fed twice a day, exercised once a day, forced to shower once a day ... and otherwise ignored.

She had known that both her father and her mother, as well as her younger brother, were in the prison with her, but she had never seen them. Since her release as part of the exchange engineered by General Tito she had learned that both her parents had been savagely beaten, but she had been unaware of it at the time. Had she known that she felt her brain might have collapsed. But she had remained in total ignorance of what was going on about her, and indeed, had had only the vaguest idea of why she was there at all.

She knew that a tall, good-looking foreign man, actually that Colonel Davis whose name had been on everyone's lips and who had become her commanding officer, accompanied by a small, blonde and quite beautiful woman, Major Fouquet, and two other men had come to see Papa, and that he had allowed them to use the attic of his house to shoot at the Germans. She had not been consulted as to whether that had been a good idea or an act of suicide. At that time, Papa had been a totally confident man.

She had not known the truth until after her exchange, when she learned that those people had assassinated the governor-general's wife. She also found out that Major Fouquet had later been captured and had actually spent some weeks in those same cells, again without her knowing it. At the time, she had been too concerned with her own survival to take much notice of what was going on about her.

The exchange had been like having the gates of heaven thrown wide. Suddenly she was free, and freer than ever before in her life, because with Papa and Mama both shattered by what had happened to them and their family, she had been left to find her own salvation. But her fate, her well-being, her very life had been taken over by that tall, dark, forceful woman who had virtually adopted her.

Jelena's first glimpse of Sasha Janitz had been on the day of the exchange, when she had lain on the ground with her hands on her head hoping to avoid being hit by the hail of bullets being exchanged by the Germans and the Partisans. Through her trembling fingers she had gazed in a mixture of wonder and horror at Sasha, standing behind her stuttering tommy-gun, strong face a mask of exultant contempt, utterly fearless – and surviving the battle, utterly unhurt. From that moment Jelena had only one ideal: to be like her heroine.

Thus she had embarked on a way of life she had never even suspected could exist, and enjoyed every moment of it. She had got up before dawn throughout the cold winter months to train with the rest of the battalion, running miles, panting and gasping for the breath that misted in front of her nostrils, feeling that her muscles were about to give way, but never surrendering, for Sasha was always there – chivvying and driving, to be sure, but also encouraging and smiling. On most days Colonel Davis and Major Fouquet trained with them, but they were remote figures who had their own quarters and were regarded by the entire battalion virtually as demigods, people who could be followed, but never emulated.

Captain Janitz was different. When the training was finished, she would take them to the rifle range and have them practise shooting, with both rifles and pistols. 'Miss that target,' she would say, 'and you will have another shot. Miss the real target, when you have one, and it will mean the end of your life.' But as yet Jelena had never shot a man, or even at a man. She had not yet been given the chance.

Sasha had also lectured them on what battle would be like. She had taken part in several desperate encounters with the Germans, often enough with the colonel and the major, when it had been kill or be killed – and all three of them were still alive, so far as Jelena knew. Some of the things Sasha had had to say had been terrifying, especially her insistence that they should always be prepared to shoot themselves or blow themselves up with a grenade before allowing themselves to be captured. 'To be handed to the Gestapo is the worst fate that can befall anyone,' she had said. 'And it is worse for a woman than a man. If you don't believe me, ask Jelena.' And Jelena had tried to look as impressively terrified as she could, while having no real idea of what her idol was talking about.

There had been other lectures, when some of the printed material handed out from the general's office had to be read – and discussed, so the orders went. Sasha had never had the time for political discussions. 'Politicians are the people who start wars,' she said. 'Like this one. Let us win this war, and then listen to the politicians – if they will let us live in peace.' Jelena had instinctively known that Sasha no longer had any desire to live in peace. But then, neither did she. She had never known that life could be so exciting, so purposeful. And so fulfilling.

Even the great unhappiness she had known when she had learned of her adored older brother's death had been alleviated by Sasha's comfort. For all the time the family had been in prison, Jelena had kept reassuring herself that young Josef at least had escaped on the day they had been arrested, and would have reached the Partisans. Her greatest joy when she had been told that she was to be exchanged had been the belief that Josef would be waiting for them. And then she had been told that he was dead. Her world had collapsed all over again. But Sasha had been there, encouraging her, making her understand that Josef had died for Yugoslavia, and for her. Sasha had been in the same mission as Josef when he had been killed, and Sasha had told her how he had died like a hero, gun in hand, shooting Germans so that his comrades, amongst them herself, had been able to escape. Josef had been a hero! That revelation had almost made her happy. It had certainly made her proud.

That night in February, when Sasha had suggested quite casually that Jelena might care to share her bed, it had never occurred to her to refuse. She had not known what to expect. She had not known to expect anything, save perhaps the strong arms of the captain about her. In the event, the captain's love had raised her to a new level of awareness, both mental and physical.

Nothing in their relationship had seemed the least irregular. Growing up with two brothers, the elder of whom had already been seeing girls when the catastrophe had struck, Jelena had assumed that in the course of time she would attract the attention of boys, one of whom she would eventually marry. That was the preordained order of things. What might actually be involved in becoming the wife of a man was a mystery she would have to unravel in that course of time; it was not a subject her mother had ever cared to discuss.

Sasha's approach had been entirely pragmatic. 'Everyone must have a partner,' she had explained. 'Both for comfort and protection. But choosing the right partner is not always an easy matter, and if you make a mistake, you can let yourself in for a lot of unhappiness. If you go to a man you are stuck with him, but if you go to a woman, that relationship is not recognized, in a man's world, as anything more than a passing fancy. So you will have time to think before you choose.'

And making the right choice was of the utmost importance in the life of a Partisan. General Tito, who was himself married, insisted upon the strictest moral behaviour by his people, and although he recognized that with such a hotchpotch of nationalities, races and religions under his command this was not always possible, he nonetheless required that when a man and a woman elected to share their lives, it was at least for the duration of the war. Promiscuity led to punishment and could even lead to expulsion from the army.

Which had made Sasha's confession that she had slept with the colonel all the more surprising. But apparently Tony Davis, and by projection, Sandrine Fouquet, occupied privileged positions.

Jelena had had no desire to sleep with anyone save Sasha. Her desire always to be at Sasha's side, to share in her every experience, had led her to that brothel, and her eventual capture by the Germans. She had been given no opportunity either to shoot herself or blow herself up. She did not know if she would have had the courage to do it even had she been granted the chance; up till that moment life had been so good. But Sasha had got away. Jelena was quite sure of that. Had the Germans captured or killed her the whole of Sarajevo would have known of it.

She had again anticipated the worst, had wondered what it would feel like to be tortured, and even worse, to stand on a platform and feel the rope being placed around her neck. She had been taken to the Ustase house and brought face to face with that dreadful man Kronic, where she had been forced to see Madame Anna lying in a crumpled heap on the floor, the air still smelling like scorched hair and flesh . . . And then she had merely been locked up, and eventually brought back to Belgrade, in the company of the officer who had been with Wassermann when she had first been arrested back in October.

Clearly she was being reserved for an even more horrible fate. She had tried not to think about it, to remember only Sasha, to convince herself that Sasha would be thinking about her, might even be dreaming of rescuing her, although she did not see how that could be possible. She was not important, like Sandrine, and even if she had been, the Partisans held no prisoner for whom she could be exchanged.

But nothing horrible had happened. Since returning to Belgrade yesterday, she had spent one night in those dreadful cells, and here she was now, at Colonel Wassermann's house, totally bewildered.

'You will not consider doing anything so stupid as to attempt to run away, I hope, Fräulein,' Lieutenant Halbstadt said. 'If you do, you will easily be caught, and then you will be severely punished. Whereas if you behave yourself, and do exactly as you are told, it might turn out very well for you.'

She knew she had to take his warning seriously, even if, for all his black uniform, he was an even more unlikely SS officer than Captain Ulrich. Like Ulrich, he was not very tall. Unlike Ulrich, he was both young and slimly built. His hair was dark, his features curiously small and fine, his eyes, the required blue, were soft. He even looked sensitive. But he was an officer in the SS, so she said, 'Yes, Herr Lieutenant.' She was prepared to wait and find out what was to be her fate.

'So, you will walk up that path, and you will ring that doorbell, and you will be admitted. I shall be with you at all times. Remember this.'

'Yes, Herr Lieutenant.'

'So, do it. Now.'

Jelena opened the door and stepped down, pausing in embarrassment. The soldiers who had arrested her in the brothel had amused themselves by taking away her long gown, and they had amused themselves further on the drive to the Ustase house. She had been expecting a far greater ordeal at the hands of the Ustase, but Captain Ulrich had refused to allow her even to be raped, and he had wanted her dressed for the journey to Belgrade. By then the brothel had been thoroughly searched, her clothes had been found, and she had been allowed to put them on. But at Gestapo Headquarters they had again been taken away and in their place she had been given one of the shapeless ankle-length blue dresses worn by all the female prisoners. She was wearing this now, and was barefoot, and she was sure that everyone on the street would recognize the dress and her appearance and know that she was a prisoner of the Gestapo, just, of course, as they would recognize the German car.

But there were very few people on the street, and those that were there hurriedly looked and then walked the other way; it was not a good thing to show curiosity, or even interest, in what the Gestapo might be doing.

She walked up the path, hearing Halbstadt's boots on the ground behind her, rang the bell and waited, resisting the temptation to look over her shoulder. The door opened, and

Jelena gazed at a tall, heavy, severe-looking woman. 'Jelena Brolic?'

'Yes,' Jelena said.

Madame Bestic looked past her at the officer. 'Lieutenant Halbstadt,' he said.

'Well, come in. Wipe your feet.'

Jelena and the lieutenant both obeyed.

Madame Bestic closed and locked the door. 'Has she been searched?'

'That was not necessary. She has come straight from the prison.'

'It is always necessary. Raise your arms, Brolic.' Jelena obeyed; she had been searched often enough before. Madame Bestic ran her hand over her shoulders and back and breasts. 'Raise your dress.' Jelena lifted her skirt to her waist, and Madame Bestic satisfied herself that there was no weapon strapped to her thighs.

'That will do, Bestic,' a voice said.

Jelena forgot her instructions and turned, sharply, to look at the woman standing in the inner doorway. She had recognized the voice, even as she now recognized the woman, although she had only seen and heard her on two previous occasions. But the first had been on that horrible day last October, when she had been arrested and put in the tram. She was suffering when the governor-general had come to inspect the prisoners. With him had been his daughter, so handsome, so magnificently dressed, wearing a black sable fur with a matching hat . . . and so filled with hatred for anyone who could even remotely be connected with the death of her mother.

The second occasion had been vastly different, the day of the exchange, when Angela von Blintoft had been waiting with the Partisans, having been their prisoner for the previous fortnight. In that time, it had seemed, the arrogant young woman of the Gestapo prison had been reduced to a frightened, half-starved waif, incongruously still wearing her fur coat, but a coat which had been torn and slashed and was hardly more than a rag. Then they had seemed almost the same age, whereas in prison Angela, three years the elder, had appeared as a sophisticate with at least ten years' seniority.

Now it occurred to Jelena that she was looking at an amalgam of the two people she remembered. Here again were the expensive clothes and shoes, the made-up face, the smoothly brushed black hair, the coldly beautiful features. But here also was an expression almost of defiance, uncertainty, perhaps even disbelief. But she wore a wedding ring, and was clearly mistress of this household.

Angela looked at Halbstadt. 'I said there were to be no guards.'

'I am required to deliver her, Frau Wassermann.'

Angela frowned at him, taking in both his good looks and his insignia – and the fact that he obviously liked what he was looking at. 'Have we met?'

'No, Frau Wassermann. Lieutenant Erich Halbstadt.'

'Oh, yes. My husband has mentioned your name. I believe you are in charge in the absence of him and Captain Ulrich. Well, thank you for delivering the young lady.'

'May I ask for how long she will be required, Frau Wassermann?'

'How long is a piece of string, Lieutenant? And she is not "required" for anything. She is to be my guest for a few days.'

Halbstadt looked dumbfounded. 'You are aware that she is a Partisan?'

'I understand that is what is claimed.'

'When she was arrested, a loaded pistol was found in her effects. That is a capital offence.'

'I assume this gun has been confiscated?'

'Well, of course. But I do not think it will be safe to trust her.'

'I am sure Madame Bestic and Rosa and I will be able to cope.'

'Rosa?'

'My maid.'

'Ah. But you understand, I am sure, Frau Wassermann, that having been left in charge by the colonel, I feel responsible both for you and for this young woman.'

Angela regarded him for a few moments. He was an extremely good-looking young man, and although he was undoubtedly older than she, he had a peculiar suggestion of innocence about him. She wondered . . . He was obviously taken with her, and over the past six months her attitude to men had changed. Once she had wanted to be dominated, even physically ill-treated – hence her attraction to Wassermann. But she had had enough of that. Now she wanted to be the dominant partner, and as that was not possible with her husband . . . and this was the first time she had been left alone since her marriage.

She wondered if she dared. Because if Wassermann were ever to find out . . . But what more could he do to her than beat her? And he was going to do that anyway, when next he was in the mood and could summon the strength. But now, too, she was about to become his accomplice in carrying out a coup which, if successful, would undoubtedly increase the esteem in which he was held by his superiors, all the way up to Himmler himself – he would have to respect her for that. As for what he might do to this boy . . . But young men who felt overly attracted to their boss's wives had to accept the risks.

'I quite understand your concern, Lieutenant,' she said. 'Why do you not come back here this evening, for dinner. With me.' She smiled at a by now totally bewildered Jelena. 'With *us*. Then you will be able to reassure yourself that she is not a danger. Would you like to do that?'

'I would like that very much, Frau Wassermann.'

'Then I shall expect you. Shall we say eight o'clock?' She held out her hand.

He bent over the offered fingers. 'I am honoured.' He

99

straightened and clicked his heels. 'Eight o'clock.' Bestic let him out, and turned back to look at her mistress.

'There will be three for dinner,' Angela said. 'Make it something good.' She turned to Jelena. 'Come with me.'

Five

The Traitor

Jelena glanced at Bestic, and received a brief nod. She walked through the hall, glancing right and left at the doors opening, on the one hand, into a well-furnished drawing room, and on the other side an equally well-furnished dining room. Then there was a kitchen and pantry, where several servants were busy preparing the midday meal – after the prison fare she'd been getting it smelt delicious – and lastly another door, which was open, that revealed a large if somewhat decrepit garden created around a lawn. On this lawn there were three deckchairs and a table containing several bottles and glasses as well as an ice bucket. The last time Jelena had known such elegance was in her father's house, the day before the murder of Frau von Blintoft. This woman's mother!

Angela had walked in front of her into the garden. Now she sat down in one of the deckchairs, legs extended; she wore stockings and high-heeled shoes. 'Would you like something to drink?'

Jelena licked her lips. Did she dare? 'It is schnapps,' Angela said. 'Very strong. It will make you relax. Pour one for me as well.'

Jelena poured the two drinks, added ice, and gave a glass to Angela, who raised it. 'Your health.'

Jelena sipped the liquid and suppressed a gasp. She had only previously tasted alcohol the Christmas before last – the 'champagne' served to the girls in the brothel was only slightly coloured aerated water – and then had been allowed only a glass of wine. This first sip, tracing its way down her throat and chest, seemed to set her alight. 'Sit down,' Angela said. Jelena obeyed. 'Life has not been very good for you, recently,' Angela suggested.

She was expecting a reply. 'Has life been good for anyone, recently?' Jelena asked.

'You have wit. I like that. You should address me as "ma'am". What have they done to you?'

'Nothing has been done to me, ma'am.'

'Well, we must try to keep it that way. Would you not like that?'

Jelena could gain no inkling of where this conversation might be leading. 'Yes, ma'am.'

'Do not be nervous of me. Finish your drink, and have another.'

Jelena looked at her glass; it was still half full. She took another sip. 'As you said, ma'am, it is very strong.'

'There is no point in drinking something that is not strong,' Angela pointed out. 'You might as well drink water.' She held out her glass. 'Fill me up as well.' Jelena obeyed, and then sat down again. Her knees felt weak. 'I feel that I know you so very well,' Angela said.

'We have never met. Until now. Ma'am.'

'But I have known *of* you for a long time. Of your family. And I knew your brother.'

Jelena's head jerked. 'Petar?' She did not see how that could be possible. And Petar had never spoken of it.

'Your older brother.'

'Josef? You knew Josef. But . . . he was killed.'

'I know. I saw him die. That is why I feel so sorry for you, and your family. That is why I am determined to help you, in any way I can.'

'Josef was killed by German soldiers while fighting with the Partisans. That is why . . .' Jelena bit her lip.

'You joined them? To avenge your brother? They are devils.'

'They are my friends.'

102

'How can you be friends with liars and murderers?'

'Liars?'

'Well, you say they told you that Josef was killed while fighting against our soldiers. Surely you know that is a lie?' Jelena stared at her, open-mouthed. 'I told you,' Angela said. 'I was there. I saw him die. And he died trying to save me. I feel so guilty about that.'

'But . . .'

'He was one of the people who blew up the train on which I was travelling. You know about *that*?'

Jelena's head bobbed up and down. Her brain was again in a fog. She could not believe what this woman was saying. And yet she was speaking so calmly, even if with considerable emotion. 'The carriage in which I was travelling came off the tracks and fell over,' Angela explained. 'I managed to crawl out. But I was captured by several of the Partisans. Your brother was one of them. When the other men saw that I was a good-looking woman, they wished to rape me. They tore off my clothes and threw me to the ground. But your brother stepped in front of me, and said he would kill the first man who laid a finger on me. He dominated them, and I would have escaped, but at that moment a woman came along. She was apparently their commander. You may know of her. Her name was Sasha Janitz. A tall woman with dark hair.'

'Sasha,' Jelena whispered.

'You know her? Has she ever told you what happened?'

'She told me Josef died heroically, fighting the Germans, holding them off so that she and the rest of the unit could escape.'

'And you believed her? My dear girl, I am so sorry. When the other men, the men who had assaulted me, told her what had happened, she turned to Josef and told him he was a Nazi-loving traitor, and then . . . she shot him. Just like that. He had no chance to defend himself. It was the most cold-blooded murder I have ever seen.' Jelena dropped her glass. 'Oh, my

dear.' Angela leapt to her feet and hurried to the girl's side.
'I have upset you. I did not wish to do that.'

'Sasha is my friend,' Jelena muttered. 'She has looked after
me for six months.'

'You mean she has amused herself with you, used you, for
six months. People like Janitz do not love. You forget that I
was her prisoner for a fortnight. Has she spoken to you of
this?' Jelena shook her head. 'Perhaps she, even she, is
ashamed of what she did to me, made me do.'

'You hate her,' Jelena said.

'Do you not hate her, now that you know the truth about
her?' Jelena bit her lip. 'You say she is your friend. You say
she loved you. Well, let me ask you this: on the night you
were arrested, did you see her? I mean after she returned to
the brothel from General von Demmich's house.' Jelena's head
moved up and down. 'What did she say to you?'

'She didn't say anything. There was no time. She knew the
soldiers would come after her . . .'

'So she escaped before they could catch up with her. But
she did not take you with her.'

'Well . . .' Jelena licked her lips.

'She just abandoned you, to save her own skin.'

'It was her duty,' Jelena said hotly. 'She had information . . .'

'If you believe that is why she abandoned you, then you
are a far more loyal friend than she deserves. But I have upset
you. Do not let us talk about Sasha Janitz any more. I am sure
that she will pay for her crimes, eventually. Let us have lunch.'

Angela had wine served with the meal; coming on top of the
schnapps, Jelena was quite drowsy by the end of it. 'I think
you need to lie down and have a good sleep,' Angela said.
'You must be at your best to entertain the lieutenant for dinner,
eh?'

Jelena allowed herself to be escorted upstairs, her brain in
a whirl. She was not certain of anything, where she was, what
she had just been told . . . Could Sasha possibly be that

devious, that cold-hearted? But she already knew that her idol could be utterly ruthless. 'Here we are,' Angela said.

Jelena looked around the spare bedroom in awe. Again, she had not known such elegant comfort since being dragged from her father's house – actually she had not known it even then.

'Take off that miserable garment,' Angela said.

'I have nothing else.'

'I will have something for you to wear when you wake up. We are much the same size. Ah, Rosa, this is Mademoiselle Brolic, our guest.'

The maid, a small, dark young woman with pert features, gave a brief curtsey.

Angela herself unbuttoned Jelena's dress and slipped it from her shoulders. 'Burn this.'

'Yes, ma'am.' Rosa took the garment and hurried from the room.

Angela turned back the covers. 'In you get,' she said. 'Have a good rest.'

Jelena got in, and Angela pulled the sheet to her neck, and then tucked her in. 'I owe your brother so much,' she said. 'So I am going to take care of you, and see that no harm ever comes to you again. Or your family. If you will allow me to do so.'

Jelena attempted a smile, and Angela kissed her on the forehead. Then she closed the door and went to her own bedroom, sat at the desk, took out her diary, and wrote: *Success. By tomorrow I will have this girl eating out of my hand.*

She went downstairs to use the telephone. Ulrich had given her the number of the officers' mess in Sarajevo, and she was through very quickly. 'This is Frau Wassermann,' she said. 'Has the colonel arrived yet? I see. Yes, I know the railway line has been blown up; he is coming by car. Very good. I will give you a message for him when he arrives. Tell him I shall be joining him in two days' time. Two days. Thank you.'

When Jelena awoke, she was for some moments unsure where

she was. Her mind was fuzzy, but gradually awareness returned to her. She was in a warm, comfortable bed – the most comfortable bed she had enjoyed for eight months – and she was being treated like royalty by the most charming woman she had ever met, a woman not greatly older than herself, but one who had clearly never endured a moment's hardship in her life.

No, that was not true. By her own admission, she had nearly been raped by the Partisans – people, she realized with a shudder, she had probably seen and even spoken with every day over the winter – and then she had been badly treated by Sasha. Would Sasha do such a thing? Sasha! Full memory came back to her, and she sat up with a start, the sheet held to her throat. The woman had said that Sasha had shot Josef because he would not let his comrades rape her. That simply could not be true. But why should Frau Wassermann make up such a story? More important, if the story was *not* true, why should the German woman be treating her so kindly? She had no cause to wish to help any Yugoslav, and she clearly hated Sasha. But she had explained why.

Jelena lay down again. Suppose she *was* acting like this because she felt guilty for Josef's death? Suppose she *could* help Mama and Papa and Petar? Would that mean abandoning the Partisans? But from what she had gathered over the winter, the Partisans knew they were beaten. They were only fighting because there was nothing else they could do, especially people like the general, and Colonel Davis and Major Fouquet, people with a price on their heads, who knew that they would be hanged if they were ever captured. Why should Mama and Papa and Petar, and herself, die with them for an utterly lost cause? Because, if this woman was telling the truth, they *could* surrender, and return to Belgrade, and pick up the pieces of their lives all over again.

Then she would never see Sasha again. But did she wish to see Sasha again? If Sasha had betrayed her, if Sasha had shot Josef . . . She sat up again, panting. Her dearest, darling brother! It was her duty to avenge her brother. As she had not known who had fired the fatal shot, she had sought vengeance on the whole German army, the whole German nation. The Partisans, Sasha, had promised her that. But if it had been Sasha herself . . . But there was nothing she could do about it. She was in the hands of the Germans, and she would never see Sasha again. Unless, perhaps, she were to escape.

That possibility had not occurred to her until now. For all Lieutenant Halbstadt's warning, it would really be very easy to do. She was not restrained in any way, and there were no sentries that she had seen. She knew Belgrade well enough, had sufficient friends here to conceal herself, and once she was out of the city she had no doubt she could make her way across even the considerable distance that lay between here and Bosnia. But did she really want to do that? Did she want to exchange this luxury for the spartan conditions in Foca? This feeling of well-being for the risk of being killed? To serve and die with people who apparently had betrayed her? Did she really wish to go back to Sasha? She did not wish ever to see Sasha again. Unless, perhaps, the Germans captured her. Then she might be allowed to watch her hang.

The door opened, and she hastily reached for the sheet. 'Don't do that,' Angela said. 'Why do you wish to cover yourself up? Are you ashamed of your body?' She wore a dressing gown, and her feet were bare. Slowly Jelena lowered the sheet, and Angela came to the bed. 'It is a very lovely body. So young, and yet so strongly muscled.' She stroked Jelena's breasts. 'And when these grow, as they will, you will have a beautiful body. You should never be ashamed of it. When you possess beauty, you should never be afraid to reveal it.' She took off her dressing gown, letting it fall to the floor. She also was naked.

Jelena caught her breath, because Angela certainly had a beautiful body.

Angela sat beside her on the bed. 'Or are you ashamed of it because of what men made you do in the brothel? Did you like what they did to you in the brothel?' Angela's voice was soft.

'No,' Jelena said, more vehemently than she had intended.

'But you went there, and you accepted it. Why?'

'Sasha . . .'

'I see. Sasha made you do it. Because she hoped to obtain information for the Partisans. And hoped that you would do so also?'

'Well . . .'

Angela stroked her cheek, and then her breasts again. 'Did Sasha make love to you?' Jelena blushed. 'Did you enjoy that?'

'She . . . she said she was looking after me.'

'Whereas she was satisfying herself. Do you prefer women to men?'

'I . . . I have never . . .'

'Had a man, outside of the brothel? Well, I can tell you, most men behave as if they were in a brothel all the time. We women need to stick together. What of this man who is coming to dinner? Did you find him attractive?'

'He is handsome.'

'Oh, yes. Well, we must be sure to amuse him.' She stood up. 'Now get up. There is a bath waiting for you. And then we must dress you.'

'I have no clothes.'

'I have said, you will wear some of my clothes, goose.'

'You would let me do that?'

'Of course. Because we are friends, are we not?'

Jelena grasped her hands. 'You won't send me back to the Gestapo?'

Angela smiled, and kissed her on the lips. 'I swear to you, by the memory of my mother, that you will never be returned to the Gestapo, little Jelena.'

'So tell me, Lieutenant, how long have you been in Yugoslavia?' Angela asked.

Halbstadt drank some wine. He was still feeling over-whelmed by his surroundings, not only by the silver cutlery and expensive glassware, the excellent food and the better wine, but also by the presence of the two women.

Angela wore a low-cut black evening gown against which her very white skin seemed to glow, her deep cleavage accen-tuating the full breasts, while her black hair, reaching past her shoulders, seemed merely an upwards extension of the gown. The Yugoslav girl, in her own way, was no less attractive. Her dark green gown was equally deep-cut, and if she had far less to offer – certainly as regards breasts – she exuded a youthful and most attractive exuberance.

As he was on his sixth glass of wine, he was finding it dif-ficult to determine which of them he would rather have in bed beside him. But what was he thinking? The one was the wife of his commanding officer, the other was an enemy of the state. And yet they sat, one at each end of the table, with him in the middle, rather like two wealthy sisters entertaining a prospective suitor. 'I came in February,' he replied.

'So you have been here just over four months. Do you like it?'

'Belgrade is a beautiful city,' he said. 'I have not had an opportunity to look at the rest of the country.'

'Jelena knows the country well,' Angela said. 'She has trav-elled into Bosnia. So have I. With the Partisans. Do you know about that?'

'Ah . . .' Everyone at Gestapo Headquarters knew about that. Just as everyone knew how this woman had visited the head-quarters often, before her marriage, and usually late at night, to be with her lover, as Wassermann had then been. Or, as others hinted, to engage in demonic behaviour at the expense of various prisoners, usually young women or girls. He could not stop himself from giving Jelena a hasty glance, but she merely smiled at him. 'I have heard something of it, Frau Wassermann.'

'I think you should call me Angela.' She rested her chin on

her forefinger. 'Although, perhaps, not in front of my husband. Did you know the colonel before coming here?'

'I had never met him. But I had heard a great deal about him.'

'I'm sure. And is it your ambition to emulate him?'

Halbstadt met her gaze, and flushed. But the wine had made him rash. 'I am sure I will never have the opportunity, or the good fortune, Angela.'

'A successful man is someone who makes his own fortune,' Angela pointed out. 'Ah, Bestic, we are keeping you up.' The housekeeper was hovering in the pantry doorway. 'You may go home. Dismiss the staff. You may clear this away tomorrow.'

Bestic looked inclined to protest. But it was very late. 'As you wish, Frau Wassermann.' She gave Halbstadt and Jelena glances that were equally disapproving, and left the room.

'We will give them ten minutes to leave, then we can relax and enjoy ourselves,' Angela suggested.

Halbstadt looked at his watch. 'Good heavens! I should be leaving, too.'

'Do you have somewhere to go?'

'Ah . . . no. But—'

'I am sure you can spare us a little more of your time.' She got up and held out her hand. A moment's hesitation, then he took it, and was led into the drawing room. Jelena followed, deciding that Angela was a more accomplished whore than any of the girls at the brothel. She still couldn't determine whether or not she was dreaming, whether she was suddenly going to wake up and find herself in that cell, with nothing but cold stone walls to stare at, and a probable beating come daybreak. If this was a dream, then she did not ever wish to wake up, no matter what she might be required to do by her new friend. New friend? She had to suppress a shudder. So far Angela had been kindness itself. But she could not convince herself that kindness was a part of her nature.

'Pour us each a brandy,' Angela said. 'The decanter is on the sideboard. Use the balloons.'

Jelena went to the sideboard, placed the three glasses in a row. Her father and Josef had often drunk brandy after dinner, but she had never watched them very carefully, so she filled the three goblets as she would have done wine glasses, then took two of them, one in each hand, to where Angela and Halbstadt were sitting together on the settee, close enough for their thighs to touch.

Angela took her glass, and then looked at it. 'Good lord! Are you trying to make us drunk?'

We already *are* drunk, Jelena thought. But she said, 'No, ma'am.'

'I see you have a lot to learn about civilized living,' Angela said. 'A brandy glass should be filled only to the point so that when it is laid on its side, the liquid just fails to spill.'

'Oh. I am sorry. Shall I pour some back?'

'No, no. As it is poured we will drink it. What shall we drink to, Erich?'

'Ah . . . success to the Reich.'

'You are going to make me suppose that you are about the most boring man *in* the Reich. Let us drink to the successful realization of our *own* ambitions. What is your greatest ambition at the moment, Erich?'

'Ah . . .' He could not stop his gaze drifting down to her half exposed breast.

'Is that all?' Angela laughed, and moved the gown aside to expose the breast even further. 'Here, help yourself.'

Halbstadt licked his lips, and glanced at Jelena, who had seated herself opposite them.

'Oh, you can feel hers afterwards,' Angela said. 'But try mine first. They are much bigger.' Halbstadt cautiously cupped the soft flesh. 'When you do that,' Angela said, 'my immediate ambition is to have you in me.' Halbstadt raised his head in alarm. 'Are you afraid to do that?' she asked.

'But . . . your husband . . .'

111

'Cannot get it up. He says it was the wound, but I noticed him failing before that. All he can use now is a dildo, and when I have pleasure from it, he gets so angry. So, will you not assist me to have some real pleasure?'

'I . . .' Again he glanced at Jelena.

'She will happily join in. Won't you, Jelena?' Jelena drank some brandy. 'But you have not told us what is *your* dearest ambition at this moment,' Angela said.

Jelena took a deep breath. The alcohol filling her system had robbed her, too, of any sense of discretion. 'My dearest ambition is to avenge my dead brother,' she said.

'Bravo!' Angela said. 'But that is not bed talk.'

When she awoke, Jelena was alone in the bed. But it was not her bed, and judging from the pervading warmth it had only recently been evacuated by . . . Angela and Erich? She wished she could remember more of what had happened, what had been done to her – or what she had done to them. But again her brain was fuzzy. Yet she still had an enormous feeling of well-being. She did not wish to move.

The bedroom door was open, and now Angela came in. She had put on a dressing gown to go downstairs, but this she now let fall to the floor as she slid between the sheets beside Jelena.

'Has he gone?' Jelena asked.

'Yes. Well, he was not much more use to us, was he? But he asked me to give you his love. He thinks you are a charmer. Well, I think you are a charmer, too. But him . . . he can hardly wait to get you back in his cells.'

Jelena's eyes opened wide. 'You said—'

'And I shall keep my promise. But it is something on which we will have to think very hard.'

'You said you would help my parents.'

'And I intend to. But again, we have to be very cautious, and plan our moves very carefully. You know my husband?'

'I have seen him,' Jelena said.

'But you have heard of him.'

'Everyone in Yugoslavia has heard of Major Wassermann.'

'He is a colonel now. Which means that he is even more powerful than he was before. And he is a mean and brutal man. I should know. I am married to him.'

'You mean he will put me back in prison?'

'He will torture you when he gets back from Sarajevo. Torturing women is the only sex he can get nowadays. And as he can't really get any sex even then, every time he does it he just gets more sadistic. He is a monster.'

Jelena preferred not to comment. Whatever this woman might say of her husband, she was still his wife.

'However,' Angela went on, 'if there is one thing he wants more than having women to torture, it is to have Davis and Fouquet to torture and then hang. Of course, Fouquet is a woman. And a beautiful one. Do you know her?'

'She is second in command of my regiment.'

'Then you must have seen a lot of her. Would you agree that she is beautiful?'

'Oh, yes,' Jelena said.

'But also cold-blooded and ruthless. She shot and killed my mother.'

'She . . .' Jelena was aghast. She knew about Frau von Blintoft's death, of course, just as she remembered that Major Fouquet had been one of the people who had visited her father's house on the afternoon of the shooting; Sandrine had actually been the one who had tied her up, but very gently and good-humouredly. Then the shooting had happened, and the major and Colonel Davis had escaped while she and her entire family had been arrested. But she had never held any grudge for that . . . nor had she ever heard the major being accused of having fired the fatal shot.

'And then she and her lover deserted you to face the wrath of my father and Major Wassermann. Just as Sasha deserted you in the brothel.'

Jelena kept her mouth shut. She had heard so many revelations about people she had counted her friends over the past

113

few hours that she had no idea what to believe. But she *did* believe what this woman had told her about Sasha's part in Josef's death; it all made so much sense of the many veiled allusions she had overheard in the Partisan camp.

'But I have been thinking about that,' Angela said. 'I am beginning to have an idea as to how we can satisfy Wassermann, help your family, enable you to avenge your brother, and enable us to be together always. Would you like that?'

'Yes,' Jelena said without thinking. 'What do we have to do?'

Angela rolled over and took her in her arms. 'It is just an idea. We will speak of it again tomorrow.'

The maid, Rosa Malic, gently awakened them with cups of chicory which she called coffee. Jelena hastily pulled the sheet to her throat, less in embarrassment at being naked than at being found in Angela's bed. But Angela was as confidently bright as always. 'Malic,' she said, 'we will be going to Sarajevo tomorrow. Pack my things. Mademoiselle Brolic will be accompanying us.'

'She has no things, ma'am,' Rosa said.

'She will wear my clothes. Sort something out.'

'Tomorrow. Yes, ma'am.'

'And draw a bath,' Angela commanded.

'Yes, ma'am.' Rosa left the room.

'Sarajevo?' Jelena asked. 'I cannot go to Sarajevo.'

'Why not?'

'People may recognize me.'

'Does that matter? You will have my protection. It is part of the plan I have worked out. While you were sleeping last night, I was thinking.'

Jelena found that hard to believe, as she had actually lain awake most of the remainder of the night, suffering heartburn at once from the brandy and the wine and the manhandling – and womanhandling – she had received, while she had listened to Angela snoring softly beside her.

114

Angela got out of bed, and began to stride around the room, throwing her long legs in front of her, untidy hair flailing. 'This is what we are going to do,' she announced. 'I told you last night that Wassermann's greatest wish is to bring Davis and Fouquet to justice. Just as yours is to bring Janitz to justice. Now, we know that all three of them are operating behind our lines in Bosnia.'

Jelena sat up. She did not know that. 'But what about the army?'

'Didn't you know? Your army has fled and are being pursued by our army, but they have left Davis and Fouquet, and Janitz and some others, behind to behave like the bandits they are. And we also know that *their* greatest wish is to kill my husband. There is the perfect scenario, don't you agree? If someone, someone they trusted absolutely, were to go to them and tell them that she knew where Wassermann would be, with only a few guards, at a certain time on a certain date, they would certainly go for it. All of them.'

Jelena held her breath. 'You wish me to do this? But . . .'

'Listen to me,' Angela said. 'And I will tell you how we shall do it.'

Rosa Malic hummed as she hurried along the street to her parents' home. In the year since the bombardment of the previous April, followed by the German occupation, not a great deal had been done to repair Belgrade, except for those areas and the houses within them that the conquerors had appropriated. The market place was still scarred and several houses nearby were merely heaps of rubble. But Rosa's parents' house had escaped with only some broken windows. As glass was difficult to obtain, these remained boarded up, but she was always glad to come home, even if for brief visits.

Coming home and seeing her father enabled her to feel that she was helping the war effort. Certainly Papa always told her that she was. Thus she had been persuaded to go back to working for Frau Wassermann, even if she heartily disliked her mistress, and had more than once felt the physical effects of Angela's bouts of ill humour. But during her first employment, when Angela von Blintoft had been living with her father in the governor-general's residence, the old royal palace, Rosa had been able to overhear many snippets of conversation indulged in by various senior officers who had come to call or to dine. These she had always faithfully repeated to her father.

He was the one who took the real risk, leaving Belgrade to wander into the mountains and make contact with the Partisans and pass the information on. According to him, what he had been able to tell General Tito had been of the utmost importance in frustrating or even defeating the German plans. Certainly she knew that it had been her ability to tell her father the exact time of departure of the train last November that had enabled the Partisans to sabotage it and take Angela captive. She didn't know what had happened after that. She had hoped, and still did, that the Partisans had given the vicious little bitch a hard time. Certainly Rosa had never expected to see Angela again, but here she was, back in Belgrade, now even more powerful and arrogant as the wife of the most feared man in the country.

When she had been sought out by that grim-faced Madame Bestic and told that Frau Wassermann wanted her back as her maid, Rosa's every instinct had been to refuse. But Papa had asked her to resume her old station, with all the promise of future revelations.

This was the first time since her return as Angela's maid that she had had anything positive to give him, and, as usual, she did not know whether it would be of the least importance. 'I am leaving Belgrade tomorrow,' she told her parents over tea. 'I am going to Sarajevo.'

'In Bosnia?' Her mother was alarmed. A Serb herself, she did not like the Bosnians.

'I am going with Frau Wassermann. She is to join her husband. They are involved in some big operation.'

'We know the Nazis have taken Foca,' Boris Malic said. 'And driven the Partisans further into the mountains. What can the Gestapo have to do with that?'

'They believe that Colonel Davis and Major Fouquet have been left behind to carry out acts of sabotage.'

'And the Gestapo hope to capture those two? They are dreamers.' Boris Malic was contemptuous; he took the greatest pride in having met the legendary pair on more than one occasion.

'But I think they have a plan to trap them,' Rosa said. 'Do you remember the Brolics?'

'Of course.' Everyone remembered the Brolics, even if no one understood why they had been considered important enough to be exchanged for the governor-general's daughter.

'Do you remember the girl, Jelena? She was at school with me. That is, she began school in the year I was leaving.'

'I remember her,' Mrs Malic said. 'A pretty little thing. But that was before she was arrested by the Gestapo.'

'She is an even prettier little thing now,' Rosa said. 'Except that she is quite a big thing. And she has been captured by the Gestapo again.'

'Then she is done for,' her father remarked.

'She spent last night sleeping in Colonel Wassermann's house. In fact, she spent it sleeping in Frau Wassermann's arms.'

Both of her parents stared at her censoriously, her mother because she did not approve of improper sexual activity, her father because ... 'You mean she has turned traitor?'

'I am not sure. I have managed to read Frau Wassermann's diary, and yesterday – that is, the day Jelena was delivered to her house by the Gestapo – she wrote that she had achieved a success.'

'What, in seducing this girl?'

'Well, Papa, it may not be a simple seduction. Jelena is accompanying us to Sarajevo tomorrow, where Colonel Wassermann and Captain Ulrich have already gone.'

Boris stroked his chin. 'And you think this may be to do with Colonel Davis?'

'I think the colonel may be interested in knowing about it.'

'If you are going to Sarajevo tomorrow morning,' Mrs Malic said, 'then no word can be got to the Partisans before you get there.' She glared at her husband to make her point; however patriotic she was, however much she dreamed of an eventual expulsion of the Germans, she never liked the idea of Boris risking his life for what had so far seemed very little gain.

'I cannot get there,' Malic agreed thoughtfully. Then he snapped his fingers. 'Kadic! He takes the mail from Belgrade to Sarajevo every week. He is leaving the day after tomorrow.'

'He will still arrive after Rosa and Frau Wassermann.'

'He will not be far behind. As the railway is out, they will be going by car, but Kadic will be using a motorbike. And whatever it is they are planning, they will not set it in motion the moment Frau Wassermann arrives in the city. There will have to be certain preparations. Kadic will have time to make contact with any Partisans that are in the district. He knows how to do that.'

'And what will he tell them?' Mrs Malic continued to be sceptical.

'Well . . . that something is brewing. That they must be on their guard.'

'Are they not always on their guard?'

'I may be able to find out what their plan is,' Rosa said eagerly. 'Tell Mr Kadic to contact me when he reaches Sarajevo, and I will tell him what I have learned.'

'It is too dangerous,' her mother complained.

'It will not be dangerous at all. I am Frau Wassermann's maid. She thinks I am a dimwit. You will write a letter for Kadic to bring to me when he reaches Sarajevo. What can be suspicious about my mother writing me a letter?'

'What can I put in a letter written today, when you are here today, that you do not already know?' Mrs Malic asked.

'Oh, Mama!' Rosa said impatiently. 'There is no need to

put *anything* in the letter. A blank sheet of paper will do. It is merely a ruse to enable Mr Kadic to speak with me. When he does that, I will give him a letter to bring back to you, but you will tell him to open my letter as soon as he is alone, and he will learn the Gestapo's plans.'

'My darling!' Angela embraced her husband, to his obvious satisfaction, even if to Ulrich's usual embarrassment. 'Here I am.' She looked with disapproval around the rather small lounge in which she was standing; in fact, it was a rather small house. 'Is this where we are to live?'

'Well, it is only for a short while.' Wassermann was looking past her at the two other young women. 'And this is . . . ?'

'Jelena Brolic. I thought you might remember her.'

'Have I ever seen her before?' Wassermann fell in with her obvious plan.

'My darling, you arrested her last October.'

'Ah. Then she has changed.'

'Entirely.'

Wassermann went up to Jelena, who suppressed a shudder. To her, this man was the epitome of all the evil in the world. Except for people like Davis and Fouquet . . . and Sasha. They were all different sides of the same coin, and deserved to perish together. But the Partisans had to come first. 'Herr Colonel,' she said.

Wassermann looked her up and down, clearly identifying her clothes as belonging to his wife. 'I would say the change is entirely for the better,' he remarked. 'We must have a talk. I believe you have met Captain Ulrich.'

'Yes, Herr Colonel.'

Ulrich clicked his heels, still uneasy about the whole thing. 'And Captain Kronic?'

'I remember the young lady very well,' Kronic said, coming up to her.

Now Jelena did give a shudder. She remembered this man and Anna . . . And when she had been taken into that dreadful

119

room, he had wanted to torture her as well. Only Ulrich had saved her from a similar unthinkable fate.

'But now she is on our side,' Wassermann reminded him.

'That remains to be seen, Herr Colonel.'

'I can assure you of her loyalty, Captain,' Angela said. 'She has entirely discovered who are her friends and who are her enemies.'

'Well,' Wassermann said jovially, 'it is splendid to have you all here. Have you had a good journey?'

'Satisfactory,' Angela said. 'What I would like is a good lunch and a hot bath. We left Belgrade at dawn, and the roads are so bad.'

'And you shall have both. And then I shall take you for a drive to show you the city. But I forgot, you already know the city.'

'I have been here briefly,' Angela said. 'I will enjoy seeing it again, shall I say, in more salubrious circumstances.'

'And so you shall, my dear. And I have a treat for you. General von Demmich wishes to meet you.'

'I thought his troops were pursuing the Partisans?'

'His troops are doing that, certainly. But the general himself believes in waging war in a civilized fashion, from as far as possible behind the front line. But as I say, he wishes to meet you. He knows your father, and claims to have dandled you on his knee when you were a babe.'

Angela made a face. She had no desire to meet anyone who had dandled her on his knee when she had been a baby, and even less a general who was still pursuing a successful career while her own father was in disgraced retirement. But she supposed there was nothing for it. 'And he knows of our objective?'

'No, no. One should never share a secret with a general. But he will be pleased at the outcome.'

'Then I will be pleased to meet him. But there is something else I wish to do: I wish to visit this famous brothel.'

'You?'

'I am curious. Will you not satisfy my curiosity? Would you not like to return there, Jelena?'

'No.' Jelena bit her lip. 'They will hate me. Please allow me to be excused, Frau Wassermann.'

'Oh, certainly. I do not suppose the general will be interested in seeing you again, anyway.'

'He has never seen me,' Jelena said quietly. 'I was not one of the girls sent to his house.'

'Well, it is probably not a good idea for him to see you now. He might just wish to resume where he left off. You have an early night. Tomorrow will be a busy day.'

'She seems prepared to eat out of your hand,' Wassermann remarked as they were driven to the general's residence.

'She is.'

'Does that mean that you have seduced her?'

'I have seduced her mind. She believes in me, and thus in what I have to tell her.'

'And her body?'

'Oh, yes. A woman needs some perks. How are we going to do this?'

'She is going to be taken to Konjic, and will escape from there.'

'Konjic?'

'It is a small town not far from Sarajevo. As it is on the main road to the coast, we are building a fortified position outside of it, to make sure the highway is not cut. We have received a report that Partisans have been seen in the neighbourhood, and there can be no doubt that it is in their interest to watch our movements, and thus the road.'

'If they are watching the road, they will see her being released.'

'She is not going to be released. She is going to escape. It will be crass carelessness. You just need to make sure she knows what to do.'

'I will see to it.' Angela considered for a few moments.

'Have you thought of the possibility that if the Partisans are watching the road and see her in this camp, they may well go in to get her? If you handled it properly, you could finish the job there and then, without involving yourself.'

'I do not think there is the slightest possibility of the Partisans going in to get her. Whatever else Davis may be, he is not a fool. When our friend gets there, there will be too many of our people about. No, the Partisans will wait on events, making no move to assist her until they are sure she has got away. Then it is up to her to convince them that she is genuine. Are you confident about that?'

Not for the first time, Angela wished that her husband could overcome his weakness for making over-elaborate plans which could so easily go wrong. But she said, 'I am utterly confident. About Jelena. Now tell me, why have you involved the Ustase?'

'Because they are there, my dear. They are to be used.'

'Is that man Kronic not the one who tortured the brothel-keeper?'

'Yes, he was. I should have thought that would titillate you.'

'Perhaps I am changing,' she said quietly.

He studied her for several moments. Then he said, 'But you are still prepared to sacrifice your little friend once she has outlived her usefulness. It will be necessary. I do not regard her as capable of either maintaining her loyalty or keeping a secret.'

'Of course. I would ask one favour, though.'

'Yes?' He was immediately suspicious.

'That I carry out the execution myself.'

Wassermann leaned back against the cushions. 'In addition to having Fouquet and Janitz to torture? Sometimes you frighten me.'

Angela smiled. 'Sometimes I frighten myself. But it is a most pleasant feeling.'

Jelena sat at the dressing table, naked, and stared at herself in the mirror as she brushed her hair. It was a small dressing table and a small mirror, as it was a small room; she was not going to be sharing Angela's bed tonight. But she was grateful for that. She had felt like a prostitute all over again when enduring her captor's – for Angela was just that – caresses in Belgrade, and had to keep reminding herself that everything she was doing was for her family, and more importantly, for Josef's memory. Now she just wanted it to be over as rapidly as possible, and until it was, to shut her mind to everything else.

As for returning to that brothel . . . She felt ill at the very thought. But as she surveyed the solemn face, framed by the hair which trickled past her shoulders both in front and behind, she could not help but ask herself what the future might hold for her. After the life she had been forced to live over the past few months, she could not envisage marriage to some ordinary young man – who would expect her to be an ordinary young woman. She had served in a brothel, and she had trained with the Partisans, and if she had not yet taken a life, she had been trained to do that too, just as she had seen lives being taken. And she had been in the hands of the Gestapo! Was normalcy ever going to be an option for her?

The door behind her opened, and she turned with a start, hands clasping her breasts and then sliding down to cover her pubes when she saw the man standing there. 'What do you want? What are you doing here? You have no business here.'

'I have business everywhere,' Kronic said, coming into the room and closing the door behind him.

'But how did you get in? There is a sentry on the front door.'

'I have access to everywhere as well. Do you think any German sentry is going to stop Captain Kronic?'

He came across the floor towards her. She looked left and right, but there was no shelter. There was not even a dressing gown for her to put on; on a warm summer's night such as this she had not thought it necessary to ask Angela for the loan of one.

'You are a sexy little thing,' Kronic remarked, standing immediately in front of her and stretching out his hand to sift some strands of her hair through his fingers. 'And you were in the brothel. There is an interesting thought.'

'If you touch me . . .' Jelena said in a low voice.

'Oh, I am not going to rape you, little Brolic. Not now, anyway. I can wait for Frau Wassermann to tire of you. I just wished to have a private word with you. You know what you are required to do?'

'I know it.'

'I just wish to be sure that you do it, and have no treachery in mind. You recall what I did to Madame Sabor?' Jelena nodded; she was having difficulty breathing. 'Well, should you attempt to betray us, then Wassermann will give you to me, whether his wife wishes it or not, and then what I did to Madame Sabor will be nothing compared to what I shall do to you. And this time Ulrich will not be able to interfere, because I will be acting with Wassermann's blessing. Remember this.' He was still holding Jelena's hair, and now he gave it a little tug; she gasped, but it was more in fear than pain. Then he left the room.

Jelena hardly slept. Her brain was a torrent of conflicting thoughts, conflicting emotions. If only it could be over and done with. If only . . .

Her head jerked when there was a tap on the door, and she realized it was daybreak She had not heard the Wassermanns return from their visit with the general, so she must have slept after all. 'Who is it?' she asked.

'Rosa.'

Jelena sat up, the sheet held to her chin. 'Come in.'

The door opened and the maid sidled into the room. Early as it was, she was fully dressed. She came to the bed. 'I am sorry to have disturbed you. But I had to speak with you.' Jelena waited. 'Do you remember me from school?' Rosa asked. Jelena shook her head. 'That is because you were very small, and I was very big. I was head girl. I remember you. You were a sweet little girl. Are you still a sweet little girl?' Jelena stared at her. 'Oh, do not worry about Frau Wassermann,' Rosa said. 'That is her way, and what can we do? We are the conquered, and must obey the whims of our masters ... and mistresses. But it will not always be so. Do you not agree?'

'I know nothing of politics.'

'But you must wish the Germans to be defeated. Don't you wish that?'

Jelena licked her lips. 'Yes. I wish that.'

'You are a good and loyal Serb. Will you tell me what it is they wish you to do?' Rosa asked.

'I do not know what you are talking about.'

'You are here. You were brought here by Frau Wassermann. She has seduced you and is treating you as an honoured guest. Yet it is known that you are a Partisan. A gun was found in your things. I heard them say this. That is a hanging offence. So is being a Partisan. But you have not been hanged, or even imprisoned. They wish you to do something for them, and you have agreed.'

Jelena wished she could think more quickly, or that she could be given more time *to* think. 'Is it any business of yours?'

'It is my business. It is all of our business. I am a Serb. You are a Serb. These people are our enemies.'

'You work for them.'

'I have no choice.'

'Well, neither do I.'

'You must pretend to work for them if it will save your life or the lives of others. I understand this. But you must never forget that it is our duty always to do everything we can to expel the invaders and save the Fatherland.'

Jelena's lip curled. 'How can we do that? They are too powerful.'

'They will not always be powerful. One day they will be defeated, and then our day will come. Then we will remember who fought with us, and who against us.'

'I have already fought with you. I am a Partisan.'

'But you are now getting ready to betray them.'

'I . . .' Jelena bit her lip.

'There is no other reason for them to have brought you here, to be treating you like this. Besides' – Rosa gave a half smile – 'you have just admitted it.'

Jelena stared at her. 'What do you want of me?'

'Tell me what it is they wish you to do.'

'I . . . if I do as they ask, they will free me and leave my family unharmed. If I do not . . .'

'Of course you must do what they wish,' Rosa said. 'But if the Partisans can be forewarned of it, when they spring their ambush or whatever it is they are planning, it will fail. No one can attach any blame to you if this happens.'

'How can you tell them what is going to happen? You cannot leave Sarajevo.'

'That is not a problem. The postman arrives today with mail from Belgrade. He is bringing a letter for me from my mother. I will give him a letter to take back to her. When he leaves here he will go on to Foca. He will have mail for the German troops occupying the town. We know that although the Partisans have evacuated Foca, there are still some of their forces in that area, and we know that they will be watching the roads, hoping to cut off any small Nazi detachments. Kadic – that is, the postman – will wear a distinguishing mark which will indicate that he has information to convey, and they will capture him, and then let him go again after he has given them my letter.'

Jelena studied her. If only she could think straight. This woman was appealing to her patriotism, but she suspected that Rosa, secure in her niche as Angela's maid, had no idea of the issues at stake. She might feel that she was helping the war effort by passing on snippets of information to the Partisans, but at no time was she endangering herself, or her parents, or her brothers and sisters, if she had any. And she had never had a beloved brother murdered in cold blood by a woman she had trusted absolutely.

At the same time, she had to be considered dangerous, because there was no saying what she would do if, now she had revealed herself, *Jelena* refused to cooperate. It really was a simple matter: survive or die. And not only did she have to survive for the sake of her parents and Petar, but she also had a duty to avenge her dead brother. So it would mean condemning another human being to death. And before death . . . She suppressed a shudder. But it had to be done. As Rosa herself had reminded her, there could be no sitting on the fence in this conflict. Her choice had been made, and had to be ruthlessly continued, no matter what the cost. Why, Sasha would be proud of her, she thought bitterly.

'Well?' Rosa inquired.

'I am to be allowed to escape so that I can go to the Partisans,' Jelena said, 'and arrange a meeting between their leaders – it is supposed that the group operating in this area is commanded by Colonel Davis and Major Fouquet – and Colonel Wassermann.'

Rosa snorted. 'Do you suppose they will fall for that?'

'I do not know the details yet. But I believe that Wassermann is prepared to make them an offer he does not think they can refuse.'

'But it will still be a trap to capture them.'

'I think so.'

'Ha! When and where is this meeting to take place?'

'I do not know. They have not told me yet.'

Rosa considered her for some minutes. 'Very well,' she said at last. 'We can at least put them on their guard. Once they know it is a trap they will be able to take steps to counter it. It may turn out very well for the Partisans. Just like your exchange last year, eh?' She ruffled Jelena's hair. 'You have been a good girl, Jelena. I shall not forget this. When the war is over, and you are accused of collaboration, I will speak up for you and tell them how you helped the Fatherland.' She left the room.

Jelena lay down again. Now she could let herself shiver,

and was seized by an uncontrollable series of shudders that racked her body for several minutes. If only it were possible not to do anything, just lie here until it was all over. But it could not be over until she had gone to the Partisans and seen Sasha again, and if she weakened, Sasha would know why and how she had come back. An angry Sasha. She knew only too well how vicious an angry Sasha could be.

And even if she survived that, if it ever came out that she had betrayed the plan to Rosa and was handed over to Kronic . . .

Her door opened again, and Angela came in. 'Still in bed? You are a lazy thing. Come on, we have a lot to do.'

'I have something to tell you,' Jelena said.

Six

The Spring

'Ah, Rosa.' Wassermann stood in the doorway of the room he had appropriated as an office for the duration of his stay in Sarajevo. 'Come in here a moment, will you?'

Rosa, on her way upstairs with an armful of clean clothes, gave him a startled glance. Like most people in Yugoslavia, she was terrified of him.

'I have something for you,' Wassermann explained. 'Put down those clothes.'

Rosa laid the clothes on the bottom step, and went into the office. Wassermann closed the door. 'It is a letter,' he said.

'A letter? Oh . . .' She could not prevent herself from turning to look at the door.

'You would have preferred it to be delivered personally?' Wassermann asked. 'But the postman – his name is Kadic, is it not? – came and went. He was in a hurry.' Wassermann went to his desk and picked up the envelope. 'Who knows that you have come to Sarajevo with Frau Wassermann?'

Rosa licked her lips. 'My mother, Herr Colonel. I told my mother.'

'As a good daughter should.' Wassermann sat behind the desk. 'But you only left Belgrade two days ago. Why should your mother write you so soon?'

Rosa blinked. She knew she was being sucked into a trap, slowly but surely. 'Something must have happened, Herr Colonel.'

'But that could be serious.' He held out the envelope.

129

Rosa took it. 'Thank you, Herr Colonel.'

'Aren't you going to open it?'

'I will open it in my room, Herr Colonel.'

'I would like you to open it now, Fräulein. If it is bad news, I need to know about it. It may be necessary to send you back to Belgrade.'

Rosa hesitated, then slit the envelope with her thumb and took out the single sheet of paper. 'It is nothing, Herr Colonel. My mother gets anxious when I am away.'

'I'm sure she does. Give me the letter, Rosa.' Rosa held out the sheet of paper. Her hands were trembling. She was finished, and she knew she was finished. She could already feel the rope round her neck. 'This is a blank sheet of paper,' Wassermann said with apparent surprise. 'Is that not strange? You stupid girl. Did you not realize that Fräulein Brolic is working for us, working for me?' Rosa swallowed. 'And you thought she was a patriot,' Wassermann said contemptuously. 'So, Fräulein Brolic told you that we are planning to snare Davis and Fouquet, and their band of brigands, and destroy them. And you, considering yourself a patriot, determined to warn them. But, as you had arranged this charade with letters and Kadic, it was not an inadvertent piece of information that you had picked up. You are a spy, Rosa. I should hand you over to Captain Kronic.' Rosa's lips quivered. 'But as this make-believe letter indicates, your mother is also a spy. I am sure that makes your father a spy, too. As well as the man Kadic, of course.'

Rosa drew a deep breath. She was done. Kadic was undoubtedly done. But Mama and Papa! 'Please, Herr Colonel . . .' She sank to her knees before the desk. Wassermann got up and came round the desk to stand above her.

'Think of them, naked, having electrodes clipped to their bodies. Hear their screams, Rosa. And now imagine yourself undergoing such a pleasurable experience.' Rosa burst into tears. 'Would you like to save their lives, Rosa?' Wassermann's tone had suddenly softened. Rosa's head jerked. 'I could employ you,' Wassermann said.

'Yes, sir. Please. Anything.'

'Well, actually, the task I have in mind will be the simplest in the world for you. You hate my wife, don't you?' Rosa's mouth opened, and then shut again. Another trap? 'Of course you do,' Wassermann said. 'I can see it in your eyes every time you look at her. You only work for her, don't you, in order to obtain information to be passed on to your Partisan friends. Is that not so?' Rosa panted. 'But you are not going to do that any more, are you? Because the very next time that I am informed that the Partisans know any of our plans, I am going to take your mother and father down to my cells, and take you as well, to watch them and listen to them scream, knowing that your turn will be next.' Rosa covered her face with her hands. 'So you will not do that. Instead, you will spy for me, and only me. You will tell me everything my wife does, and says, and, where possible, thinks.' Rosa's head rose. 'In this, you will work with Frau Bestic. She is already in my private employ, but by the nature of her position, she is largely on the outside, one might say, looking in. But you are on the inside, looking out. Aren't you?' Rosa nodded, slowly. 'This will be our little secret,' Wassermann said. 'And if you fulfil your duties with integrity, I will shelve any charges against you and your family.'

'Thank you, sir.' Rosa's voice was faint.

'So tell me, how did my wife spend her time between my departure and her coming here to join me?'

'Is your little friend ready to do her stuff?' Wassermann asked Angela when she came downstairs.

'Of course. Is it to be today?'

'For her, yes.'

'I will be glad to have it over and done with. Now tell me, Fritz, why that little bitch is still here. Why hasn't she been arrested?'

'I have decided that it is not necessary at this time.'

'She is a Partisan spy! Have you not arrested the postman?'

'Yes, we arrested him. But the fools did not properly search him. He had a cyanide capsule in his mouth, and he bit it before they realized what he was doing. He died before we could question him, and thus before he could implicate Rosa.'

'Did he not bring her the letter?'

'I have read the letter, and there is nothing the least implicating in it. So I have decided to leave her alone for the time being, and see what she turns up.'

'Oh . . .' Angela snapped her fingers in irritation. 'And I am supposed to continue employing her?'

'Of course. You will treat her the same as you have always done, until I tell you to do otherwise. Now come.' He went to the window and beckoned her. Frowning, she joined him. 'What do you think of him?'

Angela peered into the yard, where a man wearing a black uniform was standing beside the official Mercedes. Angela's frown deepened when she saw the insignia the man was wearing. 'But . . . are you being replaced? That man is an SS colonel.'

'I am glad to hear you say that. He is wearing one of my uniforms. We are roughly the same height. I think he will do very nicely.'

'You are sending a stand-in?'

'I am sure you would not wish me to risk my own life.'

'But that is brilliant. Does that man know he is risking *his* life?'

'He has volunteered for a secret and dangerous mission. If he survives, he will be commended. Now come along and meet him.'

'Why should I do that?'

'Because you will be at his side when the trap is sprung.'

Angela almost leapt back from the window. 'Me?'

'Of course. If I am officially going on a tour of inspection, and as I have no doubt that by now everyone knows you have joined me in Sarajevo, it would be strange were you not to accompany me, would it not?' He smiled at her. 'Do not worry. If you survive, you will also receive a commendation.'

Even in mid-June the sun did not clear the mountains until well into the morning. Tony and Sandrine crouched in a gully overlooking the little town of Konjic, which was situated some fifteen miles south-west of Sarajevo on the main road from the Bosnian capital to the coast.

Below them the small German encampment outside the town was just coming to life. The enemy had moved in the previous day, and had set to work to construct a fortified post. The road was an essential link in the German advance, which necessarily, in view of the large numbers of wheeled vehicles involved, had to stick to metalled surfaces, although they were fully supported from the air. Only the lightly equipped special forces could follow the retreating Partisan army directly across the mountains. The plan was, while keeping them on the run, to advance the main body to the coast, and then swing north, following one of the only other good roads in the vicinity, hoping to get beyond the mountains in time to encircle the enemy. But since learning that there was still a sizeable Partisan force in the vicinity of Sarajevo – the locals had told Tony that the Germans estimated their numbers to be in excess of a hundred – it had apparently been considered necessary to create several fortified positions along the road to safeguard the supply chain.

Tony did not know what was happening over there in the higher mountains to the north-west. Because of the danger of being identified by the German tracking devices he was using his radio as little as possible, and it was several days since last he had spoken with Tito. Then he had gathered that the army was still in being, although it was daily experiencing more hardship from the Luftwaffe in the air, and more importantly, from their shortages of food and munitions, as well as being forced to fight vicious rearguard actions whenever their pursuers got too close.

Well, Tito would by now have learned of the derailment of the Belgrade–Sarajevo train, news which would greatly help the morale of his people. Tony and his small band had been forced to lie low for several days following that triumph. The country had been swarming with patrols searching for them, and the victory had not been bloodless. One man had been killed, and two men and one of the women had been wounded. And if they had managed to replenish and even increase their armaments from the looted train, it was a constant endeavour to buy food supplies from isolated villagers, not all of whom were happy to help the guerillas, with a large German force sitting virtually on their doorsteps.

Yet despite the casualties and the hardship, morale in Tony's band remained high. They had gained a considerable victory at the railway, and if the three wounded were a continuous concern, the weather was warm with very little rain. And now it was time to hit again.

He handed the binoculars to Sandrine. 'We must have those fellows.'

She was counting heads. 'There are more than a hundred of them.'

'Yes, but the majority belong to a labour battalion. That means they are either reservists or undergoing punishment. Neither will be very keen on fighting. I make it only about a score of actual front-line troops.'

'They will be able to summon help from Sarajevo.'

'Agreed. So we must be in and out in seconds, and then into those woods up there.'

She nodded. 'It looks like as good a place to die as any. When?'

He blew her a kiss. 'We are not going to die. We will carry out the attack half an hour before dusk and then retire under cover of darkness.'

'And our objective?'

'To blow that fort up, and make a mess of the road as well.'

'They will repair it in a day or two.'

134

'Every day's delay is an advantage to Tito. Alert your people.'

He kept the women segregated from the men as much as possible, although during the first fortnight they had been so constantly on the move and thus constantly exhausted that sexual problems had not arisen. But for the last few days they had been almost sedentary, resting up and watching the German preparations; there had been no point in attacking the little fort until it was more than half completed.

So Sandrine went off to talk to her women while Tony returned to his men, about a hundred yards away. 'Is it time?' Ivanovic asked, his enthusiasm undiminished. Like them all, even the young officer was sprouting a beard.

'This evening,' Tony told him. 'We will move down the hill, keeping under cover at all times. We shall attack while the garrison is at dinner. We must be in and out in half an hour; they will undoubtedly be in radio contact with Sarajevo.'

Ivanovic nodded, and went off to talk to his men. Tony returned to his vantage point, looking down on the road. Soon he was joined by Sandrine and Sasha, as well as Ivanovic. In the gully behind them, the men and women were preparing their weapons. 'The wounded will move out now,' Tony told Sasha. 'They will withdraw up the hill to that wood back there, and wait for us. We will join them after the attack.'

She nodded and crawled away. The other three had little to say. They were well practised at their peculiar art, and merely took turns in watching the road through their binoculars, only returning to the camp for their midday meal before resuming their watch. It was past four, and Sasha had just rejoined them when Sandrine, who was using the binoculars, said, 'Transport.'

Tony sat up, took the glasses, and watched the two trucks coming down the road from Sarajevo. He had not anticipated reinforcements. Now he saw two motorcycle outriders in front and two more behind, but with the weather so warm, the normal canvas coverings for the trucks had been rolled back, and as far as he could see there were about twenty men in each. Forty men in total. Front-line troops. And . . . He frowned as he made out the flutter of a woman's long hair at the back of the second truck. He fine-focused the glasses to identify her features, then muttered, 'Holy shit!'

'What is it?' Sandrine asked.

Tony gave the glasses to Sasha. 'Look at the rear truck.'

Sasha studied it. 'Oh, God!' she said. 'Oh, God! Now I believe in You.'

Sandrine took her turn. 'Jelena? But she is dead. Or in Belgrade.'

'It is her,' Sasha insisted. 'What have they done to her?'

The glasses were returned to Tony. 'She doesn't look harmed. But she is a prisoner. She is wearing handcuffs.'

'The bastards,' Sasha said.

'They're stopping. Everyone is getting out.'

'Jelena?'

'Everyone. They're talking with the officer. They're unloading . . . It looks as if they're going to spend the night. Damnation!'

'I cannot believe it,' Sasha said. 'They are delivering her into our hands. Oh, my dearest Jelena. And I thought she was dead.'

'I wouldn't say they are actually delivering her into our hands,' Sandrine remarked. 'It is pure coincidence that she should turn up here.'

Tony said nothing as he continued to study the people beneath him. It was unbelievable luck, or unbelievable coincidence, as Sandrine had said. And he did not much believe in luck and not at all in coincidences. If the enemy thought that the mere sight of Jelena would draw him into an attack at overwhelming odds, they had to suppose him a fool. 'We shall change our plans,' he said.

'You mean we will go in earlier?' Sasha asked eagerly.

'I mean we shall not go in at all, until after those trucks have moved on.'

'What? But Jelena is down there!'

'Why, do you suppose?'

'Well . . . she is being taken somewhere.'

'She is being taken along a main highway, as conspicuously as possible, escorted by a heavy guard. It is a trap.'

'Then what are you going to do?'

'Nothing. If my estimate is correct, when we do not attack, they will merely take her back to Sarajevo tomorrow morning. So we shall postpone our attack for twenty-four hours.'

'And Jelena? Do you know what they will do to her?'

'If they were going to do anything to her, they would already have done it.'

'That is because, if it is as you say, they are trying to use her to trap us. But if their plan fails, they will have no more use for her. They will hang her!' Her voice had become strident.

'I am sorry,' Tony said. 'We have a job to do. I cannot risk sacrificing any of us to save one girl.'

'You are a bastard.' Sasha crawled away from them.

'Do you think she will do anything stupid?' Ivanovic asked.

'I doubt it. But just in case . . .' He looked at Sandrine.

Who nodded. 'I will go with her.' She also crawled away.

'Tell our people the attack has been postponed,' Tony said.

'They will not like it,' Ivanovic commented. 'And if we stay here all day tomorrow, we stand a risk of being sighted.'

'We'll withdraw to the wood as soon as it is dark.'

Ivanovic also left, and Tony continued to study the German camp. Everyone seemed in a very good humour, and their security precautions were almost nil; a couple of men lounged at the side of the road with weapons slung on their shoulders, looking up at the surrounding hills with no very great interest. Tony's interest lay in the girl. He watched her being led into the middle of the group of soldiers. She certainly looked like a prisoner, head drooping, shoulders hunched, but still there was no evidence that she was being ill-treated; as he watched her captors preparing their evening meal, he saw

137

that her handcuffs were removed, and she was given something to drink.

Sandrine arrived behind him. 'We are withdrawing,' she
said. 'Are you not coming?'

'I'll stay here a while.'

'What is so interesting down there, if we are not going to
attack tonight? It is that girl, eh? Have you ever fucked her?'

'For God's sake, Sandrine. You have a one-track mind. I
am interested in what she is doing there.'

'I thought you said that she is the bait of a trap.'

'I think she is. But it is the oddest trap I ever saw. Ah, well,
she'll be gone by tomorrow.'

They made their way up the hill to where the remainder of
the guerillas were camped. The women were preparing the
evening meal, using a carefully concealed fire made in a hole
dug in the ground and surrounded by underbrush to stop any
glow being visible at more than twenty yards. Sasha was still
in a morose sulk, but she ate with the rest. Everyone was
downbeat, having worked themselves up for combat and then
having it put off, but Tony assured them that they would have
their action tomorrow.

'What happens if Jelena and her escort are still there
tomorrow evening?' Sandrine asked as they snuggled together
beneath their blanket.

'They won't be. But if they are, we'll just have to wait
another day.'

'You are too patient. I do not think Sasha will be that
patient.'

'She will have to be or I will tie her up.'

He slept soundly, as he always did, but awoke with a start.
The night was very dark, with only a whisper of sound caused
by the wind in the trees. Then he heard shots; obviously it
had been a shot that had wakened him. He sat up, and Sandrine
stirred. 'What is it?'

Tony rested his hand on her arm as he watched a shadowy

figure coming towards him – one of the sentries. 'There is shooting down the hill, Colonel.'

'Shit! Sandrine, find Sasha. Ivanovic ...' The major was also awake. 'Check our people.'

Ivanovic hurried off, but Tony could not believe that any of the guerillas would have started something on his own. The only possible exception was Sasha, in which case ... The thought of either abandoning her or having to shoot her for disobeying orders in the face of the enemy was not something he wished to contemplate.

But a few minutes later Sandrine was back, with Sasha. 'They are shooting Jelena!' Sasha said.

'Why should they drive her out here to shoot her?' Sandrine asked. 'In the middle of the night.'

'They could be shooting at her,' Tony said thoughtfully, 'if she has made a break for it.'

'We must get down there to help her,' Sasha said.

'We are going nowhere,' Tony told her. 'In the first place, it is too dark for us to see what we are about, and in the second place, it may be an extension of their trap, and in the third place, if she has made a break and got away, we can't possibly find her until daylight. Go back to bed.'

Sasha glowered at him. 'I hate you,' she said, but she returned to her bivouac.

'Do you think they let her get away?' Sandrine asked.

'If they did, the important word is "let".'

Tony doubled the sentries, and then lay down again, having to fight the temptation to return to his earlier vantage point in an attempt to discover just what was happening. But he knew that would be both pointless and dangerous, as in the darkness he would hardly find the position and could well stumble into any searching Germans. In any event, the shooting had stopped; once he thought he heard the shrill of a whistle, but it was too far off to be sure.

And Jelena? He felt desperately sorry for the girl, as he had done ever since Sasha had returned to Foca with the news that she had been captured. Sandrine had claimed that lightning never struck twice in the same place, but it had certainly done so in Jelena's case. So it had been necessary to shut his mind to what might be happening to her or was about to happen to her, whether it was bullets slamming into her body or the rope being fitted around her neck, and only hope that she would die as quickly and as easily as possible.

Then to see her again, only a few hundred yards away . . . *Could* she be the bait of a trap?

But he could not imagine the Germans would be so blatant, would regard him as such a fool, or such a romantic, that he would attack at enormous odds just to rescue a single woman. It was far more likely that they had seen some movement up the hillside, such as a fox, and lost their heads. He knew that most of the soldiers in Demmich's army were conscripts as opposed to veterans – the veterans were all in Russia fighting the Soviets, and apparently not doing as well as they had expected, even if most observers seemed to feel that Russia would collapse before the summer was out.

The entire camp was up at dawn; Tony doubted many had slept after the interruption. He told them to remain where they were, then returned with Sandrine, Sasha and Ivanovic to the lower hill to see what was happening.

The Germans were just awakening. Tony frowned as he studied them. There was certainly no sign of Jelena, but equally there was no suggestion of the agitation he would have supposed consequent on their allowing a prisoner to escape – a prisoner regarded as being of some value, in view of the size of her escort. 'What do you make of it?' Sandrine asked, lying beside him.

'I'm damned if I know. We'll just have to wait and see.'

'But we will go in tonight.'

'We'll make a decision on that this evening. There is something going on I don't like.'

Sandrine whistled through her teeth, as she was wont to do when dissatisfied.

'Jelena is no longer there.' Sasha had been using the glasses.

'It doesn't look like it.'

'Then it *was* her escaping during the night.'

'It seems probable.'

'I would like permission to go and look for her.'

'Where?'

'Well . . . she must be somewhere about.'

'If she wasn't shot. They don't seem to be looking any more.'

'She may be lying somewhere, wounded. I wish to find her.'

Tony sighed. But he knew it would be unwise for him to push Sasha too far. 'Permission granted,' he said. 'But keep well away from the road and out of sight, and there must be no shooting. And I wish you back here by this afternoon.'

'Yes, sir.' Sasha crawled away.

'They are pulling out,' Ivanovic said.

Tony turned his attention back to the Germans. The soldiers who had arrived the previous night were certainly piling into the trucks. Half an hour later they drove away, continuing through the village and to the west – not back to Sarajevo as he had expected.

'What do you think that was all about?' Sandrine asked.

'If I knew, I'd be a happy man.'

'But you still will not make a decision about tonight?'

'Not until this afternoon. Fall out.'

Sasha had covered about half a mile from the vantage point when she heard the rumble of the engines. She made her way through the trees to look down into the valley. She could just see the encampment, and had only a brief glimpse of the road, but a few minutes later the engine sound faded; they were going the other way! Bastards, she thought, and withdrew into the trees to consider her position.

Her instincts told her that Jelena, if she *had* escaped, would have followed this less steep area to get up into the hills. She was relying on either hearing movement or being heard herself, or, in the worst possible scenario, hearing the buzz of the insects that would have accumulated on a dead body.

She walked for some time before she heard movement behind her, and swung round, tommy-gun levelled. 'Jelena?'

Jelena's dress was torn and had bloodstains, and she carried a bayonet, which was also bloodstained. That apart, she looked both unhurt and surprisingly calm. 'Sasha!'

They were in each other's arms, and Sasha was kissing her eyes and her nose, her hair and her cheeks, before coming to her mouth. 'Oh, my dearest, dearest girl. What have they done to you?'

'I would rather not speak of it,' Jelena said.

'Then you shall not. But to have you here . . . You are wounded.'

'It is not my blood. I had to kill one of them to get away.'

'Brave girl. Oh, brave girl. The colonel and Sandrine will be so happy to see you.'

Jelena looked left and right. 'They are here?'

'They are not far. How did you know I was here?'

'I didn't,' Jelena said. 'But I heard them talking in Sarajevo, and they said that Partisans had been seen in the vicinity of Konjic, so I thought if I could just get away . . .'

'And you did.' Sasha hugged her again. 'Come and see the colonel.'

The Partisans gathered round as Sasha escorted Jelena into the camp. 'Isn't it marvellous?' she asked. 'She got away from them. She killed one of them.' She held up the bayonet and indicated the bloodstains on the dress. 'She is a heroine.'

Sandrine embraced her. 'That was well done.' She looked at Tony.

'Well done indeed. Come and sit down, Jelena.' He took

her a short distance away from the camp. 'Would you like something to drink?'

Jelena nodded. 'I am so thirsty. And hungry.'

Sandrine and Sasha had accompanied them, and Sasha hurried back to fetch food and a canteen. 'Now tell us what happened to you,' Tony invited.

Jelena ate and drank, and then talked.

'You were not interrogated by this man Kronic?'

'He wanted to. Oh, he wanted to. But the man Ulrich wished to take me back to Belgrade to his boss, Wassermann.'

'But you say you were not interrogated even then.'

'They were going to. I was terrified. But then there was a telephone call from Sarajevo. From the general. He wanted me sent back there.'

'Surely he knew that you had been removed from there only a couple of days before?'

'I do not know. I do not know how Germans think. They were concocting some kind of trap for you. They felt sure you would attempt to rescue me if you had the chance. I heard Wassermann talking about it with his wife and Ulrich. They brought me back themselves.'

'Frau Wassermann is in Sarajevo?' Sandrine asked.

'Oh, yes.'

'And then they sent you along the road in an open vehicle,' Tony mused.

'As I said, they felt sure you would attempt to rescue me. But you didn't.' It was almost an accusation.

'The colonel knew it was a trap,' Sasha said, apparently now ready to support Tony's decision. 'But you escaped anyway. So all is well that turns out well.'

'Yes,' Jelena said. 'Do you wish to know about Wassermann?'

'What about Wassermann?' Tony asked.

'Well, as he is here, he is going to inspect the German positions further along the road. I heard them discussing this.'

'When?'

'He is leaving tomorrow morning.'

'I mean, when did you hear them discussing this?'

'Ah . . . on the drive from Belgrade.'

'You drove in the same car as Wassermann, and his wife, and Ulrich, and they discussed their plans, openly, in front of you?'

'Well . . . they did not know I was going to get away.'

'Obviously not. *Sprichst du Deutsch?*' Jelena goggled at him. 'But of course, they were speaking Serbo-Croat,' Tony suggested.

'Yes. Yes, that is what they were speaking.'

'So tell me about tomorrow. You say that Wassermann will be using this same road tomorrow to drive to the coast and inspect German positions there. Is he doing this on his own account, or has he been ordered to do this by General von Demmich?'

'Ah . . . he was ordered to by General von Demmich.'

'I see. What sort of escort will he have?'

'I believe three cars and two outriders.'

'That is very precise, Jelena. But that small escort was presumably arranged when he was assuming that we would have been defeated and perhaps liquidated in attempting to rescue you.'

Jelena licked her lips.

'But as we did not attempt to rescue her,' Sasha pointed out, 'he will conclude that we are not in the vicinity.'

'That's true,' Tony conceded.

'Will you take him out?' Sandrine asked.

Tony knew that to see the SS colonel dead was almost her greatest desire.

'Everyone in Yugoslavia would applaud such a triumph,' Ivanovic said, having joined them.

'That's true,' Tony agreed again. 'Will he be accompanied by his wife?'

'Oh, yes,' Jelena said. 'She is a dreadful woman.'

'You know her?'

'Well . . . yes. She was there when I was taken before him. And she drove down to Sarajevo with us. I told you this.'

'So you did.' Tony looked at Sandrine.

'Her, too,' Sandrine said.

'Oh, yes,' Sasha said. 'I would like to get my hands on her again. And this time there will be no exchange, eh?'

'Of course. Well, Jelena, you have done very well. Now go and get some rest.'

'Will we not go for Wassermann?'

'I think we possibly should. It would certainly be a great propaganda triumph if we could assassinate, or better yet, capture, the SS chief in Yugoslavia. But it will have to be done west of Konjic. That means we will have to move some twenty miles before tomorrow. Rest, and we will move out later.'

Jelena hesitated, then allowed herself to be escorted back to the camp by Sasha.

'I will alert the men,' Ivanovic said, and followed the two women.

Sandrine waited for them to be out of earshot. 'What is the matter?' she asked. She had been with Tony long enough to know when he was unhappy. 'If you are worried about what may happen when I meet Angela again, I will be very happy to let Sasha have her.'

He squeezed her hand. 'I was thinking about Jelena.'

'What about Jelena? I agree that her survival is a miracle . . .'

'Do you believe in miracles?'

'Well . . . I suppose they do happen.'

'Once in a lifetime, maybe. Not three or four at the same time.'

'What do you mean?'

'I'll agree that it is a miracle that she was not interrogated by the Gestapo. But she obviously was not; there is not a mark on her body.'

Sandrine shuddered. 'They could have used electricity.'

'Do you really suppose that a sixteen-year-old girl could

have been raped and buggered by an electrode and be able, only a few days later, to speak of it so dispassionately? The very idea made you shiver, and I would say you are far tougher, mentally and physically, than Jelena ever could be.' Sandrine scratched her nose. 'However,' Tony went on, 'it could have happened. Now let us consider miracle number two, that Wassermann, his wife and Ulrich should choose to discuss a confidential matter in front of their prisoner, and use Serbo-Croat to do so.'

'We do not know they were speaking Serbo-Croat.'

'Jelena said they were. But they would almost certainly have used German when speaking to each other, whether it was confidential or not. And I just proved that Jelena knows absolutely nothing of the German language.'

'You should have been a detective. Are you sure you are not just prejudiced against the girl?'

'Then let us consider miracle number three, that General von Demmich should have deputed an SS officer, even if he happens to be the SS commander in Yugoslavia, to carry out an inspection of German troops. You know as well as I do that the Wehrmacht, and particularly the high command, loathe the SS as much as they fear them.' Sandrine drove both hands into her hair. 'But we still have number four to consider,' Tony said. 'And that really is a miracle.'

'That she managed to get away?'

'Well, that too. But also that she escaped by killing a German soldier with his own bayonet.'

'She had his blood on both the bayonet and her clothes. And she *had* the bayonet.'

'So what did she do, carry him on her back until she was safely away, and then dump him somewhere?' Sandrine frowned. 'We both watched the Germans this morning, first of all waking up and then packing up and departing. Did you notice them loading a corpse into their trucks? Did you observe any of the angst that there would have been if one of their comrades had been killed during the night?'

'But the blood . . .'

'I have no doubt that a forensic scientist would tell you that blood came from whatever animal they slaughtered for their dinner last night.'

Sandrine whistled through her teeth. 'You think Jelena has betrayed us?'

'I think she means to. I think she has been seduced by the Germans, probably with promises of an amnesty for her family.'

'And the truth about her brother's death. Angela would have told her that. What are you going to do?'

'I think we'll go along with her. That way, if I'm right, she'll expose herself.'

'But if we know it is a trap . . .'

He gave a grim smile. 'We can lay one of our own.'

Seven

Destruction

The guerillas moved out that afternoon, breaking their journey round Konjic only for a hasty meal and a few hours' sleep. Jelena seemed content that they were taking advantage of her information, and as she spent the night bivouacking with Sasha she had no opportunity for running off, even had she intended to do so.

Sandrine, as usual, was worrying. 'How do you think they will play it?' she asked Tony in their bivouac.

'I'll be interested to find out, as they must know we'll have them under observation long before we attack.'

'So being followed by a back-up force won't work.'

'Not if we're careful. Let me brood on it.'

But he was no nearer to determining what was going to happen when they resumed their walk the next morning. By nine o'clock they had circled the town and were well beyond it, looking down on an empty stretch of road, from which a rough track, quite usable by a four-wheel-drive vehicle, led into the hills, almost to where they were grouped. Tony deputed Draga Dissilivic and another of the women to drop back and remain at the end of this track. He gave Draga his Verey pistol. 'You will allow Colonel Wassermann's transport to pass you,' he said. 'Then remain in position. If at any time you see more vehicles following, or if any vehicle, or any men, come up that track, fire the Verey pistol and then withdraw as rapidly as possible into the hills. If there is no support, and no attempt to get behind us, by the time we open fire, then join us.' Draga nodded, large features determined.

The three wounded, as before, he sent to make their way up into the wooded hills as best they could; they walked only with difficulty. And although they were capable of defending themselves they were a handicap to any rapid retreat; Tony was in fact becoming increasingly worried about them – lacking adequate medication none of them was healing as fast as he would have liked. The rest of the squad proceeded on their way, and by ten o'clock they reached a position on a hillside overlooking the road. Tony left the main body of his people to rest, going forward with Sandrine, Sasha, Ivanovic and Jelena to a ridge which afforded maximum visibility in both directions while providing adequate concealment. The sun had not yet cleared the hills behind them, and for the moment the valley beneath them was in shadow.

'What time was Wassermann going to leave Sarajevo?' Tony asked Jelena.

'I don't know. Quite early, I suppose.'

'There,' Sandrine said. An aircraft was now visible, quite high up; they watched as it circled. There had been planes before, searching for them after the raid on the train. But this one was present before they had revealed themselves.

'Of course,' Tony said. 'His aim is to have us make an appearance, then he will have established our immediate whereabouts.'

'He will still have to have men on the ground,' Sandrine argued. 'Both to protect himself and to pin us down.' Tony nodded, and felt the glow of the sun on his back as it came over the hilltops and bathed the valley in brilliant light.

'I see trucks.' Ivanovic had been using the binoculars. Now he handed them to Tony and pointed at a distant copse to the west, and therefore on the further side of their position as regards Sarajevo. Tony took several minutes to discover what the captain's keener eyes had spotted. Then he saw something gleaming amidst the trees. 'They have been careless,' Ivanovic said. 'They must have parked them yesterday afternoon when the sun was setting, and thought they would remain hidden. They did not realize that as the morning sun cleared the hills it would shine directly on them.'

Tony continued to study the wood. 'I make it two,' he said, and handed back the glasses.

'Yes,' the major said a moment later. 'Two.'

'The two which were at Konjic last night,' Tony said. 'Their back-up.'

'That is nearly a mile away,' Sandrine objected. 'We can hit and be away long before they can get to us.'

'They aren't a mile away,' Ivanovic said. 'Only their transport.' He was studying the road beneath them. On either side of the metalled surface there was a ditch filled with long grass. And now that Tony looked more closely, he could see the occasional movement. 'They must think we are either fools or blind.'

'But how do they knew we shall attack them where they are?' Sandrine commented. 'We could hit them anywhere along this valley.'

Tony glanced at Jelena. Her features were in repose, but she was biting her lip. 'I think they have it worked out.'

'So what will you do?' Sandrine asked Tony.

'Wait and see what happens. They may hope that we are around, but they don't know that yet.'

An hour passed, and then another. The sun was now almost directly overhead, and very warm. The soldiers crouched in their ditch, no doubt sweating, and the Partisans crouched on the hillside; they were certainly sweating. Tony was armed with one of the sniper's rifles he had requisitioned before leaving Foca, and he stroked the barrel as he waited. He knew that this was a somewhat clumsy trap, and thus he could not risk a general assault, but it was still a great temptation to take out Wassermann.

'Transport,' Sasha said. It was twelve fifteen. They watched two motorcycle outriders, followed by two command cars, coming down the road, the swastika flying from each bonnet.

But unlike the normal procedure, the roofs of the cars were up, as were the windows, despite the morning heat. 'That will be bulletproof glass,' Tony said.

'I still don't see . . .' Sandrine began.

'There.'

The two cars were slowing and then stopping, about half a mile back from where the Partisans were but immediately beside the group of concealed soldiers. The drivers and orderlies got down, and began setting up folding tables and chairs while others prepared lunch. Then three people got out of the first car. Tony inspected them through the binoculars. 'That has to be Wassermann,' he said. He had only ever seen the SS colonel from a distance, but it had been about this range when he had last cut him down, and that had been with an ordinary rifle, not this high-powered precision instrument. And this man was certainly wearing the uniform of an SS officer. Besides . . . 'Angela von Blintoft,' he said.

'Let me see.' Sandrine took the glasses.

'And the other man is Ulrich,' Sasha said. She did not need the glasses to identify the short, slightly rotund figure.

'How could we resist such a target,' Tony remarked.

'Frau Wassermann?' Jelena asked. 'You are going to shoot Frau Wassermann?'

'Bastards!' Sasha commented. 'You would think they knew we were here.'

'I'm afraid they do, or they are certainly hoping. Well, they've had their fun. Pull your people out, Major. It must be done very slowly and carefully. We must not let them discover our presence.'

'You do not mean to attack?'

'It's not our business to commit suicide, not even for the chance of a shot at Wassermann. We'll go back to Konjic.'

Ivanovic looked at Sandrine, who shrugged. Then he crawled away.

'You get the women moving,' Tony told Sasha. 'We'll pick up Draga on the way. Go with her, Jelena.'

151

Sasha nodded, and rose to her knees. Jelena looked from one to the other, then snatched Sasha's pistol from her holster. Sasha turned on the instant, instinctively swinging her tommy-gun. The blow caught Jelena on the shoulder, and tumbled her over the slight ridge behind which they were crouching; she went rolling down the slope, arms and legs flailing. 'Shit!' Sandrine snapped, rising.

Tony caught her arm and pulled her back down. But Sasha was also on her feet, staring down the slope, levelling her tommy-gun. 'Get down,' Tony urged her.

Jelena stopped rolling, winded but unhurt – and she had retained her grasp of the pistol. She looked back up the slope, realized that she could not now hit Sasha or any of the Partisans, aimed the pistol in the air and fired six times. Then she went on rolling down the slope. The Germans did not appear to have noticed the original scuffle up the hillside, but they certainly heard the shots. The people by the car dropped behind the vehicle for shelter, and the waiting soldiers rose from the ditch in which they had been hiding. 'The bitch!' Sasha said, firing her tommy-gun, but the range was already too great.

'Get down, and get out of here,' Tony snapped. 'Go, go, go. You too, Ivanovic.' The major was only a few feet away, and he had stopped to look back. 'You'll have to destroy the radio equipment.'

In fact, for all the relatively calm orders he was giving, Tony was as furious as Sasha, but mainly with himself, for not believing that Jelena would risk her own life to betray them. But that they were in considerable danger was obvious. The Germans were now using a heavy machine-gun, hitherto concealed in the ditch, to sweep the slope, sending bullets scything through the trees and bushes. They were also equipped with rifles rather than tommy-guns; before the three officers could regain their people Ivanovic had gone down with a shout, and from the noise beyond him it was obvious that he was not the only casualty.

'Go, go, go,' Tony shouted again when the two women turned back to look at him. 'Get your people out of here. Go up the hill.' Both hesitated, reluctant to abandon him. 'I'll be right behind you,' he promised.

Sasha looked at Sandrine, and then set off. Predictably, Sandrine dropped to the ground beside Ivanovic. 'Where are you hit?'

'In the back,' he muttered between gritted teeth.

Tony stared down the slope. He knew that his command had been utterly betrayed, that they were about to be wiped out. But, that being so . . . His fingers closed on the rifle he still held, then he looked back at the command car. He could see the SS colonel's cap peering over the roof. We shall go out in a blaze of glory, Sandrine had said. Well, he could certainly take out Wassermann, once and for all. And that might even slow up the pursuit. He levelled the rifle, aimed, and fired. The cap disappeared. Then he ran back to join Sandrine beside Ivanovic.

The major was lying on his stomach, and now they could see the blood welling through his blouse. But the wound was high up, and there did not appear to be any air in the blood – he had not been pierced in the lung. 'We must get you to shelter,' Tony said. 'Then we'll see what can be done.'

'You must leave me,' Ivanovic said. 'I can hold up those bastards.'

'Come along,' Tony said, grasping his arm to help him to his feet. Sandrine held his other arm, putting it round her shoulders, and they staggered into the trees, Ivanovic breathing stertorously.

'Are we done?' Sandrine panted. Behind them they could hear the whistles as the German infantry began their advance.

'Not until we're done,' Tony told her.

Jelena continued to roll down the hill, and now she lost possession of the pistol. She came to rest against an outcropping of rock, gasping, feeling that she was bruised from head to foot. She lay still for several minutes, listening to the firing, afraid to move in case she was hit. Then twigs crackled close to her, and a moment later she was staring at a bayonet thrust at her chest. 'No!' she screamed. 'I work for Colonel Wassermann. I warned you of the Partisan presence.'

The soldier considered for a few moments, then shouted in German. He kept his rifle pointed at Jelena's breast until he was joined by a sergeant. They exchanged comments, and then the sergeant said, 'Get up,' in Serbo-Croat.

Jelena got to her knees and then her feet. She knew she must look a sight, with her hair tangled and her dress torn, and she was bruised and cut in several places. But she had recognized the sergeant. 'I was with you last night,' she panted.

'And now you have betrayed us.'

'No,' Jelena cried. 'No. They saw you, and they would not attack. They were going to withdraw.'

The sergeant jerked his head. 'Get up,' he said again. He gave orders to the private, who again presented his rifle. 'Go with him,' the sergeant commanded.

Jelena stumbled down the hillside, the soldier at her back. Above her the firing continued, but the machine-gun had ceased its chatter. In its place there was a droning sound from overhead, and she saw two aircraft swooping over the hills and the trees. Then she faced Angela, who was white-faced and afraid – and angry. At her feet there lay an inert body in a black uniform. Wassermann? Jelena could not believe her eyes. The man's head had been shattered into an unrecognizable mess by the bullet. But Angela seemed more angry than grief-stricken. 'You silly bitch! You have ruined everything.'

'No. Please. I tried to help.' Jelena looked at Ulrich, then back at the dead man. 'I did not mean for this to happen. I swear it. I am so terribly sorry.'

'About what?' Angela inquired. 'Him? He is of no account. But I was standing next to him. Look, there is blood on my dress. That bullet could easily have hit me!'

'I didn't . . .' Again Jelena looked at Ulrich, unable to believe such callousness with regard to the woman's husband.

'You were supposed to remain with the Partisans until we captured them,' Ulrich said.

'They were not going to attack. They were withdrawing,' Jelena said. 'I tried to warn you. Listen. You think there are a lot of them. But there are only twenty.'

'Then the swine have split up. More than a hundred attacked the train.'

'No,' Jelena shouted. 'I listened to them talking. There are only twenty. There were only ever twenty.'

'Oh, let us go back to Sarajevo,' Angela said. 'Bring the bitch along.'

'But . . . your husband!'

'That is not my husband, idiot. Do you suppose Fritz would allow himself to be shot down by an outlaw? But after this fiasco, I am sure he will enjoy having a little chat with you.'

"We must wait here,' Ulrich said. 'I have called on the radio. The colonel wishes us to wait here.'

Jelena still did not understand, except that she was in grave danger. 'You said . . . You promised . . .' she stammered.

'And you failed,' Angela said coldly.

'Here is the colonel,' Ulrich said.

Several cars and more truckloads of troops were coming down the road from Konjic. Wassermann got out of the first car. Kronic was with him. 'Where are your prisoners?'

'There are no prisoners,' Angela said. 'You risked our lives, for nothing. I nearly got hit, for nothing.' She pointed at the dead body. '*He* got killed, for nothing.'

Wassermann ignored her and looked at Ulrich. 'Who are you engaging?' The sound of firing continued from above them.

'They are up there, Herr Colonel. But they were warned of our trap, and retreated before we could get to grips with them. I'm afraid this girl betrayed us.'

'I did not warn them,' Jelena cried. 'I was trying to warn

you that they were there. Otherwise they would have gone away and you would never have known.'

'If they were there, were they not going to attack us?' Wassermann asked.

'No. Because they knew it was a trap.'

'How did they know that? You told them.'

'No,' Jelena insisted, starting to cry. 'They just knew. They saw the trucks over there in the trees. They saw your men hiding in the ditch.'

'It has turned into the most utter fiasco,' Angela declared again. 'You will be a laughing stock,' she told her husband.

'You think so? They are there, not a mile away. I have called in the Luftwaffe. Major Wiedermann . . .' He turned to the Wehrmacht officer who had got out of the second car. 'You will pursue and wipe out these vermin. The aircraft will help you.' Wiedermann clicked his heels. 'Well, then,' Wassermann said. 'Let us return to Sarajevo. This is now a job for the armed forces.'

'What about her?' Angela asked.

Jelena was unable to believe that this was the same charming woman who only yesterday had been so kind to her, so loving. 'She seems to have outlived her usefulness,' Wassermann agreed.

'She knows about the Partisans, Herr Colonel,' Kronic said. 'I think she may have a great deal to tell us.' He smiled. 'To give us.'

'Oh, my God,' Jelena whispered.

Wassermann looked at Ulrich. 'It may be amusing.'

'I protest, Herr Colonel. If she is guilty of betraying us, let her be tried and hanged.'

'As she is undoubtedly guilty of betraying us,' Wassermann said, 'I think her punishment should be salutary.'

'Give her to me, Herr Colonel,' Kronic said. 'I will make her tell us everything she knows about the Partisans.'

Wassermann stroked his chin, and glanced at his wife. Angela's face was coldly impassive; she was waiting for him to implement his promise, but she knew he could not do it here, in front of so many witnesses. She had no idea that he had no intention of humouring her at all.

Jelena fell to her knees. 'Please,' she begged. 'All right, hang me. Do not let that man have me.'

'He obviously wants you,' Wassermann pointed out. 'And it is time you were treated as a woman instead of as a silly little girl, or . . .' He looked at his wife again and changed his mind about what he would have said. 'She is yours, Kronic. I do not wish to see her again. Or hear of her.'

Kronic grinned. Angela opened her mouth and then shut it again. 'No!' Jelena cried. 'For God's sake, no! Herr Colonel . . . Frau Wassermann . . . *Angela*! Please!'

'Oh, take her away,' Wassermann said. 'Major Wiedermann, I wish you every success. Indeed, I insist upon it.'

Tony and Sandrine helped Ivanovic up the hill to the original encampment. The major was losing too much blood, and he had to be attended to. Sasha and Draga were waiting for him, together with Corporal Davidovic. 'We sent the others on ahead with the wounded,' Sasha said.

'You were supposed to go with them,' Tony reminded her.

'We will go with you,' Sasha said.

There was no point in either arguing with her or reprimanding her; there was no time for that. They laid Ivanovic on the ground and took off his blouse and vest. 'He will not survive that,' Draga said.

Tony knew she was right. The bullet had made a reasonably small entry, and he was still sure it had not punctured a lung, but in its exit it had torn away half of Ivanovic's shoulder. Even if they could get him to a hospital, which was impossible, and have him patched up, he would never have the use of the arm again. 'Morphine,' he said.

Sandrine had already opened the first-aid kit, and now she handed Tony the bottle. Ivanovic was being very stoic; this was helped, Tony reckoned, by shock. But now the shock was wearing off, and he was grinding his teeth. Yet he shook his head to the morphine. 'It will put me to sleep.'

'It will dull the pain,' Tony told him. 'Do you not think that is a good idea?'

'The pain will soon be gone. But before it does . . .' His lips widened in a ghastly smile. 'I wish that rifle, and a tommy-gun . . . and a grenade.' Another grin. 'And some brandy.'

Tony gazed at him for a few seconds, then nodded. They could hear the whistles and the crackle of the undergrowth as the Germans advanced up the hill; they would all be dead in a few minutes if they did not leave now. He laid the rifle on the ground beside the wounded man. Sasha gave him a tommy-gun, and Sandrine a flask of brandy. Draga and the corporal watched them with sombre eyes.

'Godspeed to you,' Tony said. 'Come on.'

The fleeing Partisans had taken the explosives but left the radio. This was a large and heavy piece of equipment; its transport was usually the responsibility of one of the more powerful men in the squad. In these circumstances it could only be a hindrance. Tony smashed it to pieces with the butt of his pistol, then they gathered their remaining equipment and resumed their climb. No one said anything until they heard the crack of the rifle, and then another. There were shouts and more whistles, and then the chatter of the tommy-gun. And then the explosion of the grenade. 'He bought us fifteen minutes,' Tony said.

'Did you get Wassermann?' Sasha asked.

'I believe so. Now we must be sure he does not get us, even in death.'

'That bitch . . . When we catch up with her, I am going to cut out her womb before her eyes and make her eat it.'

They climbed for another half an hour. Behind them the sounds of the pursuit dwindled; there was no means of telling how many lives Ivanovic had been able to claim before dying himself, but the encounter had obviously made the Germans apprehensive of coming across any more armed, desperate and dying men or women lurking in the brush. However, all the while they heard the sound of aircraft overhead, sometimes quite low, although they could seldom see them through the trees. Then, from in front of them, they heard the sounds of several explosions.

'What orders did you give the squad?' Tony asked.

'I told them to scatter, to present less of a target,' Sasha said.

'Someone has found a target,' Sandrine commented.

They were now several hundred feet up, and the trees were beginning to thin, while the aircraft still wheeled above them. 'If we leave the trees we are dead men,' Davidovic said.

Tony levelled his glasses down the hill. There was still movement down there – slow, but sure. 'If we stay here we are dead men,' he said. 'And women.'

'It is my fault,' Sasha said. 'I trusted that bitch. You should shoot me.'

'Don't start that again,' Tony requested.

'What can we do?' Sandrine asked.

'We can't stay here. And we can't go up. So . . .' He pointed. 'We must get back down. We'll work our way round this hill and get into the next valley.'

'What about the others?'

'We'll have to try to link up with them later. They still have the gelignite.'

'And the food,' Draga said. 'We have no food.'

They made their way through the last tree fringe. Now that they were no longer climbing, they could hear the sounds of the Germans coming closer. 'How wide do you think they are spread?' Sandrine asked.

'We're going to have to find that out.'

About fifteen minutes later, Davidovic said, 'Look there.'

They looked down a shallow incline and saw four German soldiers seated on the ground around a small portable stove. 'Hallelujah,' Tony said. 'More conscripts.'

'To attack them will give away our position,' Davidovic objected.

'They know we're here, somewhere,' Tony told him. 'Not to attack them means running out of ammo, and they will have rations.' In any event, he was desperately in need of action to work out some of the angst that was possessing him. 'But we'll do it quietly, if we can.'

It was not difficult. The four young soldiers were hungry, tired, for the moment out of sight of their NCOs, and had no idea that any of the fleeing guerillas might risk turning back on them. Tony directed his people to the left and right until the lunch party was surrounded, then signalled them to move in. The click of automatic weapons being prepared was the first indication the Germans had of their impending trouble, and they raised their hands without hesitation when they realized they were both surrounded and outnumbered. The guerillas relieved them of rifles and ammunition, and also of their haversacks containing their rations and water canteens. 'Now we cut their throats, eh?' Sasha said.

'Not today. Use their belts to tie them up. Gag them with their socks.'

'You are trying to fight this war like an English gentleman,' Sasha remarked. 'One day you will be sorry for it.'

'That day we will have lost the war,' Tony told her. 'And we are not going to do that.'

As they prepared to move off, leaving the four hapless soldiers on the ground, there came a huge explosion from further down the valley.

Tony knew immediately what had happened. Stomach churning, he led his little squad towards the sound, careless now of making a noise; in any event the rumble of the explosion still echoed through the valleys. They came upon the scene a few minutes later. Here the trees had thinned, exposing the area to the sky; Tony checked his squad on the edge of the tree screen – two planes still circled overhead. They gazed at the crater, the scattered bodies, the shattered weapons.

'One bomb?' Sandrine asked in horror.

'It struck whoever was carrying the explosives,' Tony said.

'My God!'

'I thought you told them to split up?' Tony asked Sasha.

'I did. They disobeyed me.'

The planes flew away, undoubtedly satisfied that their work had been conclusive. Tony went forward. The others followed. Several of the bodies had been entirely disintegrated; only four were fully recognizable. But he reckoned there were at least a dozen dead. Out of fourteen!

'We are done,' Sandrine said.

'We were done from the moment that bitch betrayed us,' Draga growled.

'There are two left. Find them,' Tony said. 'They can't be far.' He surveyed the scene of the slaughter, then stooped over one of the dead women. Her head was a shapeless mess, but he recognized her both from her fair hair and the fact that she was a small woman, only a few inches over five feet and slightly built; her name, he recalled, had been Magda. And from a distance she could be mistaken for Sandrine. Perhaps, he realized, from even closer than that. Although both his and her portraits had been widely circulated, those had been head-and-shoulder impressions. None of the pursuing Germans could ever have seen Sandrine face to face – apart from Ulrich. But Ulrich was hardly likely to be part of the pursuit; he would have his hands full taking over from Wassermann, and, no doubt, consoling Angela. He looked up, and found Sandrine staring at him.

'Over here,' Sasha called. They ran to her. Private Soejer and one of the women lay in the underbrush. They were both shivering, and stared at them with vacant eyes. 'They are useless,' Sasha said.

'They are shell-shocked. They'll recover.'

'What can we do?' Draga asked. 'Five of us and these two, and the other wounded . . . No explosives, little ammunition, enough food for perhaps one day . . .'

'I agree that we must regard our mission as terminated,' Tony said. 'But we can still escape, and perhaps get back to Tito. This trap was laid for me – and for you, Sandrine. We are who they want. Once they are certain that they have killed us, they will call off the pursuit. So, take off your sidecap, smear it in blood. Then pull out some of your hair and stick it to the inside of the cap. Then put the cap on the ground a few feet from that woman with her head blown off.' Sandrine swallowed, but she did as he commanded. Tony selected one of the similarly unidentifiable men, roughly his own height and build, and took off his watch. It was a yachtsman's watch, bought before the war – when sailing had been his hobby – and made by Smith and Son, Southampton, as was clearly marked on the face. This he strapped round the dead man's wrist. Then he stood up. 'Let's move it.'

'Do you think they will believe it is us?'

'Yes. Because they will wish to believe it is us.'

'Well, Wassermann. That was a bit of a foul-up, eh?' General von Demmich was as jovial as he always was when he thought someone else was in a mess.

'I think it went rather well, Herr General,' Wassermann retorted.

'But you have not captured this terrible pair.'

'We have them limited to an area no more than a few miles square, cut off from any sustenance. As soon as the bombers are finished, my men will move in and clean up what is left.'

'*Your* men?' Demmich inquired. 'Those are *my* men you are using.'

'Of course, sir. I was under the impression that they had been seconded to my command.'

'Well, your command is now terminated, Colonel Wassermann. I need those men, urgently. I had supposed you intended to use the Ustase for this operation.'

'There are not enough of them, sir. If we are short of men, can we not request reinforcements?'

'No, we cannot request reinforcements, because there are none to be had. I have even been commanded to recall the troops I have been sending to the coast to get in front of the Partisans. They are needed elsewhere. As for the Ustase, you mean there are not enough *here*. But there are large numbers lying about Croatia, doing damn all. I can tell you, that is another cause for derogatory comment from Berlin, that we are not putting these people to proper use. Do you know that in Russia they are already recruiting an army of men opposed to the Soviets to fight along with the Wehrmacht? And they are going to be put into the front line. As I say, owing to the heavy casualties we suffered during the winter, and the increased Soviet resistance, there is not a man to be spared. And now this business in the mountains . . .'

'Bad news, sir?' Wassermann asked solicitously.

'It is not good news, Colonel. Tito's army has just engaged us in a rearguard battle. As usual, our commanders were taken by surprise. We have thirty-four dead and more than a hundred wounded. That casualty list is going to cause questions to be asked.'

'Indeed, sir. But isn't he still retreating?'

'I am beginning to wonder whether that is any longer an appropriate word to use. He is withdrawing, certainly. But as an army in being. Berlin is going to wish to know why we have not been able to stop him. Nor will they be pleased to learn that we have been concentrating so much time and effort, and so many men, in attempting to capture a small group of bandits here in our back yard. I can tell you, Colonel, that if Davis and Fouquet are not brought to book within twenty-four hours, I am going to have to report the lack of success.'

'They will be brought to book, sir. Do you have any precise information as to the present whereabouts of the Partisan army?'

Demmich gestured him to the map table. 'The action of which I spoke, the one fought yesterday, took place here.' He prodded the map. 'As I say, he is still withdrawing, to the north. The question is, where is he going? Back to Croatia? That is his homeland. Slovenia? That would be tricky.'

'More so for him than for us, Herr General. Slovenia is too close to Hungary. No, I think we need to look at this in a logical manner.' Demmich glared at him. 'This is because Tito is a logical man,' Wassermann went on, unperturbed. 'He may still be able to fight a successful rearguard action, but there can be no doubt that his people are taking a beating, in every sense. In those mountains they have to be short of food and shelter, and I would estimate they will be short of ammunition as well. And he will have to keep in mind that winter is just around the corner, in another couple of months. If his so-called army is caught out on those barren hills when the rain starts, followed by the snow, it will disintegrate. Now, he has been in this situation before. And what has he always done before? He has sought a base, somewhere that can be defended, where his people will be fed and sheltered by the local population, where he can regroup and recruit and prepare for another campaign. You may remember, Herr General, that last autumn he occupied Uzice, only a few miles from Belgrade. Well, we forced him out of there, so he withdrew into Bosnia and occupied Foca. Now that we have forced him out of there as well – *you* have forced him out of there – he will be looking for a similar situation.'

'Well, he won't find one in those mountains.'

'Not in the mountains. But if he comes out of the mountains . . .' Wassermann peered at the map, then prodded it with his forefinger. 'Bihac!'

Demmich leaned over the table. 'What is important about Bihac?'

'Nothing is important about Bihac in itself. But it is a town. It has houses and people and food and shelter. It lies at the foot of the mountains and is reasonably defensible. And it is a long way from our centres of strength. It also lies in the path of his retreat. I would estimate that he intends to make a base at Bihac.'

'You could be right. But if we can't catch him, how are we going to stop him? And once he gets there . . . I have been informed that even our air cover is going to have to be withdrawn to support the push to the Caucasus.'

'The way to stop him, as we cannot catch him but we know where he is going, would be to occupy Bihac before he can get there, Herr General.'

'And how am I supposed to do that? And with what?'

'As to the how, Herr General, if we act promptly, surely we can move in from the north before he, busy fighting rearguard actions as he is, can come up from the south over the mountains.'

'You are assuming that I can snap my fingers and create men by the battalion, Colonel. It simply is not possible. And if I take sufficient men from our other positions in Yugoslavia to garrison Bihac, I will leave us too thin on the ground elsewhere. That may even be Tito's plan. Meanwhile we have only your supposition that he intends to move on Bihac at all. If I put all our available strength into Bihac and he moves somewhere else, I shall lose my command. Bihac! A place no one in Berlin will ever have heard of!'

And if you cannot take the difficult decisions that are inseparable from warfare, you do not deserve to have a command, Wassermann thought. But before he could frame a reply there was a knock on the door, and Captain Vorster came in. 'Major Wiedermann is here, Herr General.'

'Wiedermann?!' Both officers turned together as Wiedermann entered the room and stood to attention.

'You are back very quickly,' Wassermann said suspiciously.

'I have returned, Herr General, Herr Colonel, to inform you that my mission has been successfully completed.'

'You have captured the Partisans?' Demmich demanded.

'I have destroyed them, Herr General.'

'You mean they are all dead? Not one of them surrendered?'

'I estimate that there may be a handful of them still alive, Herr General, but—'

'Then you have not completed your mission, Major,' Wassermann snapped. 'As long as Davis and Fouquet are alive—'

'Davis and Fouquet are dead, Herr Colonel.'

'You have proof of this?'

'I have looked on their dead bodies, Herr Colonel.'

'You killed them? I wished them taken prisoner.'

'I understand that, Herr Colonel. And that was my intention, certainly. However, they, and the retreating group of Partisans, were struck by a bomb dropped by one of our aircraft. It appears that they were carrying with them a large stock of explosives. As a result, they were blown to pieces. We found twelve bodies – or rather, the remains of twelve bodies. Another one was killed in a separate incident.'

'And Davis and Fouquet were amongst the dead? You can prove this? You saw their faces?'

'Their bodies were very badly damaged, sir. So were their faces. However, with your permission, Herr General?' Demmich nodded, and Wiedermann turned to the door to summon a waiting orderly, who carried a cloth bag, which he presented to the major. 'I have here, sir,' Wiedermann said, delving into the bag with the air of a Father Christmas distributing presents, 'one wristwatch, manufactured in Southampton, England, taken from Davis's dead body.' He laid it on the table. 'One sidecap, found beside the body of a woman who in every way answers the description I have been given of the woman Fouquet. If you will look inside the cap, Herr General, you will observe that there are yellow hairs stuck to the crown.'

The general preferred not to look inside the bloodstained cap, but Wassermann did so. 'Well, Wiedermann,' Demmich said. 'You are to be congratulated. Be sure that your name will be mentioned in my next despatch. Do you not agree, Wassermann?'

'Oh, entirely,' Wassermann said thoughtfully.

'Then you are dismissed, Wiedermann.' The major clicked

his heels and withdrew, Vorster closing the doors behind them both. 'Well,' Demmich said, returning to sit behind his desk. 'That is one problem solved, at any rate. You must be very pleased. And very relieved.' He frowned at his subordinate. 'You do not look pleased. Or relieved. You still have doubts? The evidence is here, man.' He gestured at the table. 'Incidentally, I would like those removed.' Wassermann went to the table and replaced the relics in the bag, pausing to gaze at Tony's watch for a few seconds. 'We must make sure that Tito learns of his henchman's demise,' Demmich said. 'Now, if only we could work out how to get rid of *him* . . .'

'With respect, Herr General, I have outlined how the main Partisan body should be dealt with.'

'Yes, yes. The problem is that I do not have the men to adopt your suggestion.'

'I think I may have a solution to that problem as well.'

'Indeed?' Demmich asked sceptically. 'Tell me about it.'

'In fact,' Wassermann said, 'it is a solution to two problems at once. You say there is criticism in Berlin that we are not putting the Ustase to proper use, and that there are a great number of them doing nothing more in Croatia than terrorizing the populace. And at the same time you make the point that we do not have enough of our own people to garrison Bihac. Why not have the Ustase do it?'

'Will they not merely terrorize the people of Bihac?'

'Is that of any importance to us? What matters is that they will occupy a vital position on the Partisans' line of retreat, and even more, if I am right that it is actually Tito's destination, then we may look forward to his destruction.'

Demmich stroked his chin. 'It will mean provoking something like a civil war.'

'With respect, Herr General, there already *is* something very close to civil war in Yugoslavia, between the Partisans and the Cetniks, and them both and the Ustase. If it becomes a full-scale war, well, as long as they are fighting each other, they cannot also be fighting us.'

167

Demmich snapped his fingers. 'The Cetniks! If we are to give any group our full support, should it not be the Cetniks? I was informed that you have contacts with them.'

'I had a contact in the Cetniks, yes, sir. But he has been killed by the Partisans.'

'You are not in contact with Mihailovic personally?'

'No, sir. I never have been. I do not trust him.'

'He is an enemy of the Partisans. And have not his people cooperated with us in the past?'

'The Cetniks have *pretended* to cooperate with us in the past, yes, sir. But never very effectively. I think that Mihailovic, who, as you no doubt know, is the representative of the government-in-exile on the ground in Yugoslavia, is prepared to jump in any direction that the wind happens to be blowing. In my estimation he is quite content to have us and the Partisans at each other's throats, so long as in doing that we leave him alone.'

'Hm. But to give such a position to the Ustase . . . Who would command them? This fellow Pavelic has not proved much good.'

'I agree, sir. But I think I have the very man. Someone who has cooperated extensively with us in the past, and who I know personally has the determination and the ruthlessness to carry out such a task.'

'Do I know this person?'

'Yes, indeed, sir. I believe you have entertained him to dinner in your house.' Wassermann could not resist the temptation to remind the general of that unhappy occasion.

'Captain Kronic? The man is a thug.'

'So is Tito. Set a thug to catch a thug, sir.'

Demmich considered for a few moments. 'Would he accept such a charge?'

'I am certain of it. He would have to be given the appropriate rank, of course.'

'What rank?' Demmich was suspicious.

'Well, if he is going to command virtually a regiment of the Ustase, he will have to be made a colonel.'

'Do I have that authority?'

'I am sure the governor-general would agree, sir. Once the circumstances are explained to him. He is as anxious to be rid of Tito as anyone.'

'Hm. Yes. I shall have a word with the governor-general.'

'By phone, sir. We must act with all possible haste.'

Demmich nodded. 'I shall telephone him today. I shall tell him this is your recommendation.'

'Thank you, sir.'

'However . . .' Demmich pointed. 'If I am to give you credit for this ingenious plan, you will also have to take responsibility for it. You have succeeded, however fortuitously, in ending the careers of Messrs Davis and Fouquet. It is now your responsibility to end the career of Tito. I shall make sure that Berlin knows this.'

Wassermann picked up the bag, faced the desk and clicked his heels. 'As you say, Herr General. Heil Hitler!'

PART THREE

THE TRIUMPH

For Freedom's battle once begun,
Bequeath'd by bleeding Sire to Son,
Though baffled oft is ever won.

George Gordon, Lord Byron

Eight

Frustration

'Do you think we should make any effort to find those remaining Partisans, Herr Colonel?' Ulrich asked, standing before Wassermann's desk.

Wassermann was putting his papers into his briefcase in preparation for leaving Sarajevo. 'I don't think that is the least necessary. We were summoned here to do a job, and we have successfully accomplished that. Davis and Fouquet are dead. So we are told. Those brigands who have survived will cause us no trouble, especially as they have lost their explosives together with their comrades. I doubt they will continue to survive for very long, certainly without Davis to lead them.'

'Yes, sir. I suppose ... well, that there is no doubt that Davis *is* dead.'

Wassermann looked up. 'What makes you say that?'

'I ... well ... I have been inspecting the watch, and the cap. They were both taken from bodies which had been blown to bits by the explosion, but they are both unmarked. I know there is blood on the cap, but that could easily have been put there. I have to say, Herr Colonel, that I find it somehow strange that we should have spent more than a year looking for that man, and the woman, had them slip through our fingers time and again, and then suddenly, almost without warning, they are both killed together in a single moment. That is uncanny.'

'It is not the least uncanny, Ulrich. Nor did it happen suddenly and without warning. It happened as a result of the trap we laid for them, and into which they fell.' His tone was aggressive, because he also had felt there was something suspicious about the watch's appearance.

'I would still feel happier had we looked upon their dead bodies. As you may know, sir,' Ulrich said, 'my occupation before the war was that of detective-inspector. In that capacity, I was required to investigate several murders.'

'I did know that, Ulrich.'

'The point I wish to make is that while it is possible to obtain a conviction for murder without a body, it is very difficult. Without a body, you see, there is no absolute guarantee that a crime has been committed, that the apparent victim has been killed. There have been several cases in criminal history where someone has been convicted of murder, and indeed been executed, only to have the supposed victim turn up a few months or even years later.'

Wassermann studied him for several seconds. Then he said, 'And the cap, and the English watch?'

Ulrich took off his cap and laid it on the desk. Then he unstrapped his watch and laid it beside the cap. 'Am I now dead, sir?'

Wassermann picked up his phone. 'Connect me with Major Wiedermann.' He tapped his fingers on the desk while Ulrich replaced his watch and cap. 'Ah, Wiedermann. Good morning. I wonder if you would be good enough to tell me what happened to the bodies of Davis and Fouquet? Yes, I understand that they were virtually destroyed. But you were able to take the watch from Davis's wrist, weren't you? I see. On the spot. Yes, I can see that the crater was a ready-made grave. Yes. I wish to see the bodies for myself. Yes, this morning. I need to return to Belgrade as quickly as possible. So, we will require a squad of six men equipped with shovels. And be sure that they have strong stomachs, eh? Yes, I said we. I wish you to be present. No, no, Wiedermann, I am not in the least doubting your account of what happened. But it is a matter of form. In my report I must state categorically that I have seen the bodies myself. Yes. Half an hour.' He replaced the phone. 'These

174

Wehrmacht officers, always fearing that we are trying to do them down. Get your gear together, Ulrich. We shall proceed directly to Belgrade when we have viewed the bodies.'

'Yes, sir.' Ulrich clicked his heels and left the office. Wassermann picked up his stick and his briefcase and followed. Two orderlies were bringing down the luggage, followed by Angela and Rosa.

'Well, my dear,' Wassermann said. 'I imagine you will be glad to see the back of this place.'

'I will always be glad to see the back of Sarajevo,' Angela said. 'I hope you do not intend to return.'

'It is not my intention,' Wassermann agreed.

They went into the yard, where two command cars and a truck waited, as did Major Wiedermann, who looked astonished, and disturbed, to see the two women. 'With respect, Herr Colonel,' he said, 'I do not think this is an occasion for ladies.'

'Ladies, perhaps not,' Wassermann agreed. 'My wife, yes.'

He held the door for Angela, and she got into the back of the first car. Wassermann sat beside her. Ulrich, Rosa and Wiedermann got into the second, and the little cavalcade drove out of the yard, the truck bringing up the rear, 'One day I am going to scratch out both of your eyes,' Angela remarked.

'I was only trying to be amusing.'

'We do not share the same sense of humour.' She looked left and right as they turned on to the street. 'Why are we going west? I thought we were returning to Belgrade.'

'We are. But there is a little detective work that needs doing first. I am sure you will find it interesting.'

She glanced at him. 'What has happened to Brolic?'

'I am sure that, whatever it is, she is not enjoying it.'

'You promised me that I would have the final say in the matter.'

'So that you could enjoy a last tender moment? I decided that would not be a good idea. Besides, she is serving a useful purpose.'

'Having her pubic hair set alight? What can she possibly have to tell you now?'

'Nothing. But I doubt anything is being done to her pubic hair. At least as regards matches. Kronic seemed quite taken with her.'

'The idea makes me feel sick. It would have been better to shoot her.'

'But she was a necessary gift, my dear. Colonel Kronic is now taking over a position of great responsibility. He has to be kept happy.'

Angela snorted, and looked away. They were out of the town now, and half an hour later were through Konjic. 'We are not returning to the place of the ambush?'

'Don't you wish to?'

'I never wish to see it again. I could have been killed.'

'But you weren't. One should always look on the bright side. Actually, we do not need to go that far. There.'

He pointed to the rough track leading off the road. 'I really do not wish to have to walk any further than is necessary.'

The track was very bumpy and they were thoroughly jolted when the driver at last braked. 'I do not think I can go any further, Herr Colonel.'

The other vehicles had stopped behind them, and Wiedermann came up to their car. 'It is in that valley over there, Herr Colonel.'

'How far?'

'Perhaps another mile.'

Wassermann pulled a face. 'Come along, my dear.'

Angela looked at her high-heeled boots. 'You expect me to walk a mile?'

'I am going to,' he pointed out. She also got out of the car, and they were joined by Ulrich and the six soldiers. 'You will remain with the drivers, Rosa,' Wassermann told the maid, who gave a little bob of the head.

The walk was certainly difficult for a man depending on his stick for balance. The ground was uneven, and it went up and down. More than once Wassermann would have fallen had Ulrich not held his arm, and several times the party had to stop to permit him to rest; Ulrich had thoughtfully brought along a bottle of schnapps with which to alleviate his discomfort.

'The Partisans fled over those hills,' Wiedermann explained. 'But you see, as they got higher, the trees thinned and they were exposed to our aircraft. Thus they were forced to turn away into this valley. But by then they had been spotted, and the planes were able to carry out low-level runs at them. Of course, hitting the man carrying the explosives was a stroke of fortune, but we would have got them in the end. We have arrived.'

They had reached a break in the trees, and in front of them lay the wreckage of the Partisan group – discarded backpacks, broken tommy-guns, articles of clothing. Wiedermann led them to the discoloured earth of the filled-in crater. 'You will dig here,' he told the sergeant in command of the squad. 'It is only a few feet down.'

Ulrich opened the satchel he was carrying and produced four gas masks. 'If you would like to put these on, Herr Colonel, Frau Wassermann.' Angela looked at him in amazement. But the six soldiers had also donned gas masks. 'It is roughly twenty-four hours since these people were killed,' Ulrich explained. 'And the weather is warm.'

Angela put on the mask, as did the men. The soldiers were now digging vigorously, piling the earth beside the original crater; already a leg had been uncovered. Angela at last understood what was happening. 'Do I have to be here?' she asked, her voice muffled by the mask.

'I'm afraid you do,' Wassermann said. 'You may be needed.'

Two of the soldiers were now in the shallow pit, sifting the earth aside, uncovering more bodies. 'This one,' Wiedermann said. One of his men seized the corpse by the ankles and pulled it clear. 'This is the woman.'

Angela turned away, and Wassermann held her arm. 'I wish you to look at it.'

'Oh, really, Fritz, that is horrible.' Angela inhaled loudly through the mask, and stared at the body; the clothes were covered in dirt, and the shattered head . . . 'Ugh!'

'Maggots,' Wassermann explained. 'We shall all look like that one day, my dear. Even you.'

'I feel sick. I wish to go back to the cars.'

'Just tell me who this woman is, and then you may leave.'

'This woman?' Angela's forehead creased above the mask. 'How should I know who she is?' She shuddered. 'Was.'

'She is your old friend Fouquet. Do you not recognize her?'

Angela looked at the corpse again. 'That is not Sandrine.'

'Of course it is. She is the same height and build, and her sidecap was found beside the body.'

'Let me look at her hand.' Wassermann nodded, and one of the soldiers extended the dead arm, raising the hand. 'I thought you had met her,' Angela said.

'I met her.'

Angela snorted. 'But I suppose you did not waste the time looking at her hands. Sandrine has perfect hands, with long, slender fingers.'

Wassermann peered at the dead hand; the fingers were short and stubby. 'Shit!' he commented.

'Just as she had the most perfect feet,' Angela said. 'Except that the soles were scarred. She told me they had been badly cut when she was escaping from Belgrade in April of last year.'

'Show us her feet,' Wassermann said. The boots and socks were pulled from the woman's feet. Several of her toes were calloused. But the soles of the feet were smooth. Wassermann turned to Wiedermann. 'Show me the man.'

Wiedermann looked over the several other bodies that had been disinterred. 'That one.' He pointed.

Wassermann stood above it. 'Well,' he remarked, 'I don't suppose anyone here knew Davis well enough to comment on his feet.'

'Excuse me, sir,' Ulrich addressed Wiedermann. 'From which wrist did you take the watch?'

'From the left.'

Ulrich bent over the body. 'This man has never worn a watch on this wrist.'

'How do you know that?' Wassermann asked.

Ulrich picked up the hand. 'There is no mark, Herr Colonel.'

'But the watch was on his wrist,' Wiedermann protested.

'How long after the explosion did you get here, Herr Major?'

'Well . . .' The visible part of Wiedermann's face flushed. 'It must have been about an hour. We did not know they had all been killed, you see, and were proceeding cautiously.'

'An hour,' Ulrich said. 'With respect, Herr Colonel, will you look at your own wrist, without your watch?' Wassermann frowned, and unstrapped his watch. 'During the months you were in hospital, sir, did you wear that watch?'

'Of course I did not.'

'So, sir, you have really only been wearing that watch, day in and day out, for the past few weeks. Yet there are distinct marks on your flesh. There is even a slight difference in colour, from the number of times you have been in the sun with your sleeves rolled up. This man's wrist is completely unmarked, and there is no colour contrast.'

Wassermann stared at the evidence for several seconds. Then he said, 'I wish to God you weren't a fucking forensic genius, Ulrich. Tell your men to reinter these cadavers, Wiedermann, and then join us.' He walked away from the grave, and stripped off his mask. Angela and Ulrich followed him and did likewise.

'What a fuck-up,' Angela said. 'You mean you actually believed you had got them?'

Wassermann glanced at her. 'We did get them, and you had better remember that. Ah, Wiedermann. I wish you to listen to me very carefully. General von Demmich has already forwarded a report to Berlin informing them that due to your untiring efforts Davis and Fouquet have been brought to justice. Because of this, he is recommending you for your actions.

There may even be an Iron Cross in it for you. Were the truth of the matter ever to get out, not only would your hopes of a medal be dashed forever, but your hopes of promotion also. You know the workings of the minds at OKH as well as I do. One false claim, or misrepresentation of the facts, goes in a man's record and stays there for the rest of his career.'

Wiedermann swallowed. 'I believed that it was them, sir.'

'What you believed is immaterial. OKH deals in facts. Or it likes to think it does. Therefore, as far as the rest of the world can ever know, Davis and Fouquet lie buried in that pit. The fact that they are not in that pit is known only to the four of us, and must remain our secret for the rest of the war.'

'Yes, Herr Colonel. But . . . if they are not dead, will they not reappear at some stage, and give us the lie?'

'I am going to take steps to make sure that does not happen,' Wassermann said. 'We will return to Sarajevo now. Your men can follow when they have finished filling in that hole.'

'You said we were going back to Belgrade,' Angela complained.

'We are. But I have someone to see first.'

Wassermann followed his tapping stick into the building appropriated by the Ustase as their headquarters in Sarajevo. Very few of the people he encountered had ever seen him before, but they stood to attention in respect to the black uniform. 'Where is Colonel Kronic?' he demanded.

'I am here, Colonel Wassermann.' Kronic stood at the top of the stairs. Wassermann blinked at him, and then looked at his watch. It was eleven in the morning, and Kronic was still wearing a dressing gown. 'If you will give me five minutes to dress, I will come down,' Kronic said.

'I will come up.'

'Ah . . .' Kronic looked as if he would have objected, but Wassermann was already on his way, his stick tapping the steps, and although Kronic was now technically of an equal rank thanks to his unexpected and still dazzling promotion, he knew that in fact there was no officer in the German army, and even less so in their auxiliary forces, who was of equal rank to a colonel in the SS – except for those ranked even higher within the Schutzstaffel itself.

Wassermann reached the top. 'You have an office?'

'Ah . . . in here, Herr Colonel.' The door was open. Wassermann entered an untidy room, at the rear of which there was another door, also open. Kronic attempted to get past him to close this door, but Wassermann prevented him, and stood in the opening to look into an equally untidy bedroom, an even untidier bed, and what could be described as a yet untidier girl, who sat up at his entry, attempting to gather sufficient of the sheet to hide her nakedness. 'You said I could have her,' Kronic reminded him. 'I am going to interrogate her, but it is best to soften them up.'

'He has raped me,' Jelena said. 'Again and again and again.'

Wassermann walked across the room. He hooked the ferrule of his stick into the sheet and flicked it away from Jelena's trembling hands. If what Rosa had told him was true, that most attractive body had been shared by both his wife and that little swine Halbstadt. 'You do not seem to have offered much resistance,' he remarked. 'I see no bruises.'

'He threatened me. He said he would . . .' She bit her lip.

'Set fire to your crotch? Perhaps you would enjoy that as well. Stay there.' Wassermann returned into the outer room, and Kronic closed the door. Wassermann sat beside the scarred desk. 'Why are you still here?'

'Well, there has been so much to do. There have been arrangements to be made. Phone calls to local commanders. My forces have to be assembled. I am leaving this afternoon.'

'To go where?'

'I am going first to Banjaluca. We have a unit stationed there. Then I am going to Zagreb, where our main forces are concentrated. From Zagreb we will move down on Bihac.'

'How long will this take?'

'I anticipate that our advance units will be in the town in

a week, and that we shall be fully concentrated in another week.'

'What will be your strength?'

'At least a thousand men.'

'You realize that Tito is supposed to have between three and five thousand? And that the Wehrmacht can offer you no assistance? Nor can the Luftwaffe.'

'Tito may have had a few thousand men when he left Foca. Retreating, crossing those mountains, harried by your army and your air force, I estimate he will hardly have half of that now. And we will have the better weaponry and unlimited ammunition . . . You said we would have that.'

'You are being granted access to whatever you require from our arsenal in Zagreb.'

'And we will be behind fortifications. If I could also have a squadron of tanks . . .'

'You are required to *defend* Bihac, not conduct an offensive.'

'The tanks would provide me with artillery. At present I have none.'

Wassermann stroked his chin. 'It might be possible. Do you know Hans Gruber?'

'I have met him. But . . . he is in hospital.'

'He is due to be discharged in a few days' time. In view of the beating he received from that Partisan bitch he is to be invalided home. However, I happen to know that he is very unhappy about this. He is desperate to have another crack at the Partisans, and the woman Janitz in particular. Well, it seems very likely that she is dead, killed in the explosion that wiped out Davis's command, but there is no need for him to know this. I think he may well volunteer to join your force, and as there is no prospect of *him* going to the Russian front, I should think General von Demmich will probably give him permission to do so. In those circumstances, the general might well be prepared to release six tanks.'

'That would be splendid. Then I would have a real fighting force.'

'I hope you are right. Now there is something, an additional task, that I require of you, in the most complete secrecy.' Kronic looked interested. 'I have just discovered that our assumption that Davis and Fouquet are dead was a mistaken one.'

Kronic raised his eyebrows. 'I thought you had incontrovertible evidence?'

'We did. Unfortunately, the evidence was provided by Davis and Fouquet themselves.'

'Then . . . where are they?'

'I have no idea. I can only make a further assumption. We do know that your little friend in there claims there were never more than twenty of them. We also know that thirteen of them were killed. That leaves too small a group to operate effectively, especially as several of those survivors must be carrying wounds. We also know that their store of explosives has been destroyed. All of these factors lead me to feel certain that they will now have aborted their mission and that they will be trying to rejoin Tito.'

'Well,' Kronic said, 'perhaps they will perish in the mountains.'

'I would very much like to think that would happen.'

Kronic leaned back in his chair. 'I do not have the men to mount a pursuit of Davis and Fouquet and also garrison Bihac.'

'I appreciate that. But do you not have contacts in the Cetniks?'

'Ah . . . perhaps,' Kronic said cautiously. 'Don't you?'

'My principal contact got himself killed during the winter. And having been back in Yugoslavia only a few weeks I have not yet had the opportunity to make any fresh ones. However, knowing as we do that the Cetniks have a headquarters around Ravna Gora – that is, about fifty miles north-west of Sarajevo – it occurs to me that this is virtually on the road from here to Zagreb. The road you are about to take.'

'That is true,' Kronic said thoughtfully.

'Situated as they are, the Cetniks are well placed to send a party into the mountains without anyone knowing about it. I am sure they have many local contacts amongst the people there, people who regard Mihailovic as the proper leader of the Yugoslav resistance and would therefore be prepared to give his men any information they may have on the whereabouts of the Partisans, or a small group of Partisans.'

'That is true,' Kronic said again. 'Am I allowed to tell my contact who they are actually looking for?'

'Is that necessary?'

'I think it would be a help. I happen to know that the Cetniks as a group, and my contact in particular, hate Davis and Fouquet much more than they hate the Germans. With respect, Herr Colonel.'

'Explain. I know that Davis and Fouquet served with the Cetniks briefly, after their escape from Belgrade in April of last year. I have never learned why they left to join Tito's people. Presumably it was because they are Communists.'

'I do not believe they are Communists. They abandoned the Cetniks because Mihailovic would not accept Croatians in his force. Indeed, I understand that he wanted to execute a Croatian woman who was with them, a woman who happened to be Davis's fiancée at the time. But my man – his name is Maric – has a more personal reason for hating Davis and Fouquet. Because he fears them.'

'Explain.'

'Maric was a member of the assassination squad that entered Belgrade last October to murder the governor-general. Your wife's father.'

'I was there,' Wassermann said. 'But that was a Partisan squad. You say this man is a Cetnik.'

'He is now. At that time he was serving with the Partisans. However, as you may remember, the assassination squad, which included Davis and Fouquet, attempted to make their escape through the sewers. Your people pursued them. Maric offered to remain behind and hold off the pursuit, giving them instructions as to how to get out. But it was a betrayal. The directions he gave them led them directly into the hands of your people. Maric figured – correctly, as you see – that once you had the other members of the squad you would cease looking for him, and so he would get away.'

'So did Davis and Fouquet,' Wassermann observed. 'But they lost Kostic. I can see that they would have it in for Maric.'

'More than that,' Kronic said. 'Do you remember that your people did eventually get hold of Fouquet?'

'I remember very well,' Wassermann said. 'I had her in my hands, and before I could do anything about it I was hit.'

'But you didn't actually capture her yourself.'

'She was captured by the Cetniks, and handed over to us. They were looking for the reward we had offered.'

'Did they get it?'

'No, they did not. As I say, I was wounded, and the matter was left in Ulrich's hands. I know he reported to Berlin and recommended that the reward be paid, but before a decision had been reached, my wife – Fräulein von Blintoft, as she then was – had been captured in turn, and the governor-general, her father, had arranged for her to be exchanged for Fouquet. So the Cetniks never got a penny.'

'Well, I don't know who actually delivered Fouquet to you after her capture, but the man who made the capture in the first place was Maric. He was a corporal then. He is a captain now.'

'It's a small world. So, she has two reasons for hating him.'

'And he has every reason for wishing to dispose of her. Is the reward still extant?'

'Certainly.'

'Would you care to double it?'

'I have not the authority to do that. I would have to refer the matter to the governor-general.'

'Do you think he would agree?'

'It would mean admitting to him that Davis and Fouquet are still alive and free. However . . .' Their deaths had been confirmed, and indeed trumpeted, by Demmich. As he had reminded Wiedermann, Wassermann was well aware how jealously the Wehrmacht guarded its reputation, and especially that of its officers, with greater determination the higher the officer's rank; they might condemn a man utterly for a false claim, but until that falsehood was proven and made public they would do everything in their power to protect him. The news that Fouquet and Davis were still alive after they had been reported dead would be an even blacker mark on Demmich's record than it would be on Wiedermann's. Thus the governor-general would almost certainly be prepared to go to some lengths to retrieve the situation before it became public knowledge. 'I think he could be persuaded.'

'It was ten thousand marks, was it not? Each. Which is now to be doubled. I will persuade Maric to undertake the task of finding these people. But the reward will be paid to me. I will give Maric his share.'

'Has anyone ever told you, Kronic, that you are a scoundrel?'

Kronic grinned. 'I am sure many people hold that opinion of me, Herr Colonel. But then, I am sure many hold it of you, too.'

Wassermann stood up. 'I look forward to hearing from you. And not only as regards Davis and Fouquet. I wish to hear that you have defeated Tito's army, and driven it back into the mountains. However, as regards Davis and Fouquet, I will require photographs of their bodies, and their faces must be clearly identifiable.'

'Very good. And what if they are taken alive? Do you wish them returned to you?'

'Certainly not. I wish the photographs of their dead bodies.'

'So, if they are taken alive, you are willing to leave their disposal in my hands.'

'Yes, Kronic. As long as it is done in private.'

Kronic grinned. 'Is the woman as beautiful as they say?' He held up his finger before Wassermann could speak. 'I am a scoundrel. But be truthful, would you not like to have

Fouquet, stripped naked and tied to, shall we say, a bed before you?' He glanced at Wassermann's crotch. 'That is, supposing you were able.'

'One day I am going to strangle that little toad with my bare hands,' Wassermann remarked, sitting beside Angela as they drove back to Belgrade. They were alone except for the chauffeur; Rosa and Ulrich were in the second car. 'And whoever has been gossiping about me to him.' He glanced at his wife. 'How well do you know him?'

'I never met him until the day we arrived in Sarajevo.'

'Have you ever had a conversation with him?'

'He is not the sort of person with whom I would choose to have a conversation; I found him utterly distasteful. And to think that you have allowed him to get his claws into poor Brolic . . .'

'Poor Brolic, is it? I thought you wanted to execute her?'

Angela shrugged. 'I would not have ill-treated her.'

'Merely put a pistol to the nape of her neck. What do you have under that so attractive tit of yours? I am sure it is not a heart.'

'I am a realist. Is Kronic going to execute her?'

'I don't think he is. Not for a while, at least.'

'You mean he is going to continue torturing her?'

'Not in the sense I think you mean. He is going to go on putting more into her than his claws.'

'The idea is repulsive.'

'Is it? Once upon a time, I seem to remember, you enjoyed having things put into you. By me.'

'Yes, my dear. I was very young and inexperienced. But now that you are no longer, shall I say, interested . . .'

'You turn your attention elsewhere? Are you pleased that Sandrine is alive?'

'I would not like to think of her being blown up by a bomb. I am very glad that did not happen. She was such a lovely person.'

'Well, she is going to be captured, and executed. Kronic is going to take care of it.'

At last Angela turned her head. 'You would let that little rat . . .'

'He is very keen. But he has promised me a photograph of her dead body. I will let you have a copy, to put on your dressing table.'

'Are you really as vicious as you pretend to be?'

'I am far more vicious than you even suspect. Have you any idea what it is like to have to watch the world of beautiful women surrounding you, possessing all the feelings and instincts of a man in the prime of life, and being unable to do anything about it?'

Angela rested her hand on his. 'I am so terribly sorry, Fritz.'

'You are a lying bitch.'

'I am your wife. If there is anything I can do to help you, you have but to say.'

'Well, then,' he said, 'you can begin by telling me about Halbstadt.'

Angela sat at the desk in her sitting room. 'Come in, Bestic.'

The housekeeper entered. It was the day after her employers' return from Sarajevo, and Wassermann had already left for the office. Bestic had no idea what had happened, but she gathered that the trip had not been a total success.

'Are the menus prepared for today?' Angela asked, her voice quiet.

'Of course, madame.'

'Very good.' Angela indicated the envelope on the desk. 'That is your next week's wages.'

Bestic raised her eyebrows. 'Today is Tuesday, madame. I am usually paid on Friday.'

'I am paying you now. You are sacked. Get out of my house.'

Bestic looked down her nose. 'You cannot sack me, madame. I am employed by the colonel. I will wait for the colonel to come home.'

'You will not. You are a deceitful bitch. You have been spying on me. You are a Serbian guttersnipe. But all Serbs are guttersnipes.'

'And what are you, madame, but a German whore?'

'You . . . you dare to speak to me like that?'

'Are you afraid of the truth, madame?'

'You . . . you . . .' Angela pulled open the drawer, and snatched out the Luger pistol that lay there. 'Get out before I shoot you.'

Bestic's lip curled. 'You will not shoot me, madame. You have not the guts for it. You would hang. Even you.'

Angela squeezed the trigger.

Nine

The Reunion

Tony surveyed the remnants of his command. He was flanked by Sandrine and Sasha, Draga and Davidovic. Soejer and Katerina, the two survivors of the explosion, had slumped to the ground. The three original wounded were also seated. 'Are we finished, Colonel?' asked one of the men.

'Our mission is finished, yes,' Tony said. 'We have no more explosives, and we have lost most of our people.'

'Will we surrender?' the wounded woman asked. Her bandages were bloodstained; her wounds had opened during the scramble up and down the hills.

'We will not,' Tony said. 'We are going to follow the army, and attempt to rejoin it. We will take you, but it is going to mean walking several miles every day, and I do not know how often we will eat.'

'We will be a hindrance,' the woman said. 'I am dying, in any event. My wound is putrefying.'

Tony glanced at Sandrine. They had in fact been aware of the smell since rejoining the casualties. 'There will be a doctor in Konjic,' Sandrine suggested.

'Konjic is full of Germans,' the wounded man pointed out.

'The Germans are outside of the town,' the woman said. 'The people in Konjic will help us. I am Bosnian. They will help us. We are no more use to the army. Is that not right, Colonel?'

'You are our comrades,' Tony said. 'If you wish to come with us, we will help you for as long as we can.'

'Then we will all be killed. We will go into Konjic.'

Tony looked at the two men. Their shoulders hunched, but they knew that the woman was right. 'You are brave people,' he said. 'Now, let us divide up what we have.'

'No,' the woman said. 'You will need everything. Leave us two of those German rifles and a dozen cartridges. And three grenades.'

Sasha doled out the weapons. 'We shall not forget you,' Sandrine said.

The woman looked at Tony. 'Was our mission a success, Colonel?'

'We did what we were commanded to do. That is a success.' He saluted them, and his little band did also.

They could not risk crossing the road until after dark, and so remained concealed amidst the rocks. There were still German soldiers beneath them, but these were mainly cleaning up the mess. 'There are only twenty of them,' Sasha said. 'We could go down there and kill them all. I wish to do that.'

'There is no point in trying to convince them that we are destroyed as a fighting force,' Tony said, 'and then demonstrating that we are very much alive.'

'You have iced water in your veins,' she grumbled. 'I have blood.'

'Stefan was my comrade,' Davidovic said.

Tony sighed. 'They were all our comrades, Corporal. But we have a duty to those of our comrades who are still alive and fighting. If you wish to rejoin Stefan, you are welcome to do so.' Davidovic hunched over his gun.

Sandrine lay beside Tony. 'They will get over it.' She spoke French so that the others would not understand her.

'I'm not sure they will, at least not in a hurry.' He remembered the retreat from Uzice, when more than once they had had to abandon their wounded when the Germans got too close – and in the Partisan army, abandoned wounded are expected to commit suicide rather than be captured. The women had

191

been affected for days. Now the men were equally affected. And him? If he did have iced water in his veins, this war had put it there.

'You know I will support you,' Sandrine said. 'Just tell me one thing: *was* the mission a success?'

'No.'

'We blew up a train. And we killed Wassermann.'

'One train. And I'm not sure that was Wassermann. If it was a trap laid by him, he would hardly be likely to expose himself like that.'

'He exposed Angela.'

Tony gave a savage smile. 'Perhaps he felt sure I would not shoot a woman. Even that woman.'

'I would have shot her,' Sandrine said. 'Had I the rifle.'

'I should have shot that girl,' Tony said. 'The very moment she turned up.'

'Then you would have lost Sasha.'

'Instead of which I have lost sixteen good men and women.' He looked at Soejer and Katerina, who continued to sit staring vacantly. 'Or eighteen.' He squeezed her shoulder. 'Rest up. We are going to have to move all night.'

As soon as it was dark, and the Germans had returned to Konjic, they crossed the road. They had no idea where they might find the Partisans, their only certainty being that Tito had intended to move north-west, so they travelled in that direction, using Tony's compass to home in on Bihac as Tito had commanded, even if the others, including Sandrine, did not yet know that was their destination.

Progress was very slow, both because they could only safely move by night and because they had consumed all their food in forty-eight hours. They had experienced this before, on the retreat from Uzice the previous winter, when they had been reduced to cooking all manner of plants not generally regarded as edible. This time, too, the women did wonders with such things as nasturtium seeds, but Tony knew they had to keep up their strength, and he and Sandrine, both excellent shots, brought down the occasional rabbit to enhance their diet. Mostly, however, they depended on the various small villages they came across. On these occasions the initial reluctance of the locals to risk involvement with a Partisan patrol was invariably overcome by the sight of the gold coins supplied by Tito. The villagers were also a continuous source of information, confirming that the Partisan army had indeed passed that way, and that various German units had followed.

Tony was apprehensive of encountering a German force too large to be tackled, but in fact after they had been on their way about a week he realized that the aircraft they had seen so much of earlier were totally absent, and the following day, as they hid in a gully, they observed a body of soldiers, at least a hundred strong, tramping through the adjacent valley, but marching east instead of north-west.

'Do you think they have been defeated?' Sandrine asked.

'They don't look like defeated troops,' Sasha objected.

'Then they must have completed their task,' Davidovic said. 'And either captured or killed the general.'

They looked at each other in consternation. 'We'll believe that when it is confirmed,' Tony said.

He looked over his small command. They had now spent nine days trekking across the mountain, sticking to the valleys where possible. But each valley was higher than the last, and now they were surrounded by towering peaks. Up here it was always cold once the sun set, but as they spent the nights moving this had not been a problem, and in fact they had been amazingly lucky with the weather, which, apart from the odd summer shower, had stayed fine and warm during the day. Yet the going had been very hard, and Tony had only maintained morale by constantly reminding them that they were closing on the army.

Soejer and Katerina had largely recovered, at least externally, from the shock of the explosion and of seeing their comrades blown to pieces. They had gradually regained their hearing, and were still subject to nervous twitches, but they could talk and even on occasion laugh, and they were able to take their places both on watch and in preparing food. He doubted they would be a problem, simply because their mental horizons were for the moment concerned only with survival.

Similarly, Draga was not a very imaginative woman. Besides, she had campaigned with him so often that she had the utmost faith in his judgement. The same could be said of Sandrine, who he knew would go wherever he commanded, and do whatever he commanded too, without a moment's hesitation.

He could not be so certain about Sasha. She also had fought at his side on several occasions, in situations even more desperate than this, and she had never failed him or let him down in actual combat; only when the lives of some of her girls had been at risk had she made decisions of her own which had more than once been costly. Now four of her women were dead. But there was also the Jelena factor; it was eating away at her mind, Tony knew. She had certainly loved the girl; whether it was as a sister or a sexual companion or simply out of a sense of guilt at having executed her brother he had no idea. But it had been her eagerness to welcome Jelena back into their ranks that had led to the disaster. He knew that was weighing heavily on her mind, and while he felt she would keep going, there could be no doubt that she was in an emotionally volatile state.

Davidovic worried him the most. The corporal had also proved his worth in combat, but he was a silent, withdrawn man, and he was equally unhappy at having to abandon his comrades. Like Sasha, he was existing on a desire to avenge their deaths, which could only be achieved by rejoining the army and resuming the fight. If any of them got the idea that the army no longer existed . . .

The absence of aircraft meant they could move during the day, and thus both travel faster and cover more ground in every twenty-four hours. But equally they grew steadily more exhausted, their exhaustion compounded by their poor diet. Meanwhile their clothes were in rags and their boots holed.

Yet they knew they were on the right track, and closing on the army. More than once they came across little groups of graves, and discarded equipment. And after they had spent a month in the hills they came to a village where they were told that the army, or what was left of it, had passed that way only the previous week. 'How many?' Tony asked the mayor.

He shrugged. 'Maybe a thousand.' Sandrine blew through her teeth. The mayor nodded. 'Many deserted even here.'

'And the Germans?'

The mayor grinned. 'There are no Germans. There is no necessity for them. The Partisans are finished.'

'Shall I shoot him?' Sasha inquired.

'He's entitled to his opinion,' Tony said. 'We need food.'

'There is no food. Your army took it all.'

'You must have heard them coming. You will have hidden enough. We will buy it off you.'

The mayor's eyes gleamed. 'You have money?' Tony felt in his haversack and took out a gold coin. He had only five left. But if what this man had told him was true, they would have caught Tito up in another ten days at the most. The mayor examined the coin. 'You have more of these? Let me see them.'

'Let me see your food,' Tony countered.

The mayor looked at the group, taking in their ragamuffin appearance, but also their tommy-guns and the pistols on their belts and the strings of grenades round their necks, and decided that it would be safer to do business with them than to attempt to rob them. 'Bring out the food,' he told his people.

They left the village, where they had also been able to buy beer, in a mixture of elation and despair, carrying enough food to last them several days. 'Are we really going to catch the army up?' Katerina asked.

'Within a week,' Tony promised. 'We are travelling at least three times as fast as they are.'

'What army?' Davidovic asked sourly.

'Even a thousand men are an army,' Tony told him. 'And once we get to Bihac, we will be able to recruit, and re-arm.' He hoped.

'Bihac?' Sandrine asked. 'Is that where we are going?'

'That's where the army is going,' Tony said.

A few evenings later they bivouacked on the edge of a small wood that was close to a precipitous cliff face. This looked west, and Sandrine stood with Tony to gaze at a splendid vista as the sun sank into the mountains, while below them was a sheer drop of several hundred feet into the next valley. 'There are times when it is good to be alive,' Tony said.

'Any time is good to be alive,' Sandrine countered. 'But that drop gives me the shivers.'

It was almost dark. He held her hand as they turned away from the cliff edge and returned to where Draga had lit a fire. 'Let's—' He checked when he saw movement in the trees. 'Down.'

'They're behind us, too,' Sandrine said.

'Shit! Katerina . . .' She had been on watch, but there was no sign of her.

'I have twenty men here,' a voice called. 'Armed with automatic weapons. You are surrounded. Stand up with your hands on your heads.'

'Maric!' Sandrine whispered. 'My God, Maric!' Her hand tightened on her tommy-gun. Tony shook his head. 'He will not take me again,' she said. 'You promised that would not happen.'

'Would you rather die?'

'Yes,' she said fiercely. 'I would rather die.'

'And I am asking you to live. At least until we can get even with the bastard.'

'You have ten seconds to surrender,' Maric said. 'Or we will fire into you.'

Tony looked left and right. Soejer had already laid down

his rifle. Draga and Davidovic were waiting to be told what to do. Sasha was breathing heavily, and was stroking her tommy-gun, clearly about to explode. Tony felt the same way, but their position was untenable. They were surrounded on three sides; the fourth was the cliff edge. They could not see their enemy, but they themselves were totally exposed against the sunset. To attempt a shoot-out would mean their deaths. Tony stood up, leaving his tommy-gun on the ground.

'That is very sensible of you, Colonel,' Maric said. 'Now drop the pistol as well. And the knife and the grenades.'

Tony took off his belts, and laid them beside the tommy-gun.

'Very good. Come along, ladies.'

Sandrine stood up, leaving her weapons behind.

'As beautiful as ever,' Maric remarked. 'I am so happy that you have survived, mademoiselle. Till now.'

Sandrine said nothing, but, although they were not touching, Tony thought he could feel the hatred emanating out of her.

'Come along,' Maric said.

Both Davidovic and Soejer stood up, hands on their heads. A moment later Draga followed their example.

'And you,' Maric told Sasha.

Sasha stood up. She had discarded her tommy-gun and belts, but Tony saw that she was holding a grenade in her right hand, which she pressed against her hair as she put her hands on her head; it was invisible at a distance. 'No,' he muttered. 'Don't be a fool, Sasha.'

The Cetniks emerged from the trees, weapons levelled. They came from both sides, twelve on the right and eight on the left. Maric, a short, dark man with a thick moustache and a straggly beard, was with the larger group. 'What a coup,' he said. 'Do you know, Colonel, that we were never paid for delivering Mademoiselle Fouquet to the Germans last November? But I am reliably informed that the reward is still outstanding. In fact, it has been doubled. You are now worth twenty thousand marks each. Is that not a great compliment?'

Tony watched him approach. At the same time he saw, out of the corner of his eye, Sasha moving away from them and towards the cliff edge, for the moment ignored by the Cetniks, who were concentrating on Sandrine and himself; he did not suppose any of them had ever seen Sasha before, or even heard of her. He had no idea what she was thinking of doing. He couldn't believe that she was going to jump, and in any event, he didn't know how he could stop her, or if he had any right to do so, in view of what Maric was saying. But what Maric was saying surely did not apply to her, or any of the others. 'You mean to hand us over to the Germans?' he asked. 'Then you have no interest in our companions.'

'None. Except that they are Partisans. They will die with you.'

'Die? How can you claim the reward if we are dead?'

'That is how the Germans, at least Wassermann, want you. Dead. All they wish is a photograph of your body. And of yours, mademoiselle.' He slapped his haversack. 'I have a camera here, to take your pictures. Do you know what I am going to do? When I have shot you, mademoiselle, I am going to strip you naked before I photograph you. But I have a better idea. I will strip you naked first, eh? Because we have some unfinished business, do we not? And anyway, it is too dark to take a photograph now. You will amuse my men, and me, until tomorrow morning.'

Sandrine looked at Tony. She was breathing heavily and was clearly just as wound up as Sasha. But Sasha moved first. She now walked away from the group fast and reached the cliff edge. 'That woman!' said one of the Cetniks.

Maric swung round. 'What do you think you are doing?' he demanded.

'Dying,' Sasha said. As she spoke she pulled the pin of the grenade.

'Silly bitch,' Maric commented, assuming that she was going to blow herself up.

But Sasha had drawn back her arm, having counted to two. 'She's going to throw it!' someone shouted.

'Scatter!' shouted someone else.

Maric raised his pistol and fired. Sasha gave a shriek and disappeared over the cliff, but the grenade was already flying through the air. 'Down!' Tony shouted, grabbing Sandrine's arm and forcing her to the ground. The sound of the explosion ripped through the evening, followed immediately by a chorus of screams and shouts. For the moment the Cetniks were entirely preoccupied – and the Partisans had nothing to lose, as they had just been condemned to death. Tony and Sandrine had dropped beside their weapons, as had Draga and Davidovic. None of them looked at any other for either orders or support; they merely grabbed their guns and started firing, while Tony threw two more grenades.

Maric went down in the first volley, as did several of his men. Others fell to the grenades. Of the remainder, most took to their heels. Only one or two attempted to return fire. Their panic-stricken shooting was mostly wild, but at such close range they could not entirely miss. Soejer fell with a shriek, Draga cried out, and Tony felt a dull thud somewhere in his body, without at the moment feeling any pain. But now Sandrine was on her feet, tommy-gun moving to and fro as she sprayed the remaining Cetniks. When her gun clicked empty she picked up Tony's to finish the job, moving closer to her victims, Davidovic at her elbow.

The shooting stopped, the echoes winging away into the gathering night. 'Finish them off,' Sandrine said to Davidovic. 'Not him.' She pointed at Maric, who was moaning and writhing on the ground. 'I wish to speak with him.' She knelt beside Tony. 'Is it bad?'

'It hurts,' he said. The shock was wearing off.

She tore open his shirt. 'I do not think it is so bad.' She pulled his shirt right away from the arm and he grimaced with pain, his head jerking when he heard the crack of the pistol Davidovic was using to dispose of the wounded Cetniks. 'You see,' Sandrine remarked, running her hand over the rear of his shoulder, 'the bullet is sticking out. It went right through, above the heart and below the shoulder blade. You are very lucky. You are always lucky.'

'Listen,' he said. 'See to Draga.'

She turned her head. 'Draga is dead.'

Davidovic stood above them. 'Will the colonel die?'

'Of course he will not die,' Sandrine said. 'Now, I am going to give you some morphine, then I am going to take the bullet out.'

Tony did not object. The evening was now swinging round and round his head as the pain took hold, and the sips of morphine sent his mind whirling away through space. Yet he could still think. 'Listen,' he said.

'Sssh.' Sandrine was bending over his back, her tongue between her teeth. 'You have stronger fingers than me,' she told Davidovic. 'Pull it out.' Davidovic obeyed. Tony gave a shout of pain, and then subsided. 'That is good,' Sandrine said. 'Now, I will put antiseptic on it, and then I will bind you up. The antiseptic will be painful. You must take some more morphine.'

Even that didn't help all that much. 'You are a master of understatement,' he muttered through gritted teeth.

'And you are a master of getting yourself wounded,' she said. 'Is this not the fourth time? It is a bad habit.'

'Listen,' he said. 'Is Maric still alive?'

'Can you not hear him? He is making a terrible noise. I will deal with him in a minute. Then he will make even more noise.'

'Listen,' Tony said again. 'Find out how he knew where to find us.'

Sandrine frowned. 'You think we were betrayed?'

'We're supposed to be dead, remember?'

She went on bandaging him with experienced expertise, and tied the last knot. Then she gave him water to drink. 'Now you must rest. Davidovic, go through all these bodies. We need all the food and water they are carrying, and any bullets that will fit our guns. Also any grenades they may have.'

'Yes, Major.' Davidovic went off.

'You are a natural leader,' Tony muttered, fighting off the waves of unconsciousness.

'I always knew this,' she admitted. 'But I have always been content to follow you. Now I am acting as your deputy. I will think as you would think, and act as you would act. Until you are ready to take command again.'

'Then Maric . . .'

'Oh, yes, Maric.' She moved away from Tony to stoop beside the wounded Cetnik, peering at him in the gathering gloom. 'You are not in good shape,' she told him. 'You have been shot in the stomach.' Maric's hands were pressed to the wound, but the blood and muck were seeping through his fingers. 'You are going to die. But it may take a little while. Think of it, Maric, you are never going to rape a woman again. And you will die without achieving your lifetime ambition, to rape me. Does that not make you sad?'

'Morphine,' he groaned. 'For the love of God, mademoiselle, give me some morphine.'

'I do not think there is any love of God in you,' Sandrine said. 'And I am very sure there is no love in God for you. Shall I make your dying more painful yet?'

'Mademoiselle, I beg you . . .'

'But I shall not – if you tell me why you came looking for us, and how you knew where to look for us.'

Maric inhaled, a dreadful sound. 'It was Kronic who told me where to come.'

'Kronic? The Ustase captain?'

'He is a colonel now.'

'And he knows we are alive? How?'

'Wassermann worked it out.'

'So he is still alive. Faults on both sides. And he worked out that if we were alive, we would try to rejoin Tito by the most direct route. That makes sense. But you were still lucky to find us in these mountains.'

'We found out where you were from a village you visited

four days ago. We have been stalking you since then.'

'But if Kronic knew that we were alive, why did he send you after us instead of coming himself?'

'Because he has been given a command. He commands in Bihac. Mademoiselle, morphine. I am begging you.'

The words had penetrated Tony's fogged brain. 'Bihac! Kronic has been given command of Bihac? Why?'

'It lies across Tito's line of retreat,' Maric panted. 'Colonel, sir, I beg you . . .'

'What force does he command?'

'Over a thousand men.'

'Kronic has been given command of German troops?'

'His people are all Ustase. He has rallied almost the entire force. And he has been given a squadron of tanks . . .'

'The Germans have given the Ustase tanks?'

'No. They have placed the tanks under his command to hold Bihac, but they are manned by Germans, and are under the command of a German officer, a Major Gruber. Colonel, I am begging you. The pain . . .'

'Has he anything more to tell us?' Sandrine asked.

Tony had been trying to sit up. Now he lay down again. 'I do not think so.'

'Then I will put him out of his misery. Happy dreams, Maric.' She put her pistol muzzle to his head and squeezed the trigger.

Tony swallowed, but reflected that she had actually done Maric a kindness, as there was no way they could end his pain other than by death. And besides, the man, in selling her to the Gestapo, quite apart from betraying them in the Belgrade sewers, had caused Sandrine endless hours of pain and misery. But still, when he remembered the utterly feminine and dainty young woman he had known in Belgrade two years before . . . War did that to people. He still intended to marry her, if they both survived, but he increasingly found it difficult to imagine her settling down to a life of domesticity in a Somerset village, or even in central London.

'We must leave here,' Davidovic said. 'We cannot bury all of these bodies. The weather is warm. By tomorrow this place will stink.'

Sandrine chewed her lip. 'We will have to carry the colonel.'

'You are a woman,' Davidovic said; he had clearly been considering the matter. 'I have made the decision. We cannot stay here. If the colonel cannot move, then we will leave him a canteen of water, some food, a pistol, and a grenade. Those are the rules.'

There was a click, and Tony raised his head. Sandrine had drawn her pistol with lightning speed and presented it to Davidovic's forehead. 'Drop your weapons.'

'You cannot kill me,' Davidovic protested. 'Without me you are nothing.'

'If I let you live it will be as a beast of burden. I am in command. Drop your weapons, or I will blow you apart.' Slowly Davidovic discarded his guns and his knife, followed by his grenades. 'Now get over there.' Again slowly, Davidovic withdrew. He was, for the moment at least, overawed by her aggressive determination – and he had the evidence of her ruthlessness before his eyes. 'Stop there,' Sandrine commanded. 'Sit.' Davidovic sat on the ground. 'And stay sitting.'

'Sandrine,' Tony said. 'This will not work. You cannot tend me and watch him at the same time. You will have to sleep, some time. And word must be got to Tito, as rapidly as possible. If he just marches into Bihac, believing it is undefended, he will be cut to pieces.'

'I know,' Sandrine said. 'But I will not leave you. It is a pity Draga did not survive.'

'Or Sasha. She saved our lives.'

'I know. She is a heroine.'

'And Katerina.'

'I will send Davidovic to look for her in the morning. But . . . what is that noise?'

'A bird call.'

Sandrine listened, and they both heard the wailing cry again.

'That is a human voice!' Sandrine said, looking right and left as she got to her feet.

'It is from over the cliff,' Davidovic said. 'It is a ghost.'

'Help!' came the cry. 'Help me!' Sandrine ran to the cliff edge.

'For God's sake, be careful,' Tony shouted. 'And you, don't move,' he told Davidovic, levelling his pistol as the corporal made to get up.

Sandrine had dropped to her stomach and was peering over the edge into the gloom. 'Who is down there?'

'Me!' Sasha shouted. 'Help me!'

'Where are you?'

'I am hanging from a tree.'

'How far?'

'Oh . . . six feet.'

'You only fell six feet?'

'What does it matter how far I fell?' Sasha demanded. 'If I fall from here I will be killed.'

'I thought that was what you wanted. I thought you had been hit.'

'I was not hit. And I did want to die. Now I want to live. Get Tony.'

'Tony cannot help you,' Sandrine said. 'It will have to be me. And Davidovic. Come here, Davidovic. Cover him, Tony.'

Tony kept his pistol aimed at the corporal as Davidovic went to the cliff edge. 'If she goes over, you die,' he said.

'He's not dead?' Sasha asked, her voice anxious.

'No,' Sandrine said. 'Hold on just a moment.'

'I have been holding on for half an hour,' Sasha pointed out.

Sandrine pushed herself up and returned to Tony's side, began buckling belts together, using Draga's and Soejer's as well as Tony's, and then taking some from the dead bodies, to make a strong rope some twelve feet long. This she took back to the cliff edge, first of all making it fast round her waist.

'For God's sake, be careful,' Tony begged again.

Sandrine sat down, digging her heels into the earth before throwing the belt-rope over the edge. 'Can you reach it?' she called.

'Move it,' Sasha said. 'To and fro.'

'Do it,' Sandrine told Davidovic. He obeyed, kneeling at the cliff edge.

'Again,' Sasha shouted. 'Got it.'

'Make a noose under your arms,' Sandrine said. 'And say when you are ready.'

'Ready,' Sasha said a few moments later.

'Now, Davidovic, you are going to pull her up. Just remember that if either she or I fall, the colonel is going to shoot you. Are you ready, Tony?'

'Yes,' Tony said.

'Then start pulling,' Sandrine said. Davidovic looked over his shoulder to make sure that Tony was alert enough to actually fire the gun; Tony waved it at him to leave him in no doubt. Then he and Sandrine began reeling up the belts. It seemed to take forever – Sasha was a fairly heavy woman – and Tony had a constant fight to stay awake as the morphine gained control of his brain, but at last Sasha scrambled over the edge, bleeding from a variety of scratches, her clothes even more torn than before.

'You have more lives than a cat,' Sandrine told her. 'You and the colonel both.'

'Is there any brandy left?' Sasha asked. 'I would like some brandy.' Sandrine gave her some, and she drank and then knelt beside Tony. 'Are you bad?'

'I've been better. We thought you were dead.'

'I thought I was dead, too. I wanted to be dead. I did not wish to be raped and then murdered by these thugs.' She looked around herself. 'Now I am glad I am alive.'

'So are we,' Sandrine said. 'Let's get away from this place.'

The two women and Davidovic between them managed to

carry Tony a quarter of a mile upwind of the little battlefield, further into the concealment of the wood and beside a stream rushing down from the mountain. While they did so, Sandrine brought Sasha up to date, including Davidovic's attempt to take command. 'That is mutiny in the face of the enemy,' Sasha declared. 'Are we going to shoot him?'

'The enemy were all dead,' Davidovic protested. 'Anyway, you cannot shoot me. You need me to help you with the colonel.'

Tony had nodded off during the movement, painful as it was; now he again opened his eyes. 'There are things that need to be done.'

'You must have some more morphine,' Sandrine said. 'You are in pain.'

'Later. Now listen. First, a search must be made for Katerina, as soon as it is light. She may be lying wounded somewhere.'

'That will mean returning to that place of death,' Davidovic objected.

'It must be done. Then a message must be got to General Tito, as quickly as possible. We cannot wait for me to be able to move.'

'We are going to carry you,' Sandrine said.

'That will take too long. He must be warned, as I say, as quickly as possible. Certainly before he gets to Bihac. Or even near it.'

'What is so urgent?' Sasha asked.

'He must be told that Bihac is no longer an open town, but is occupied by a battalion of Ustase supported by a panzer squadron. He must be told that the garrison is commanded by Colonel Kronic, who until very recently was in charge of the Ustase section in Sarajevo.'

Sasha nodded. 'I have met this man. Well, nearly. He was at General von Demmich's house.'

'Right. The panzer squadron is commanded by a Major Hans Gruber, who has only recently been discharged from hospital . . .'

Sasha giggled. 'I know Gruber as well. I mean really. Then I put him in hospital. So he has recovered. Well, well. I am glad of that. Although after the way I hit him I would not have expected him to return to active service so quickly.'

'That is a good point,' Tony said. 'He may not actually be fit for command. But the general must be warned that the town is garrisoned and cannot simply be occupied. I put this in your charge. All of you.' He sank to the ground, exhausted.

'You are now relieved of your command,' Sandrine said. 'Your business is to get well, not give orders. I will give the orders. I am going to remain here with the colonel. You, Sasha, and you, Davidovic, will take the message to General Tito. You will also inform him that the colonel and I are here, and need rescuing.'

'I will deliver the message and come back for you,' Sasha said.

'If General Tito gives you permission,' Sandrine reminded her.

'Oh, I am not going to desert,' Sasha said. 'I wish to be with the army when we attack Bihac. I would like to see Hans again. But him . . .' She jerked her thumb at the listening Davidovic. 'I do not want him along. He will either try to kill me or rape me the moment my back is turned.'

'Well,' Sandrine pointed out, 'I do not wish him to stay here, for the same reason.'

Sasha looked at the corporal. 'You are not very popular.'

'You are bitches, both of you,' Davidovic said. 'I would not touch either of you if you begged me to.'

'That is very sensible, because we are not going to beg you to,' Sasha said. 'We are going to have to kill you.'

'You cannot do that!'

'Well, what are we to do? You cannot come with me. You may not wish to assault me, but you will certainly try to kill me to stop me from reporting your attempted mutiny. You cannot stay here with the major and the colonel, for the same reason. We cannot simply send you away, because you will come back, no doubt when the major is asleep.'

'I will give you my word . . .'

'Your word is of no value, because you know, and we know, that you will break it.'

'Colonel, sir!' Davidovic appealed. 'Have I not served you faithfully? When I sought to take command it was because I felt I was the best of us to do so, with you wounded.'

'The colonel is asleep,' Sandrine said.

'I am awake,' Tony said.

'You should not be,' Sandrine told him crossly.

'I do not think we can execute the corporal out of hand. He has been a good soldier. But I also accept that he is guilty of mutiny, and that he probably can no longer be trusted. As of this moment he is under arrest. You will take him with you, Sasha.'

'Me? He will attack me.'

'No, he will not. You will take him as your prisoner, with his wrists bound together. If you from time to time choose to release his wrists, you will bind them again as you consider it necessary. Equally, if you think it necessary, you will bind his feet at night. He will not be armed. Now listen to me, Davidovic. If you behave yourself, and obey Captain Janitz in everything, when the army is reached she will release you and she will not prefer charges against you. If, however, you attempt either to escape or attack her or disobey her in any way, she will deliver you to a court martial. Do you understand this?'

Davidovic looked at Sasha, who smiled at him. 'You are to be my slave,' she said. 'I have always wanted to have a slave.'

At first light Sandrine and Davidovic returned to the battleground to search for Katerina. 'You think she will be all right?' Sasha asked, sitting beside Tony and holding a canteen to his lips. He had slept fitfully, and was parched; the pain was considerable, but he had refused any more morphine until his orders had been implemented.

'She will be all right,' he said. 'She is tougher even than you, Sasha.'

'I know this,' Sasha agreed. 'I respect her. Sometimes I wish I could be her. Such beauty, such self-possession, such determination . . .' Her lips twisted. 'Such love.'

'Don't sell yourself short,' Tony recommended.

'I caused all of this to happen, by trusting that little bitch. I loved her, Tony. Will you believe that?'

'I believe that.'

'Now, if I ever see her again . . . Will I ever see her again, Tony?'

'I should think that is unlikely, at least until the war is over. She will be back in Belgrade.'

'Working for the Germans,' she muttered. 'For that other bitch, Angela Wassermann.'

'Forget her,' he advised. 'Get that information to Tito.'

'Kronic,' she mused. 'I remember him. I remember what he did to Anna. Do you know about that?' Tony shook his head. 'He set fire to her crotch. Jelena told me. Anna and I were friends as girls. Oh, she was ten years older than me, but she loved me.' She glanced at Tony. 'She taught me everything I needed to know. And then, to be publicly hanged, after . . .'

'Forget her, too. Until we have taken Bihac.'

'Then I will get my hands on Kronic,' she said. 'And Gruber.' She gave another giggle. 'I gave him head. That is all he wanted.' Another quick glance. 'Does Sandrine give you head?'

'When she is in the mood.' He grinned. 'When I am not wounded.'

Sasha sighed, and looked up. 'They are back.'

Davidovic was several yards in front of Sandrine: she was taking no risks. 'Katerina is dead,' she said as they came up. 'They cut her throat. They must have taken her by surprise.'

Tony's turn to sigh. Of his original twenty-two, he was down to four. Mainly thanks to Jelena's treachery. He wondered what *he* would do if he ever caught up with her. But that was as unlikely a scenario as Sasha doing so. 'Move out,' he said.

They bound Davidovic's wrists, and divided the food; Sasha donned her various belts and weapons, then stood to attention. 'I will be back in a fortnight. With help.'

'We'll be waiting,' Sandrine said.

They watched the ill-assorted pair disappear through the trees. 'Do you think she will make it?' Sandrine asked.

'Yes. As you said, she has more lives than a cat.'

'We all have more lives than a cat, or none of us would still be here. Just let's hope her luck holds out long enough for her to get back to us.'

'Don't you like it here?' he teased. 'We have all the mod cons, and each other.'

'As long as it doesn't rain. Shit!' The first drops began to fall.

The rain lasted long enough to soak them, but was then replaced by warm sunshine. Sandrine spread their clothes out to dry, then went for a bathe. Bathing was a passion with her, one she had not been able to indulge very often over the past couple of months. 'This feels so good,' she said, and filled a canteen to bring the water ashore and wash him in turn. 'How do you feel?'

'Just looking at you makes me feel better.'

She stuck out her tongue. 'You're sure you wouldn't rather be looking at Sasha?'

'I told you, remember. There is too much angst.'

'I can feel that way too,' she pointed out. 'I felt that way yesterday. The very sight of that thug made my skin crawl.'

'You said he never made it.'

'He never got inside me, if that is what you mean. But he handled me . . . ugh! I rank him lower than Wassermann. Will we get Wassermann?'

'One day.'

'How long will that day take to come?'

'I have no idea. Just be sure that it will. Listen, we're being given a break from the war. Let's enjoy it, and worry about Wassermann later.'

'We shall honeymoon,' she announced.

'Without a wedding . . . and without sex?'

'We shall think of something,' she assured him.

It turned out to be more of a honeymoon than he could ever have hoped, even without sex. The weather stayed fine – allowing for the occasional rain shower – and warm, except at night. But then they huddled close to each other under their blankets. They had all the water they could use, and actually, with careful management, sufficient food to last them a fortnight, thanks to the rations taken from the dead Cetniks, who, lured by the thought of the reward, had been equipped for a lengthy hunt in the mountains. Sandrine also went hunting every few days, and invariably brought back a rabbit.

'Did you ever in your wildest imagination when you were a journalist in Paris suppose you might one day live like this?' Tony asked.

'No. But I always wanted adventure. That is why I took the Belgrade posting.'

'And jumped with both feet into this.'

'I didn't jump. I was pushed. But if I hadn't, I would never have got together with you. Do you realize that if it hadn't been for the war, I might have married Bernhard Klostermann?'

'Bernhard always struck me as being quite a decent fellow, until he was overtaken by events.'

'But I would have been a German *Hausfrau*, standing on street corners and shouting "Heil Hitler!" and wearing neat little white blouses and black skirts.'

She looked down at her torn pants; the knees had gone, the turn-ups were frayed, and there were slashes in the thighs. 'Never mind,' he said. 'One day you'll again be walking down the Champs Élysées, wearing high heels and chic clothes.'

'Will I, Tony? Will I?'

'You have my word. I will take you there myself.' He raised his head. 'Shit! Company.' Sandrine rolled on her stomach, gathering her tommy-gun as she did so. 'Easy,' Tony said. 'It's Sasha. And . . .'

Walking at Sasha's shoulder, at the head of several men, was the burly figure of General Tito.

Ten

The Battle

'Well?' Tito demanded.

The surgeon finished his inspection. 'This was well done,' he said. 'It is healing very nicely.' He raised his head to look at Sandrine. 'You are to be congratulated, mademoiselle.'

'Ha! He gets hit so often I am in constant practice.'

'When will he be fit for duty?' Tito asked.

'I'm fit for duty now,' Tony protested.

'You mean battle?' The surgeon shrugged. 'As the colonel says, he could fight now. *Could,*' he emphasized. 'I would give it another fortnight.'

'Very good. Stretcher-bearers!'

'I can walk,' Tony said.

'No doubt. But you will get better more quickly if you are not exhausted.' He snapped his fingers and Tony was placed on the stretcher and lifted. Tito walked beside him as he was carried over the uneven ground. 'I want you well in that fortnight. Is what Captain Janitz had to tell me true?'

'Maric knew he was dying.'

'Those bastards are smarter than I thought they were. However, the Ustase . . . they are not regular troops.'

'There are still a thousand of them, at least. And they will be behind fortifications. And they will have that stiffening of panzers.'

'Only six, you say.'

'From our point of view, sir, that represents heavy artillery,

213

as we have nothing to reply with. May I ask how many men we muster?'

'I have three hundred men.' Tito grinned. 'And five hundred women. They have been less prone to desert. They are waiting for the return of their commanding officer, which is why I want you back on your feet before we attack.'

'You mean to attack, at such odds?'

'I have no choice. Winter is only two months away. I must gain shelter for my people. *Your* people, Tony. Besides, we are considered defeated. That is the main reason for the desertions, not the hardships we have suffered. Men and women will suffer anything if they believe they are winning. So we must win. Once we have Bihac, our people will come flooding back, and more besides. And I have a surprise for you. We have a genuine – what do you say in your army? – pukka liaison officer, sent from Cairo. A Major Johnstone. Do you know him?'

'Peter Johnstone? He was with me in Belgrade. I haven't seen him since the night the city was bombed.'

Tito nodded. 'That is what he said about you.'

'But why have we got a liaison officer *now*, when in the eyes of the world we are beaten, when they wouldn't send us one before?'

Tito tapped his nose. 'A combination of politics and common sense. The politics is a growing realization that the Nazis have bitten off more than they can chew in Russia. You know that they are at Stalingrad?'

Tony frowned, partly from the jolting he was suffering as the stretcher-bearers stumbled and kicked stones. 'Isn't that on the Volga? If they get across that, there's not a lot left to stop them.'

'That is true. But they are not going to get across.'

'What makes you think that? It's a river, not the English Channel.'

'I am not speaking of the river. It is the city that matters. It used to be called Tsaritsyn. But it was renamed after our glorious leader. He intends to fight for it. I said that the Germans were *at* Stalingrad, not that they have taken the city. If we can hold them there, with winter only a few weeks away . . . Their advance ground to a halt last winter. It will do so again. And all the while we, I mean the Soviet forces, are getting stronger. So your British have decided that they will recognize us, because Stalin wishes them to do so. The other factor is that they have been doing their sums, and have realized that if the Germans have been making such enormous efforts to destroy us, they must regard us as important. The British are following fashion. In any event, your friend will be delighted to see you. Like me, he thought you were dead.'

'Is he going to resupply us with munitions?'

'Yes. Once we have taken Bihac.'

'Back to square one.'

'We will take Bihac, Tony. I have an idea. It is the panzers that are the key. Now I am going to hurry on ahead. You will be with us in two days' time. And we will make our plans.'

He was replaced by Sasha and Sandrine. 'You did a splendid job,' Tony said to Sasha.

'I did my duty. I am glad to see you looking so well.'

'Snap. Did Davidovic behave himself?'

'As far as he was able.'

'You mean he did give you trouble. How long did it take you to reach the army?'

'Eight days.'

'And when did he start giving you trouble?'

'He tried to give me trouble almost the moment we were out of your sight,' Sasha said.

'But you dealt with it.'

'I shot him. As soon as we were out of earshot.'

Tony looked at Sandrine, who shrugged. 'He had it coming.'

'Well?' Kronic asked the captain of the patrol.

'I saw no Partisans, sir. Some of the peasants we spoke to

said they were camped in the hills about ten miles away, but I did not go that far.'

'If our masters would allow me the use of a single aircraft,' Kronic grumbled. 'Well, as long as they keep ten miles away they cannot do us any harm. But I wish to be informed if there is any indication that they are trying to get round us.' The lieutenant saluted and left the room, to be replaced by Gruber. 'Ah, Gruber,' Kronic said. It amused him to be able to address an officer in the Wehrmacht so casually. 'Our friends appear to have come to a standstill. Well, that is not bad for us, eh? But it is possible that they might attempt to get round us. In that case, we will need to use your panzers.'

'My panzers are to be used defensively,' Gruber said. 'They are facing the south-east, the direction from which we expect the enemy to attack.'

'Yes, but if they are needed elsewhere . . .'

'They will not be needed elsewhere. Tito has no idea we are here. He will march right up to us, unsuspecting. I look forward to this.' Gruber still moved and spoke hesitantly, and suffered from recurring double vision as well as violent headaches. 'I wish to destroy them. Have you heard the news?'

'Stalingrad has fallen?'

'Not yet.'

'Well, then, Cairo has fallen?'

'Again, not yet. This is from Belgrade. Colonel Wassermann's wife is in gaol, charged with murder.'

'What did you say? Murdering who? Not her husband?'

'No, no. Her housekeeper.'

'A German?'

'No, no. A Serb.'

'You are telling me that a German lady is being charged with murdering a Serb? I do not believe it.'

'It is true.'

Kronic scratched his head. 'What is the world coming to? Thank you, Herr Major.' Gruber saluted and left the room. Kronic continued to stare after him for some moments. Of all the crazy situations . . . And where did it leave him? If he was enjoying his new rank and powers enormously, he was well aware that he owed his position entirely to Wassermann, and were Wassermann to be removed from office it was extremely unlikely that his successor would continue the arrangement – he was very aware of the dislike and contempt felt by the German regular army for the Ustase.

He was also worried that he hadn't yet heard from Maric. It was now six weeks since he had set the Cetnik on the trail of Davis and Fouquet. He could not believe it would have taken this long to catch up with them. Suppose Maric, having been told by Kronic himself of the increased reward, had gone behind his back and done a separate deal with Wassermann to receive the money direct? They were all bastards, not to be trusted.

He got up and went into his living quarters. The maidservant he had appropriated hastily bowed. He ignored her and strode through to the bedroom. Jelena sat in front of the mirror, brushing her hair. Although it was mid-morning, she was naked and had clearly just got out of bed. She spent most of every day in bed, waiting to be fed or for him to come to her. In many ways she reminded him of a cat, who would give her allegiance to anyone who would feed her and stroke her; certainly she had entirely abandoned any attempts to resist him – rather she seemed to welcome his attentions. While he found her endlessly desirable. This was partly because of the sensation of power she gave him. He could enjoy her to the utmost, but he could also end her life by a snap of his fingers, or, if he chose, a twist of his wrists, without anyone attempting to stop him or even criticize him.

But today was different. Today she had an added interest for him. 'How well did you know Frau Wassermann?' he asked.

Jelena half turned her head, then looked back into the mirror. 'I only knew her for a few days.'

'But you agreed to work for her, for the Germans, against your friends.'

'She . . . The Germans promised to grant an amnesty to my parents. And my brother.'

'Have they done that?'

'Well, no. My parents, and my brother, are still with the Partisans. And then . . .'

'The plan failed.'

'It didn't fail. They were all killed. Davis and Fouquet . . . and Janitz. Is that not true?'

Kronic placed his hands on her shoulders and gently squeezed her neck. He enjoyed having secrets as much as he enjoyed having power. 'Then the Nazis betrayed you in turn. Do you hate them?'

'I . . .' Jelena closed her mouth. 'Have I the power to hate anyone?'

'Even me, eh? Well, you know, everyone gets their just deserts in the end. Your pretty ex-employer is being tried for murder.'

Jelena swung round violently. 'Angela?!' She bit her lip. 'But . . . not her husband?'

'Do you know, that same thought crossed *my* mind when I heard the news. But it seems to have been her house-keeper.'

'Madame Bestic? But why?'

'That has not been established. You called Frau Wassermann "Angela" just now. Did you know her that well? Were you lovers?' The colour drained from Jelena's cheeks. Kronic laughed, and sat on the bed. 'Tell the truth. I will not punish you. I find the idea exciting.'

'She . . . she is insatiable.'

'And do you think that this Bestic was one of her lovers?'

'I cannot believe that. She . . . well, she was ugly. And she and Angela hated each other.'

'Interesting. Come here and lie down.'

Jelena obeyed. 'What will happen to her? Frau Wassermann?'

'If she is found guilty? If the sentence is carried out here in Yugoslavia, she will probably be hanged. If she is taken back to Germany, she will be beheaded.'

'My God!' Jelena could not envisage either possibility.

'It is an attractive thought, isn't it? Unfortunately, I do not see the Germans allowing her to be convicted. At least in Yugoslavia.'

'I have the Reichsführer for you, Herr Colonel,' the secretary said.

Wassermann regarded the telephone with apprehension before speaking. 'Wassermann, sir.'

'Ah, Colonel.' Heinrich Himmler's voice always sounded as if he were speaking through a sieve. 'An unhappy business.'

'Yes, sir. I apologize for asking you to intervene, but—'

'We are speaking about your wife. Yes, indeed. I have heard from the governor-general.'

'Yes, sir. It is his decision that she should be tried by a civil court here in Belgrade.'

'So he tells me. Well, as he points out, it is a civil crime.'

'Yes, sir. But a German woman being tried in a Yugoslav court will surely be bad for morale.'

'I do not see how it affects *our* morale as a nation, Wassermann, or as an occupying power. General Hartmann feels that *not* having Frau Wassermann tried in Belgrade for a civil crime would have a bad effect on the morale of the Yugoslavs.'

'With respect, Herr Reichsführer, are we concerned with the morale of the Yugoslavs?'

'We need to be, Colonel, with regard to the pacification of the country. That is not happening as fast as it should. We have now been in complete control of Yugoslavia for close on eighteen months, yet there are still substantial guerilla forces in the field against us. Oh, I agree that you have done well finally to eliminate Davis and Fouquet, but as long as Tito and his people are at large they remain a considerable problem.'

'Tito and his people will be destroyed before Christmas, sir.'

'I am very glad to hear you say that so confidently, Wassermann. But I am sure you will agree that it would facilitate our task of eliminating *all* resistance – I am thinking now of the Cetniks – if we could convince a majority of the Yugoslavs that we deal with our own malefactors as stringently as we deal with theirs.' Now Wassermann regarded the phone with distaste. Those people in Berlin knew so little about conditions in the countries they so carelessly set out to dominate; Himmler apparently honestly thought that there were such people as 'Yugoslavs' as opposed to the reality of Croats hating Slovenes, Bosnians hating Albanians, and Serbs hating everybody.

'You see, Wassermann,' Himmler went on, as if addressing a small child, 'Yugoslavia cannot be considered in the same light as Russia. Russia has been earmarked for years by the Führer as the area into which Greater Germany must expand, must find living space, eh? The Führer has no interest in the Balkans, except as docile satellites of the Reich. I am sure you understand this. Believe me, I am very sorry about your wife's behaviour, but General Hartmann tells me that she just seems to have lost her temper with that woman. Nor has she denied this. Is that correct?'

'Yes, Herr Reichsführer.'

'Well, you see . . . When is the trial to begin?'

'If it takes place here in Belgrade, within a fortnight. She has already been in prison for six weeks.'

'She has not been ill-treated, I hope?'

'No, sir. I have seen to that.' He drew a long breath. 'Is there no circumstance, Herr Reichsführer, in which I could take over this case as a military matter?'

'Your loyalty as a husband does you great credit, Wassermann, but I'm afraid I cannot think of any, except . . . Well, if you could discover evidence that your wife acted as she did because this woman had turned out to be a spy working for the Partisans . . .' He paused.

'Yes,' Wassermann said thoughtfully.

'The evidence would have to be incontrovertible,' Himmler said.

'Yes, sir. I understand.'

'Very good, Wassermann. Good day.'

The phone went dead, and after a few moments Wassermann replaced it on its hook. A lifeline? Could he risk taking it? But then, could he risk *not* taking it? Angela had made her position perfectly clear. If she was forced to go on trial before a Yugoslav court she intended to shock the world. He did not suppose that publicly recounting tales of his sadism would do very much harm, but to tell all the eager reporters and gossip-mongers of his sexual inadequacy, of the way he had been cuckolded by his own officers, of her numerous female lovers, and above all, of his dishonesty in the matter of the trap for Davis and Fouquet. That would not only ruin him, but it might irreparably damage the entire German administration in Yugoslavia. The governor-general had no idea that Angela knew anything about that, much less that she had inspired it. Nor was there any temptation to tell him, make him understand the implications of her threat, because then his anger would be directed at his police chief.

It had been a temptation to point these facts out to Himmler. Himmler would undoubtedly have rallied round and taken over to save the reputation of his people, but he would never forget, and when the whole business had been forgotten by everyone else, one morning at dawn there would be a knock on his door . . .

Wassermann shuddered. He would have to save himself. He left his office, nodded to an always sympathetic Ulrich, and was driven home. He entered the house, ignored the greeting from his new housekeeper, and went upstairs. He said, 'Rosa!'

She appeared from the spare bedroom; she was always close at hand within the house, having succeeded Angela as the receptacle for his sexual frenzies. 'Herr Colonel!' As always, she was breathless and trembling.

'Ah, Rosa,' Wassermann said genially. 'I have decided that the time has come for you to earn your keep.'

Rosa would have supposed that she had already earned her keep – almost every day for the past six weeks – but she began to unfasten her dress.

'No, no,' he said. 'Not that, now. There is a part I wish you to play, a role, a story for you to tell. Come and sit here beside me, and I will explain what you have to do.'

'So there it is,' Tito said. 'We have sufficient food for one more week. And we have sufficient ammunition for one all-out assault.' He pointed at the sky – the meeting was being held in the open air – where dark clouds were gathering to the west. 'And winter is coming closer; our position will be untenable then. Now, I have always known that these were difficulties we would have to face. But I also knew before we began our retreat that if we could reach Bihac before we ran out of food and before the onset of winter we would survive. We have done this. What I did not calculate was that the Germans would learn of our plans, or work them out for themselves – I do not know which is the truth – and occupy the town before we got there. But for the information provided by Colonel Davis, we would have walked straight into a trap. However, the strategic situation is unchanged. We must take Bihac, no matter what the opposition. And it may even have improved our overall prospects. Certainly the Ustase will not be short of arms and ammunition; if we can capture their reserves along with the town . . .' He paused to look over the grim faces in front of him.

'If only we had sufficient men,' Astzalos growled.

'But we are not going to fight soldiers,' Tito said. 'We are going to fight scum.'

'Who are fortified, and are supported by a regiment of panzers,' someone said.

'A fortified position is only as strong as the men defending it,' Tito said. 'Our problem is the panzers. And it is not a regiment; Colonel Davis tells us that there are only six tanks. But I agree that they are the key.'

'You wish a forlorn hope to infiltrate the town and put them out of action,' Tony said. 'I will need a squad of ten.'

'I'm sorry, Tony,' Tito said. 'Before I convened this meeting I had a talk with Dr Trifunovic, because I knew you would wish to volunteer. He says you are not yet fit enough.'

'With respect, sir—'

'With respect, Colonel. Much as I have regard for your ability, you must understand that for you to undertake to lead such a mission, and to be unable to play your full part, would be to endanger the lives of your comrades as well as the success of the operation. In any event, your face is on too many posters. You would be arrested in minutes.'

'I will lead the squad,' Sandrine said.

'Now, hold on a minute,' Tony protested.

'I'm afraid your face is also too well known, Major Fouquet,' Tito said.

'I will go,' Sasha said. 'I will take nine of my women. The Ustase will never suspect us.'

'Are you out of your mind?' Tony demanded. 'Didn't you tell me you knew this man Gruber, the one commanding the panzers?'

'I have no intention of going near the panzers until we are ready to strike.'

'And what about Kronic? You said you met him at Demmich's house.'

'I have even less intention of going near Kronic.' She turned to Tito. 'I can do it, General. You know I can.'

Tito stroked his chin. 'You realize it is virtually a suicide mission?'

'Not for me,' Sasha declared. 'I have more lives than a cat. Ask Sandrine. And I have only used up a few of them. I will do it, General.'

'Well, then,' Tito said. 'Now, Major Vronic actually lived in Bihac at one time. He has drawn a plan of the town. As when he was there was a few years ago now, he cannot vouch for its total accuracy, but it is all we have. I have had my printing machine run off copies.' One of his secretaries passed them out. 'We may assume that the perimeter has been fortified, at least with barricades, and I imagine that the tanks have been placed here at the south-east corner, as it is the direction from which they will expect us. Now here is the central square, and the town hall. Captain Vronic estimates this is the most likely situation of the Ustase Headquarters, simply because it is, or *was*, the only building with adequate communications. We will assume that he is right. Now, Saturday is market day. That will be your opportunity to enter the town, Captain Janitz, because people will be going in from all over the surrounding countryside. I leave it to you to decide what weapons you will carry and how you will conceal them, remembering that the Ustase will be searching everybody. You will remain in the town overnight. Your strike will be immediately before dawn on Sunday. Now, there can be no doubt that Kronic knows we are here, and will have patrols out to inform him when we move and in what direction. That means our advance will have to be timed very carefully. On Friday night we will push forward three small units to a position within a mile of the town. These units will remain concealed throughout Saturday, but the moment you attack the tanks on Sunday morning, they will enter the town in your support. One of the units will complete the destruction of the tanks, if that is necessary. The remaining two will occupy the headquarters building, and hold it. This should cut communications both within the city and with the ouside world. The rest of the army will move as soon as it is dark on Saturday night. We shall have to advance cautiously and if possible soundlessly, and thus it will be slow. But we would hope to be within two miles of the town by dawn on Sunday. Thus we will be able to support you within an hour after that.' He looked around at their faces.

'I assume we will be allowed to lead one of the advance parties,' Tony said.

Tito grinned. 'Very good, Colonel. And you, Major Fouquet. Colonel Astzalos, you will command the third squad. Colonel Davis will be in overall command. Now, gentlemen, and ladies, I have only one final word. This is our last throw of the dice. If we do not succeed in taking Bihac, this army is lost. And with it, Yugoslavia.'

'We will take Bihac, General,' Sasha said.

'I must say,' Peter Johnstone remarked as he dined with Tony and Sandrine, 'our General Tito has a most devoted band of followers.' Like Tony, he had known Sandrine in Belgrade before the war, and was clearly amazed by her transformation.

'I hope you will report that to London,' Tony suggested.

'Oh, I shall. And are you as devoted as the rest of his army?'

'I would say he is the finest man I've ever met.'

'Even if he is a Communist?'

'I'm talking about the man, not his politics.'

'Oh, quite, old man. But how do you suppose things will turn out after the war? Will he be taking his orders from Moscow?'

'I would say that depends on the orders.'

'He seems pretty committed.'

'He is. But he is even more committed to Yugoslavia.'

'You mean to his concept of how Yugoslavia should be – and should be governed.'

'Well, I suppose both you and I have our own ideas of how England should be, and should be governed, after the war.'

'Absolutely. But if, shall we say, you are a Socialist, and you wish to get rid of the Tories, you will merely vote against them at the next election. You will not, I assume, intend to influence the outcome of that election by freely using your tommy-gun.'

Tony glanced at Sandrine, who was listening with interest;

he knew she was a far more political animal than himself. 'Are you expressing the views of London, old man? If so, why are you here?'

'I really would not like you to take offence,' Johnstone said. 'I do represent the views of London, yes. And I am here to make my recommendations as to how the war can best be waged in Yugoslavia. I can tell you that from what I have seen and heard since arriving here, I intend to tell them that Tito is our best bet.'

'You have seen the Cetniks?' Sandrine asked.

'I was with Mihailovic, briefly. I had met him before, when I was stationed in Belgrade. So had you, Tony.'

'Yes,' Tony said.

'And as I say, I regard Tito as a better bet. Although we need to bear in mind that Mihailovic remains the choice of the government-in-exile as commander of the resistance forces.'

'It was Mihailovic's people who tried to murder us,' Sandrine said.

'At his command?'

'They were his people.'

'Yes, but I gained the impression that he does not have such a grip on his people as does Tito.'

'I still regard him as responsible,' Sandrine insisted.

'Quite. As I was saying, assuming you take Bihac, I will recommend that you be given all the material assistance we can spare. However, London will need to be convinced that such arms and ammunitions that are supplied will not be used for unlawful or revolutionary purposes after the war.'

'I don't see how anyone can guarantee that. We can only put our trust in Tito's integrity.'

'Who is an avowed Communist. I am expressing London's point of view.'

'I thought we were all on the same side,' Sandrine said.

'At the moment, we are. However, it occurs to me that the best man to convince our superiors that Tito can be trusted is yourself, Tony.'

'You mean they want me back. Do they intend to put me on trial for the murder of Frau von Blintoft?'

'London is prepared to accept that that was an incident outside of your control.'

'And Major Curtis?'

'Everything I have been able to find out leads me to believe that he was, as you claim, killed by the Cetniks. I certainly intend to put that in my report. The fact is, old man, that London feels that it is time you had a change of duty.'

'Is that an order?'

'At this moment, no. Just a heavy hint.'

'And how would this be done?'

'You'd be picked up off the coast by submarine. It's quite straightforward, really. That's how I came in.'

Tony glanced at Sandrine.

'Oh, Sandrine will be welcome to accompany you.'

'I hate submarines,' Sandrine said.

'Have you ever been in one?'

'No.'

'Well, then . . .'

'I hate Hell,' she pointed out. 'And I have never been there, either.'

'The fact is,' Tony said, 'the way I have been shot up over the past eighteen months, if I go home to England I am going to be stuck behind a desk, which would just about drive me mad. I'd rather see this one out.'

'That may not go down very well at GHQ,' Johnstone suggested.

'Well, as we have agreed, all things depend on us taking Bihac,' Tony said, and turned his head as Sasha approached them. She wore the shapeless ankle-length dress of a Yugoslav peasant woman, with a shawl over her head.

'How do I look?'

'Like someone the average man would run a mile to get away from,' Sandrine suggested.

'That is what I intended.'

'Where are your weapons?' Tony asked.

Sasha gathered her skirt to her waist, and Johnstone hastily averted his eyes: she wore no underclothes. But strapped to the inside of her right thigh was a Luger, while a knife was strapped to her left.

'And your grenades?' She opened her cloth bag.

'They will certainly look in there,' Sandrine objected.

'They are welcome. Look for yourself.'

Sandrine did so, and recoiled. 'What in the name of God . . . ?'

'Cut garlic, and overripe onions.'

'It is still one hell of a risk,' Tony said. 'All it takes is one inquisitive sentry with a poor sense of smell . . .'

'Bah,' Sasha said. 'As the general said, these are not German soldiers. They are scum. They will only wish to search the pretty ones, and I am taking two very pretty girls, who will be quite unarmed.'

'But you are also a pretty woman,' Sandrine objected.

'You think so?' Sasha grinned at her, and again Sandrine recoiled. She had blacked out half of her teeth. 'And, you see . . .' From her pocket she took a black patch with an attached cord, which she fitted over her left eye. 'And here . . .' She indicated the bent stick she was carrying, and leaned on it. 'What do you think, Major Johnstone? Am I not a repulsive old hag?'

'Well . . .'

'So, now we are leaving. All I wish' – she looked from Sandrine to Tony – 'is that you will be in close support.'

'You have it.'

'Then will you not give a poor little old lady a farewell kiss?'

Both Sandrine and Tony obliged. Sasha regarded Johnstone speculatively, and then left.

'She is a very brave woman,' Johnstone remarked.

'All of my women are very brave,' Tony said.

'And will she be able to carry out this mission?'

'Sasha? Oh, yes. She will carry it out. I only hope she has at least one of those nine lives left.'

Tony and Sandrine spent Saturday assembling their squads, as did Astzalos. They were going to command twenty personnel each, and it was essential that every member of each squad knew exactly what he or she had to do. Because of the preponderance of women to men, the three units were composed of both sexes. All had to be volunteers – not that there was any shortage of those. But Tony was surprised to find Petar Brolic standing before him, fully equipped as a soldier. He had seen the boy around the camp often enough, but only as a labourer. 'How old are you?' he inquired.

'I was fifteen yesterday, sir. I have been given permission to fight.'

'And you wish your first fight to be your last? Do you know how dangerous this will be?'

'War is dangerous, sir.' He had obviously been listening to Tito.

'Do your parents know what you are doing?

'My parents do not know, sir.'

'Well, then . . .'

'May I ask, sir, is it true that my sister betrayed you? That is what they are saying.'

Tony sighed. 'Yes, it is true. But your getting killed will not atone for that.'

'It is my duty to make up for it if I can, sir. Will you take me?'

'Very well. Report to the sergeant.'

Johnstone was sitting beside him. 'Don't you yearn for the orthodoxy of a company of British soldiers?'

'As I remember, they had their problems.'

'But none quite so personal as that. Do you think he will be any good?'

'I'm prepared to gamble on it. You're welcome to come along and see how he turns out.'

'I'd like to, believe me. But I have been forbidden, by your boss.'

'Why?'

'I think he feels that, having lost Curtis, to lose another liaison officer only a few months later might upset London. '

'I suppose that's a valid point.'

'But I will wish you all the luck in the world.'

They shook hands, and Tony went in search of Sandrine; they had spent the previous night locked in each other's arms.

'You realize this is the first time we have gone into battle separately, at least by intention,' he said.

'Don't you think I can do it? I am as good as Sasha.'

'I know you can do it, because you are better than Sasha. But you can still stop a stray bullet.'

'If you live, I live. I feel it in my bones.'

'And if I die?'

'Then we both die.'

He kissed her. 'Remember to keep your head down.'

Tito was there to see them off. 'Win this one, and we win the war,' he told them.

Jelena sat up to the tolling of the bell. Saturday! Market day! A day to be enjoyed, because it gave her a reason for leaving the Ustase Headquarters.

When she had first come to Bihac, she had been afraid to leave the building at all. She did not suppose anyone knew who she was, but they certainly knew she was a Serb, and not a Bosnian or a Croat. Equally, they knew she was Colonel Kronic's woman, a far more solid reason for hate; Kronic and his men had not been in Bihac a week before there had been several summary trials and executions. In fact, the Ustase ruthlessness had made her position safer, as everyone was terrified. As to what would happen if the Partisans, or any other patriot force, were to overrun the town . . . It was a thought that made her shudder. But having survived so much over the past few months, she was beginning to feel that she had a charmed life.

In any event, Kronic had given her a small automatic pistol, a Walther. 'If you are ever in danger of being captured by the enemy,' he said, 'use this – on yourself.'

It did not seem to occur to Kronic that she might use the pistol on him. But she knew she was not going to, unless she was prepared immediately to turn the weapon on herself; to be tortured to death by the Ustase had to be the most unimaginable fate possible.

As for Sasha, she was surely dead. Jelena still felt desperately confused and unhappy about the whole situation. She had truly worshipped her, as a woman and as a fighting machine, and as a heroine. To dicover that she was nothing more than a vicious animal . . .

And Angela! Now *there* was a vicious animal. She wondered if Kronic would let her go to Belgrade for the trial. She could even be a material witness. But to what? What could have made Angela shoot that dried stick of a housekeeper? It was better to forget her, as she had to forget Sasha.

And her family? Them too. Her plans for the rescue and rehabilitation of her family had come to nothing. If she had learned one thing from the frightful events of the past year, it was that only survival mattered, regardless of who had to be trampled underfoot to ensure that survival.

She put on one of the new frocks Kronic had bought for her, with matching high heels and a slouch hat which flopped over her right eye. For such an uncouth man he had a surprising taste for being well-dressed himself, and for seeing his mistress similarly well-dressed. Jelena had never owned such fine clothes.

She had to pass through the office to gain the courtyard. Kronic was seated at his desk, glowering at various reports. 'Where are you going?' he inquired without raising his head.

'To the market. Did you not hear the bell?'

'That was two hours ago.'

'Well, it will be in full swing now.'

He looked at his watch. 'It will be time for lunch in an hour.'

'I will be back in an hour.'

'Well, take two men with you.'

'Oh, Felix, do I have to? It makes me so conspicuous.'

'You are already conspicuous. Yes, you have to. I do not want to have to investigate your murder. I have too much else to do. Get out.' He pointed with his pen. 'But take two men with you.'

'Yes, Felix,' she said docilely, and left the room.

Kronic picked up the report and read it again. Von Paulus's Sixth Army had fought its way into Stalingrad, but now could not get back out. Every man was needed to help keep open both the supply lines and an escape route. Equally bad were the reports coming out of North Africa, where Rommel was being so starved of men and matériel – especially tanks and petrol, which were needed for the Russian front – that he had ground to a halt only sixty miles short of Alexandria. Of course, the reports also claimed that once he was re-armed Egypt and the Suez Canal would fall. But the fact was that the German armies had been even closer than sixty miles from Moscow last winter – and the Russian capital had not fallen. Meanwhile it also seemed certain that the British were building up a considerable army in the desert. To make matters worse, Rommel was now back in Germany, a sick man.

Kronic was not the least concerned about the various German problems. He had no doubt that they would win in the end; they had done nothing else for the past three years. What did concern him was the recurring nightmare that with Wassermann in eclipse, and the war not going according to plan, some general, either in Belgrade or Berlin, was going to wake up one morning and ask his adjutant, 'What in the name of God is a panzer squadron doing sitting on its ass in some remote Yugoslav town when it can be put to good use somewhere else?'

Because he knew in his heart that the people of Bihac were less afraid of him and his people, for all the ruthless cruelty with which he had overawed them, than of the visible presence of the mighty Wehrmacht. Equally did he have a suspicion that Tito, out there in the mountains, might know the situation within the town, and, as he was also well-informed about world affairs and how the wider war was going, might also be waiting for the panzers to be withdrawn before attempting an assault.

Jelena went down the stairs, her calf-length skirt swishing, her heels clicking. The various clerks and lounging soldiers all looked at her appreciatively; she grew prettier by the day as she approached her seventeenth birthday. 'I need two men to accompany me to the market,' she announced. 'The colonel's orders.'

Several stepped forward, and Jelena selected the two youngest and best-looking. They walked one on either side of her as she crossed the courtyard and went under the archway on to the street and made her way to the market. People hastily got out of her way, even if they refused to look at her. Then she was amidst the stalls, fingering the various items – there were quite a few attractive leather handbags or belts as well as brightly coloured blouses and skirts. Kronic gave her a liberal allowance, and she selected a handbag, hung it on her shoulder, walked round the next stall, and found herself looking at an old woman with one eye, walking with the aid of a stick.

Jelena stood absolutely still, feeling the hair on the nape of her neck prickling. As soon as she saw her, the woman turned away from her and vanished into the throng. Jelena tried to think. An old woman, with one eye, and a stick, and a shawl over her head. However, Jelena's last glimpse of the woman walking away suggested that she didn't really need the stick. And her face, despite the eye-patch . . . Sasha! It had been Sasha! Sasha wasn't dead after all. She was alive, and unhurt, and in Bihac! And she had looked straight at her!

Jelena's knees felt weak, and she nearly fell. One of her bodyguards caught her arm. 'Are you all right, mademoiselle?'

What to do? Denounce her? But her principal memory of Sasha was of the woman with a tommy-gun, defying the world. From what she had been told, she had escaped from General von Demmich's house, and then the brothel, thanks to uninhibited violence. She had no idea if Sasha could possibly have a tommy-gun concealed under her dress, but she would certainly have something, and she would not hesitate to use it. To denounce Sasha in the middle of the market would mean that a great number of people would be killed – and one of the first would probably be herself!

'Mademoiselle?' the soldier asked again, anxiously.

'I must get home,' Jelena said. 'I do not feel well.'

'Shit!' Sasha muttered. 'Shit!'

'That was Brolic,' said Marita, her second in command. 'I thought she was dead, or locked up.'

'Well, obviously she isn't. That bitch! She is sent to haunt me.'

'You think she recognized you?'

'She looked straight at me. And then hurried off.' Sasha peered past the stall behind which she had taken shelter.

'What are we to do?'

Sasha squinted at the clock tower; it was just coming up to noon. Tony and Sandrine and Astzalos would be in position, but they would not be expecting action until tonight, and then were only intended to act as support until the Partisan army arrived, and *they* were still ten miles away. But there could be no doubt that Jelena would denounce her as soon as she felt it was safe to do so; that was a matter of minutes.

Tito had warned her that this could be a suicide mission. She did not wish to die, but . . . 'We go in,' she said. 'Now.'

Jelena hurried back to headquarters, the two bewildered Ustase men behind her.

In the downstairs hall she encountered Major Gruber. 'Fräulein?' he asked. 'You have been assaulted?'

Jelena ignored him and ran up the stairs. 'That was quick,' Kronic remarked as she entered the office.

'Sasha!' Jelena panted.

Kronic raised his head. 'Sasha?'

'Sasha Janitz! The Partisan! You must remember her!'

'Janitz! She is dead.'

'She is alive and in the market place, right this minute.'

'Are you out of your mind?'

'I saw her!' Jelena shouted. 'And she saw me!'

Kronic stared at her for a moment, then picked up his phone. 'Get me—' There was an explosion, followed by the rattle of gunfire. He got up and ran round his desk to go to the window. Jelena preferred to remain where she was, against the inner wall. 'We are being attacked!' Kronic bellowed, and then staggered back when there was a deeper explosion, followed by another. The glass shattered. Jelena dropped to her knees.

A bugle was blowing, men were shouting, women were screaming. And then there was a fourth explosion, louder than any of the others. By now smoke was rising in a thick cloud from the fortified south-east outskirts of the town. Kronic leaned out of the window. 'Get out there!' he shouted. 'Kill the bastards!' He turned round, buckled on his belt, and ran down the stairs. Jelena remained huddled against the wall, trembling.

Kronic burst through the outer hall, and found some of his men hastily assembling in the courtyard. 'Follow me!' he shouted, and led them out of the yard and on to the street. People were milling about, but they separated to allow the armed irregulars through. Kronic was running now, down the couple of streets that separated the headquarters from the perimeter, where he found a scene of utter chaos.

Four of the tanks were burning. Dead bodies were scattered about, several of them women. His men were firing indiscriminately in every direction. And Gruber was staring at the

235

ruins of his squadron with a confounded expression. 'Women!'
he complained when he saw Kronic. 'A bunch of women!'

'How did they get so close?'

'They just strolled up, led by a one-eyed old hag. My men
were amused to see them. Then one of them suddenly climbed
on to one of my tanks, took a grenade from her satchel, and
dropped it through the hatch. The others all tried to do the
same.' He gestured at the burning vehicles. 'How did they get
into the town with those arms? They had pistols as well.'

'Market day,' Kronic said savagely. 'Are they all dead?'

'I don't know. But my tanks! They are ruined. I am ruined!'

'We have three prisoners, sir,' said a Ustase lieutenant. 'Two
are wounded.'

Kronic followed him across the open space to where several of his men were standing, pointing their rifles at the three
women lying on the ground. One of the women was obviously very badly hurt, surrounded by a growing pool of blood.
Another was also bleeding, but not severely. The third was
unhurt.

Kronic stood above her, bent, and jerked the shawl from
round her head. Then he plucked the black patch from her
eye. 'Sasha Janitz,' he said.

Sasha dragged her skirt to her waist to draw her knife from
the concealed sheath – she had lost her pistol – and struck at
him. But the lieutenant kicked the weapon from her hand –
and then kicked her as well.

Tony listened to the explosions, watched the smoke rising from
the perimeter earthworks. 'What has happened?' asked
Martina Drozic, his second in command, a heavy-set young
woman with auburn hair. 'They were not supposed to go in
until tonight.'

Tony used his binoculars in an attempt to see, but the distance was too great, although there could be no doubt that
he was looking at exploding and burning fuel, which in that
place had to be vehicles, and which in that position strongly

suggested tanks. Sasha had carried out her mission. But why hadn't she waited until the appointed time? 'Send a runner back to the army,' he told Martina. 'Tell General Tito that at least some of the tanks have been put out of action. Tell him that I propose to advance our entry to the town to dusk tonight. Ask him to make all possible speed: there is no longer any reason to conceal our movements.' Martina nodded. 'Then send another runner to Colonel Astzalos and Major Fouquet, and ask them to join me here for a conference, but to do nothing until after we have met.'

Martina crawled away, and Tony settled down to wait, wondering what had happened to Sasha. And more importantly, what had happened to make her commit suicide? Obviously, despite her assurances, she must have run into either Gruber or Kronic. That had to be carelessness more than bad luck. But Sasha, as brave as a lion . . . He simply could not imagine her being dead.

Predictably, Sandrine arrived before Astzalos. 'Sasha is in trouble,' she said. 'We must help her.'

'We will. We'll go in as soon as it is dark.'

She gazed at him with wide eyes. 'You say we are to do nothing until it is dark? That is nearly six hours away.'

'We cannot cross that open space in daylight. We would be shot to pieces long before we gained the houses. Strictly speaking, we should not move at all until the army comes up. If those tanks are out of action, they are not going to be repaired by tomorrow morning.'

'We are supposed to support Sasha.'

'That was assuming she would make her move in the middle of the night, and have some chance of defending herself.'

'She could still be—'

'Do you hear any gunshots?'

Sandrine glared at him. 'I agree with Sasha. You have iced water in your veins.'

'I'm trying to win a war.'

'And suppose they have taken her alive? Do you know what they will do to her?'

Tony squeezed her hand, and looked up as Astzalos joined them. 'There has been a foul-up,' Astzalos said.

'There has been a development,' Tony corrected.

'Our plan has been wrecked.'

'I don't agree. I would say the tanks have been wrecked. I have sent a message to the general, asking him to make all possible speed. The Ustase will be distracted by what has happened. If he takes the risk and leaves as soon as he gets my message, he should be here by midnight at the latest. We will move in at dusk.'

'What, sixty men?' He glanced at Sandrine. 'And women? That will be to commit suicide. If you are so sure that the tanks are out of action, why do we not wait for the army?'

'For two reasons. One is to make sure the tanks are blown, all of them. The other is to rescue our people.'

'What absurdity. They are all dead.'

'We need to make sure of that, too. Here are your orders. At dusk we will advance across the open ground. Be sure to use all available cover, even if they are distracted by what has happened, they will still be expecting an attack. Astzalos, you will make for the tank emplacements.' He prodded the town plan. 'There. You will destroy the remaining tanks. Sandrine, you and I will make for the Ustase Headquarters.' Another prod. 'Here. It is only two streets away from the perimeter. We will take it over and hold it until relieved.'

'And Sasha and her women?'

'If any have survived and are prisoners, that is where we will find them. Astzalos, as soon as you have made sure that all of the tanks are out of action, you will join us at the head-quarters building.'

'If we can get there,' Astzalos grumbled. 'The whole town will be alerted.'

'My estimate is that the whole town will be in a state of panic. It is our business to keep it like that until the army arrives.'

*   *   *

'You!' Gruber said. 'You unutterable bitch!'

The Ustase soldiers had pulled Sasha to her feet. Her face was twisted with pain from the kick she had received. 'My people need help,' she said.

Gruber glanced at Kronic. 'That one is of no use to anyone,' Kronic said, indicating the woman who was severely hurt. 'Shoot her. Bring this one.' He pointed at the other injured woman.

'You cannot do that,' Sasha protested.

Kronic stepped up to her and hit her in the stomach. She gasped, and would have fallen had she not been held. For a few seconds she could not breathe. 'Bring them to headquarters,' Kronic told his men. Marita was dragged to her feet and her arms were pinioned, which brought a fresh moan of pain. Sasha was also dragged up and bound, and then pushed along the street. This was deserted, as the population had hastily taken shelter. Kronic and Gruber stood together, surveying the burning tanks and the slowly assembling remnants of their crews. 'You have two left,' Kronic said.

Gruber nodded. 'I must get them out of here.'

'Do what?'

'I cannot lose my entire squadron.'

'Your orders were to defend Bihac.'

'As long as it could be defended. Now . . .'

'It can still be defended.'

Gruber threw out his arm. 'The entire Partisan army is out there, moving towards us.'

'We do not know that. And even if they are, we still have our fortifications, and your two guns. Let them come. We will defeat them.' He put his arm round Gruber's shoulders. 'We will alert all our people, and have them in position for when the assault comes. Then we will win.'

'That bitch caused this! I am going—'

'Patience, my dear Hans. You will do anything you wish to her. I promise. But first, let us prepare for battle.'

*　　*　　*

Sasha and Marita were pushed up the stairs and thrust into Kronic's office. Released by her guards, Marita promptly sank to her knees; Sasha gazed at Jelena, who had risen and stood by the desk. 'Another betrayal,' she said.

'You are an enemy of the Reich.'

'The Reich,' Sasha sneered. 'So, you are a German now. Listen. Marita is hurt.'

Jelena came round the desk, making sure the guards were between her and Sasha, and stood above Marita. 'She does not look badly hurt to me.'

'I do not think it is a serious wound. But she is losing blood. She needs a doctor. Will you have one brought?'

'I do not give orders here.'

'You just lie on your back and receive them. Marita was your comrade, once. Will you just stand there and watch her bleed to death?'

'So were you my comrade, once,' Jelena said. 'And you are both going to die. Perhaps she is the lucky one.'

'You are the foulest lump of shit that ever dropped to the ground,' Sasha said.

'And you murdered my brother,' Jelena reminded her. 'I am going to watch you die. Stay here with them until the colonel comes,' she told the guards, and left the room.

Jelena joined Kronic and Gruber for lunch in the town square. By now some order had been restored, although people remained highly nervous, and if any of them were tempted to remark on the success of the Partisan raid, none of them dared do so.

'Have you seen her? Janitz?' Kronic asked.

'Yes. What will you do to her?'

'She will be interrogated. We need to find out Tito's plans.' And what has happened to Davis and Fouquet, he thought. But he had told neither Jelena or Gruber about that.

'Do you think they will attack us?'

'Undoubtedly. But they sent their suicide squad in too early.

Or they themselves are too late. They have to come at us across open ground, and there is no sign of them yet. We will be ready for them.'

'And what will you do with Sasha? That is, when you have finished with her.'

Kronic chuckled. 'You mean, if there is anything left for us to do something with. We have two choices. We can execute her privately, in which case we can prolong her agony for as long as we wish. Or we can hang her publicly. We need not use a trap, but it will still be reasonably quick.'

'I would like her to die slowly, in private,' Jelena said.

Kronic laughed, and ruffled her hair. 'Who is my little terrier, eh?'

'I hope you are not serious,' Gruber remarked.

'Don't tell me you will intercede for her? Did she not send you to hospital? Did she not destroy your tanks? Did you not wish to torture her yourself?'

'She deserves a beating, certainly,' Gruber said. 'And then execution. I could not condone anything else.'

'May I remind you, Major, that you are not in command here. And that your ability to aid in the defence of Bihac has been sadly reduced. But I will compromise. You may have her first, to beat her to your heart's content. When you are finished, I will take over to ask her a few questions. After that, we will see about her execution.'

Gruber got up. 'I will make a full report to Belgrade of everything that happens, Herr Colonel.'

'That is your prerogative, Major.'

Jelena watched him walk away. 'Will he make trouble for you?'

'If he can. But to do that, he first has to survive the coming battle. All we have to do is make sure he does not do that. Finish your meal, and you may come with me on my rounds.'

It was half past five when they returned to the headquarters, and the autumnal sun was already sinking into the west behind the mountains, shrouding the town and the valley in gloom. Jelena was exhausted, and apprehensive. The Ustase were not used to discipline, and rounding up all of his personnel and making sure they knew where they had to be and that they might have to fight a pitched battle had been a difficult job even for Kronic.

They found Marita alone in the office with one guard. Someone had actually bandaged Marita's wound; she had been hit in the thigh, but the bone was not broken. Now she was in a totally collapsed state from shock and loss of blood. 'She keeps begging for water,' the guard said.

'Well, let her beg. Where is the other one?' Kronic asked.

'She hasn't got away?' Jelena added, at once frightened and anxious.

'Major Gruber took her,' the guard said.

'That man is a menace,' Kronic said. 'Took her where?'

'I do not know, sir.'

'Well, send someone to find him. And her. I want her here.' He went to a table on which there were several bottles and glasses, and poured himself some wine.

'Please,' Marita begged. 'For the love of God, I am dying. Please give me a drink.'

'If you are dying,' Kronic pointed out, 'that would be a waste. Would you like me to help you on your way?'

'If Sasha has somehow escaped . . .' Jelena said.

'Not even Gruber would be that stupid. He is amusing himself. Well, he has had his fun. Now it is our turn. Now—'

He swung round at the sound of a shot.

'In there.' Gruber pushed Sasha through the doorway of his quarters. His orderly, standing just inside the door, came to attention. 'Get out,' Gruber said.

The orderly left, and Gruber closed and locked the door. Sasha waited. Her hands were still bound behind her back, and she was helpless. She also knew that she was going to die. She wished she could have died in the raid on the tanks, but as Sandrine had said, she had more lives than a cat. Only now she had used up her last one. And before she died . . .

Gruber stood in front of her, and smoothed hair away from her eyes and face. Then he took a handful of the material of her dress and pulled it. 'When last I saw you, you were better dressed than this.'

'I have known better times.'

'Why did you hit me like that?'

'I needed to get away.'

'And now you are back again. Do you know what Kronic and that little witch of his mean to do to you?'

'It will not be nice.'

'You can say it that calmly?'

'If it is my fate to die in agony, then it is my fate to die in agony.'

He pushed her against the bed, making her sit down, and then sat beside her. 'Would you not rather live?'

'As what?'

He stroked her hair again, then her cheek, then her breast through her gown. 'No woman has given me such pleasure.'

'I thought you wished to beat me?'

'I did, when I saw what you had done to my tanks. But now I forgive you. It was a very gallant action. Listen, I can save your life.'

'Kronic wishes me dead.'

'Kronic is a shit.'

'He commands here.'

'But he does not command me. I am an officer in the Wehrmacht. Oh, he may rant and rave, but he dare not lay a finger on me. So, I will tell him that you are my prisoner, and that I consider you important enough to be taken back to Germany for interrogation.'

'Then I will be tortured there.'

'No, no. When I leave here, I am to be retired – because of what you did to me, eh? You will live with me.'

Sasha's eyes widened. 'You can do this?'

'Of course. I have an uncle who is the Führer's closest confidant.'

'Göring is your uncle?'

'No, no, not that fat slob. My uncle is Martin Bormann.' He could see that the name meant nothing to her. 'Have you never heard of him?'

She shook her head.

'Well, all the world will hear of him one day. Many people consider that he is the Führer's natural successor. So you will be safe. Now, my sweet girl . . .' He turned her round to release her wrists, then unbuckled his belt.

'I would be better after I have had a drink,' Sasha said, rubbing her hands together to restore the circulation and wincing at the pins and needles. 'And a bath.'

'That is true. And you are worth waiting for. The bathroom is through there. I will pour us a drink, and we will toast the future.' He took off his belt, draped it across a chair, and went to a table on the far side of the room, where there was a bottle of schnapps.

His back was to her. Sasha gazed at it, and then at the holster hanging from the discarded belt. He was really such a nice man. And he trusted her. But he was an enemy. And she had a great deal to do before she died.

She moved forward and quietly drew the Luger. Gruber turned back towards her, a glass in each hand. 'Here is to—' He stared at the gun. 'I am offering you life.'

'I am sorry,' Sasha said. 'I can only offer you death.'

'You bitch!' He dropped both glasses and ran at her. Sasha shot him through the chest.

Kronic ran out of his office, the sentry at his heels. 'Sound the alarm!' he shouted. 'Call out the guard.' He knew instinctively that it had been Janitz. That fool Gruber . . .

He ran down the stairs and across the courtyard, with several men now behind him. Gruber's quarters were on the far side of the hollow square. He ran into the lobby and up the stairs, and encountered the orderly, who was standing outside the door. 'What has happened?'

'I do not know, sir. The door is locked.'

'But Major Gruber is in there?'

'Yes, sir.'

'With Janitz?'

'With a woman,' the orderly said uncertainly.

Kronic summoned his men, who were waiting on the stairs. 'Break it down.' He stood aside to let them pass him, and was surrounded by a huge gush of sound.

Tony's squad moved forward as soon as it was dark, crawling across the open ground before the town. He knew Sandrine was to his left and Astzalos to his right, although he could not see them. There were only a few lights visible; it seemed that Kronic had imposed a blackout as well as a curfew. Thus there was little noise from in front of them, and they had very nearly reached the barricades when they heard a shot.

'Some idiot!' Martina panted.

'That came from inside the town,' Tony said.

Whoever had fired the shot, it had distracted the sentries, who were muttering at each other. Before they knew what was happening, the Partisans were on them, firing their tommy-guns and hurling their hand grenades. The Ustase screamed their terror and ran in every direction.

The noise spread as Sandrine's and Astzalos's people went into action. Tony had memorized the town plan, and dashed down the street towards the town hall. Thanks to the curfew the street was empty, and there were no armed men to be seen. But there were sentries at the arched gateway to the town hall courtyard. These fired, and one of the Partisans fell, then they too were overwhelmed by the tommy-guns as Tony led his people into the yard.

'Break that door down!' Kronic shouted over his shoulder. 'But take the bitch alive.' He ran back down the stairs and emerged into the courtyard. 'Sound the alarm!' he bellowed. 'All units prepare to resist attack.' He ran across the yard, and stopped when he saw the people coming towards him, hardly visible in the darkness, but surrounded by spitting fire. He turned to run for the headquarters building, and went down as several bullets thudded into his back. He gasped for breath and inhaled only choking dust. The Partisans trampled on his body as they ran by.

Sasha stood above Gruber's body for several seconds. Then she raised her head to look at the door, which had been splintering under the blows of the men outside. But these now ceased as the noise from the courtyard swelled.

She checked the pistol; there were still eleven cartridges in the magazine. She drew a deep breath, threw the door open, and ran down the steps, gun thrust forward. But there was no one there. She burst into the yard, and came face to face with Sandrine, who was just leading her people through the gate. 'Nine lives!' she shouted. 'Nine lives!'

Sandrine gave her a hasty embrace, then ordered a barricade to be set up at the gate. There was a heavy machine-gun in the yard, and this was dragged forward to command the archway. From inside the building there were screams and shouts. More important, from the south-east perimeter there came two loud explosions. 'The last two tanks,' Sasha said.

Tony came down the stairs, followed by several of his people. Two of them were dragging Jelena. 'Got her just in time,' he said, and showed them a little pistol. 'She had this, but not the guts to use it.'

The girl was weeping. 'Please,' she begged when she saw Sandrine and Sasha. 'He made me do it. Kronic. Ask him . . .'

'You have just tripped over his body,' Sandrine told her.

Jelena turned, then gave a little shriek and a jump when she saw it lying there.

'Hang her,' Sasha said. 'Hoist her up nice and slow.'

Tony hesitated, and looked at Sandrine. But there was no

pity there. He felt none himself. But . . . 'I am sorry,' he said. 'She will have to stand trial. We are fighting to re-establish the rule of law. Thus we have to act within the law.'

'You and your laws,' Sasha grumbled.

'She is responsible, directly or indirectly, for the deaths of eighteen of our people,' Sandrine said. 'Maybe nineteen, if you include Davidovic. But you are right, Tony.'

'Please,' Jelena said. 'They made me do it. They . . .' She peered at the faces surrounding her. 'Petar! Oh, Petar! Help me, Petar.'

Her brother came forward. 'They told me you were dead.'

'They are going to hang me. Please, Petar . . .'

'You betrayed us. You betrayed Yugoslavia.'

'Petar . . .'

'But I cannot have my sister hanged.' Petar levelled his rifle and shot her in the breast.

'Well, Wassermann,' Himmler said over the phone. 'Is your wife safe and well?'

'Yes, Herr Reichsführer, I am pleased to say.'

'And none the worse for her ordeal?'

'No, sir,' Wassermann lied.

'You must be very relieved. Now, tell me about Bihac.'

'I have not actually read the full report, sir.'

'I have received a report from General von Demmich. It would appear that the Ustase, as usual, were completely worthless.'

'I'm afraid that does seem to have been the case, sir.'

'General von Demmich says that using them was your recommendation.'

'Well, sir, we were short of men.'

'Thus we now have a situation in which, far from being destroyed, as you promised would be the case, the Partisans have found a secure base in which to spend the winter and recuperate. And, incidentally, they have managed to lay their hands on the very large arsenal of guns and bullets we supplied to the Ustase.'

'Well, sir . . .'

'General von Demmich also informs me that far from being dead, it appears that Davis and Fouquet are alive and indeed led the assault.'

Wassermann swallowed. 'I am afraid that is correct, Herr Reichsführer. The information given to me by Major Wiedermann was over-optimistic.'

'Yes. Major Wiedermann is being transferred to the Russian front. But you, Wassermann . . .'

Wassermann held his breath.

'I don't suppose you would be of much value on the Russian front. But I am forced to come to the conclusion that we returned you to duty prematurely. You will return to Berlin for a new and less onerous appointment.'

'But . . . Davis and Fouquet . . .'

'Would seem to have outwitted you. Again.'

'But who will command here in Belgrade?'

'I propose to give Ulrich a chance to see what he can do. I am gazetting his promotion to major now. Is he there?'

'He is here, sir.'

'Put him on the line.'

'Yes, sir. Will I see you when I reach Berlin?'

'Perhaps. I am a busy man, Wassermann, as I am sure you appreciate.'

Wassermann handed the phone to the obviously curious Ulrich. 'Congratulations . . . Major,' he said, and left the room.

Wassermann went upstairs to the bedroom. Rosa was pottering about as always.

'Come here,' Wassermann said.

She approached him cautiously. Although she was now largely reconciled with her mistress – having falsely given evidence condemning Bestic at Angela's trial – she was unsure of her position viv-à-vis her master.

'I have been recalled to Berlin on an urgent matter, Rosa,' Wassermann said. 'It may be a little while before I return.'

Rosa's jaw dropped. 'But if you are not here, Herr Colonel . . .'

'You will be in no danger. I have given Captain Ulrich instructions that you are to be protected, and you will be paid a pension. So as long as you behave yourself, and keep your mouth shut, you have nothing to worry about. But remember, I know that every word you said at my wife's trial was a lie. Should you betray me, I will have you hanged beside your mother and father. Do you understand this?'

Rosa's head bobbed up and down.

'Very good. I will see you again before we leave.' He went down the stairs and out the garden door.

Angela was seated in a deckchair on the lawn, drinking schnapps. Not only had her weeks in prison left no physical mark, but also the way in which she had been extricated from a potentially fatal situation had made her aware of her power.

Wassermann stood above her. 'We are returning to Berlin.'

She raised her head. 'Whatever for?'

'Orders. My spell of duty in Yugoslavia has been completed.'

Angela stared at him for several moments. Then she burst out laughing. 'You have been sacked! You! The great Wassermann. Sacked!'

'Bitch!'

She held up her hand as he moved towards her. 'Just remember that if you lay a finger on me, ever again, I am going to tell the world exactly what a liar and a cheat you are, exactly how you got me off that murder charge.'

Wassermann glared at her, his fingers opening and shutting.

'So Davis and Fouquet have triumphed again,' Angela remarked.

'They have *survived* again,' Wassermann said. 'This war is not over yet.'

'I'll say goodbye,' Peter Johnstone said. 'I'm expected on the coast in three days' time. I have to say that it has been quite an experience.' He looked around; he, Tony, Sandrine and Sasha were standing in the courtyard of the town hall, and all around them were the sounds of the Partisan army putting the town back together, repairing its defences. 'Quite a triumph. You're sure you won't change your mind and come with me?'

'We'll see it out,' Tony said. 'Will you be coming back?'

'I certainly hope to. I'd like to see the end as well. But in any event, I'm going to make sure you get what you need to reach that end.' He shook hands with Tony, embraced Sandrine, hesitated for a moment, and then embraced Sasha as well. 'Till the next time.'

They watched him walk away to join his escort for the trek over the mountains to the coast. 'Do you think he will do it?' Sandrine asked.

'Yes,' Tony said. 'For the first time, I really feel we are going to win.'

An orderly stood beside him. 'The general requests your presence, Colonel.'

'Work to be done,' Tony said. 'Carry on, Major Fouquet.'

'Well,' Sandrine said, 'let us put our girls to work, Captain Janitz. They must be fit and ready for the next battle.'